EIGHT MINUTES TO SUNRISE

#5 TILDAS ISLAND SERIES

TAMSEN SCHULTZ

Copyright © 2021 by Tamsen Schultz

Published by Devil's Gate Press, LLC

Cover Design by Melody Barber

Edited by Edited by Rebecca and Woody Fridae, Cameron Yeager

E-Book ISBN: 978-1-955384-00-1

Print ISBN: 978-1-955384-05-6

ALSO BY TAMSEN SCHULTZ

THE WINDSOR SERIES

THE PUPPETEER (Prequel)

1) A Tainted Mind (Vivienne & Ian)

2) These Sorrows We See (Matty & Dash)

3) What Echos Render (Jesse & David)

4) The Frailty of Things (Kit & Garret)

5) An Inarticulate Sea (Carly & Drew)

6) A Darkness Black (Caleb & Cate)

7) Through The Night (Naomi & Jay)

8) Into The Dawn (Brian & Lucy)

WINDSOR SHORT STORIES

Bacchara, Chimera, and The Thing About London

THE TILDAS ISLAND SERIES

1) A Fiery Whisper (Charlotte & Damian)

2) Night Deception (Alexis & Isiah)

3) A Touch of Light and Dark (Nia & Jake)

4) This Side of Midnight (Anika & Dominic)

5) Eight Minutes to Sunrise (Beni & Cal)

THE DOCTORS CLUB SERIES

1) Cyn

2) Six

3) Devil

4) Nora

To everyone who is helping us all get to the light at the end of pandemic tunnel.

ACKNOWLEDGMENTS

It's hard to believe that my second series is complete. I've had so much fun writing these stories and I've loved bringing Damian, Alexis, Jake, Dominic, and Beni (and their significant others) to life. It's also given me a chance to live (even if only in my mind) in the tropics during this time of COVID—but hey, I'll take "travel" any way I can get it.

As always, thank you to Stephanie, my intrepid and talented PA, Woody and Rebecca Fridae for the great development feedback, Cameron Yeager for the additional editing, and Melody Barber for the cover artwork.

So, what's next, you might ask? To set your mind at ease, none of these characters will be gone forever. I just can't do that to "people" I like, so don't be surprised to see some familiar names crop up in subsequent stories—in fact, both Beni and Lucy have already popped up in book one of my next series, The Doctors' Club, and I'm sure they won't be the only ones who will make an appearance.

Last, thank you to each and everyone of you who has picked up one or many of my books. Maybe you read to escape, maybe you read for entertainment, or maybe you read for dozens of other reasons. Whatever the reason, nothing makes me happier than knowing my stories are a part of that.

CHAPTER ONE

CALVIN MATTHEWS STOOD in the shadows of the doorway leading out to the veranda of The Shack, a local watering hole owned by former SEAL Isiah Clarke. He watched as the woman he'd come to see, Benita Ricci, lifted her rum and took a sip.

Sitting at a table with her four FBI teammates, Clarke, and the liaison between the FBI and the local police department, Beni was listening to her colleagues debate whether or not he, Calvin Matthews, the Vice President of the United States, was guilty of all sorts of heinous crimes. Crimes that ranged from funding the development of a designer drug to murder.

"I don't want to think Matthews played the American people so much," Damian Rodriguez said. Rodriguez was a former Army Ranger and one of the agents on the special FBI task force with Beni.

"No one does," Anika Anderson, the police liaison, said. "He and President Cunningham were a breath of fresh air when they ticketed up. I can't remember the last time we've had a political team in office that genuinely seems committed to the people of the United States."

"But power and money do funny things to people," Alexis

1

Wright interjected. And Agent Alexis Wright would know. She was an agent, but she was also the daughter of Jasper and Vera Wright. Her parents were powerful people. Not politically powerful, but in the world of music and entertainment, Jasper and Vera Wright were royalty.

"Uh, yeah, I can vouch for that," Jake McMullen added before taking a large swallow of his rum. Cal wasn't quite sure what the agent, and former surfing pro, meant by the statement, but the rest of the team nodded.

"He's not involved," Beni said, finally stepping into the conversation.

Everyone looked at her and Cal held his breath, waiting to hear what she'd say next.

"I don't want to think he is, either, Beni, but Shah is right, we have to consider it," Dominic Burel said. He was the fifth agent assigned to the task force and his comment was referring to their director, Sunita Shah. "The elite in both parties benefit when the country is divided, and with his connections, there's no doubt that he'd be one of them."

Beni took another sip of her drink then shook her head. "We'll do what we need to, but I'm telling you, he's not involved. Matthews is..." She paused and Cal found himself leaning on the balls of his feet, anxious to hear her opinion of him.

"Have you seen his record?" she continued. "There's no way he would have invested in the work that he invested in and fought the fights he fought for those unable to fight for themselves, if he didn't believe in what he was doing. His life's work is completely antithetical to everything we've investigated. Human trafficking rings by a man who singlehandedly brought about the regulation and protection of sex workers in Chicago? Or a drug lab from a man who, when mayor of Chicago, fought for drug clinics and rehabilitation centers that reduced the number of drug related crime and deaths dramatically?" She shook her head and Cal didn't fight the little thrill that shot through his body knowing she'd followed his career so closely. "I'll do what I have to do," she said. "But I don't believe anything that points to Matthews being involved."

Cal knew the power of a well-timed entrance and, with her last words, he stepped into the room. Six sets of eyes jumped up and settled on him. The expressions on their faces ranged from wary to unreadable to surprised. But not Beni. She had her back to him and had no idea he was standing less than eight feet from her. Though, how she didn't feel the energy arcing between them—the way it always had—was beyond him.

When no one responded, her head came up and she scanned the table. Then slowly, she turned.

"I can't tell you how glad I am to hear you don't doubt me, Benita," Cal said.

Her eyes widened. "Cal," she managed to choke out. Then she raised her glass to her lips as if to down it, only to find it empty. Blinking at the tumbler, she set it down, rose from her seat, and faced him. "What are you doing here?"

"I received an interesting call from Director Shah this morning," he said. "Thought I'd come down and talk to her myself. We had a very informative discussion about an hour ago. Then she told me *you'd* be here. So, I'm here." That wasn't quite the whole story. He'd been looking for an excuse to reach out to Beni for years, Shah's call had just provided the opportunity.

"Where's your Secret Service?" she asked, glancing behind him.

He grinned. "Worried about me?"

She rolled her eyes and a little bit of the girl he'd known all those years ago peeked out. "You're second in line to leading this great country we call our own. Yeah, I'm worried," she said.

His grin spread into a smile. "I figure with five FBI agents, a retired Navy SEAL, and one of Tildas Island's finest—not to mention the two CIA spooks behind the bar—I'm pretty safe here. But they're outside, watching the entrance and exits," he said, his team having briefed him on the situation prior to his arrival. Before she could say anything more, he moved into her space. "I've missed you, Benita," he added quietly.

Her eyes searched his, no doubt looking for any hint of deception on his part. She wouldn't find any. He *had* missed her. But she'd been the one to leave him—without a word—sixteen years ago and he couldn't blame her for not trusting his honesty.

"I—" She started to say something, but he cut her off. Sliding his hand behind her neck, he pulled her forward, slanted his mouth over hers, and kissed her. Kissed her in the way he'd wanted to for years. Kissed her with everything he had, trying to wipe away the years they'd been apart.

And god help them both, she kissed him back.

Time passed, but lost in the feel of her, in the sense of belonging and rightness, he couldn't say how much. Maybe seconds, maybe minutes. Then abruptly, she pulled away. He didn't let her go far, though. His eyes burned into hers as he held her tight, one hand still at her neck, the other at her waist.

"I let you go once before, Benita Ricci," he said. "You can be damn sure I'm not going to do it again."

Beni's hazel eyes widened at his proclamation and to be fair, he couldn't really blame her. He hadn't meant to say those words—and for a man who was considered one of the best orators of the modern era, that was saying a lot—but he wasn't about to withdraw them.

His hands cupped her jaw as the kiss he'd laid on her still sizzled between them. Yes, there was no question in his mind that Benita Ricci was never going to be out of his system. It had been sixteen years since she'd left him without a word or a backward glance. Once the hurt had receded, he had tried to convince himself that whatever it was that had been between them had been nothing more than teenage hormones. He knew better now, though. He'd always known better if he were honest with himself. It had just been easier to chalk up what they'd shared together—what Beni had thrown away—as a hormonal reaction than something more.

Seeing her now, though, well, it changed everything. He was no longer willing to accept all the lies he told himself about their past. Nor, for that matter, was he willing to accept all the lies she probably told herself. Because holding her now, feeling the energy arcing between them, her pulse racing under his thumb...well, there was no way that what he was feeling, even after all these years, was only one sided.

He leaned in and brushed another gentle kiss across her lips then drew back and stepped away. She'd tensed as he'd moved toward her, and though she'd allowed the kiss, she was one beat away from withdrawing from him in every way. And he couldn't have that.

"Why don't you introduce me to your friends and colleagues, Benita?" he asked, taking another step back and letting his gaze touch on the group of people at the table.

Everyone had risen from their seats and were watching him and Beni closely. The scrutiny could have been because of who he was, but it was just as likely that they were preparing to come to their friend's defense if need be. Judging by the looks directed at him, he'd bet it was close to a 50/50 split, with Isiah Clarke, Anika Anderson, and Damian Rodriguez on Team Beni and Dominic Burel and Jake McMullen on Team Vice President. Not surprising, Agent Alexis Wright was watching the scene, her head cocked slightly to the side, appearing to be withholding judgment.

"Benita?" He dropped his gaze back down to her to find her studying him. Gone was the slightly dazed look that had graced her face after he'd kissed her, and while this look wasn't hostile, it was calculating. Not a coy or cruel calculation, but he could practically hear the questions and thoughts forming in her head. She'd always been intelligent—exceptionally so—but the years that separated them had infused that intelligence with experience and confidence. And fuck him if it wasn't even sexier than it had been all those years ago.

He cleared his throat and stepped around Beni, holding his hand out to Isiah who stood closest.

"Calvin Matthews," he said. "And you're Isiah Clarke. Thank you for your service and it's a nice place you have here."

Isiah studied him for a long beat and Cal considered whether he was debating stepping into the protector role. Not that Beni needed protecting, especially not from him, but the vibes Isiah was throwing off let Cal know he was treading on thin ice. The former SEAL was *not* impressed by the fact that the vice president had just waltzed into his bar and kissed one of his friends.

Alexis placed a hand on Isiah's lower back and that seemed to signal something between the couple. Isiah held his hand out. Relief trickled through Cal at this first step of acceptance, as tentative as it was. Until he realized he still had five more of her friends to meet.

Damian and Anika treated him to the same scrutiny as Isiah, and while Jake, Dominic, and Alexis were a little more welcoming, they weren't exactly gushing at his arrival. Then again, until moments ago, they'd been discussing whether or not he was orchestrating a series of major crimes all with the intent of toppling the current political structure in the United States. Maybe their reserve wasn't solely on Beni's behalf.

"Well, this looks fun," a voice spoke from behind him. "I can see this is a tougher crowd than usual for you, Cal."

"Serena," he said, greeting the former CIA asset who now worked at The Shack.

"What are you doing here?" she asked.

He shrugged. "I just had an interesting meeting with Director Shah. Looks like Duncan Calloway, or someone who's hired him, is trying to bring down my administration by framing me for a shit ton of crimes—including human trafficking, designing illegal drugs, and the sale of your identity as a CIA asset—all so that the hostile, divided two-party system can be restored and those at the top can go back to making a shit ton of money off the backs of everyone else. Calloway was always an ass, but he's really outdone himself this time."

Both Damian and Isiah drew back at his explanation, though Cal wasn't sure if it was the substance of his summary or the casual delivery of it that caused the reaction. His response *was* nonchalant, but it wasn't forced or feigned. He wasn't guilty of any of the things Shah had told him the team had uncovered in the last eighteen months, and, more to the point, he trusted them, especially Beni and Director Shah, to prove that. He had every faith in them, so while the situation wasn't ideal, it wasn't worth getting too worked up about.

Serena studied him, an inspection he was more used to than he'd care to admit. Four years ago, when the Republican Presidential Nominee, Anne-Marie Cunningham, had chosen him, a Democrat, to be his running mate, foreign policy had been his biggest weakness. Then one day, Serena had, literally, appeared on his doorstep to help. To this day, he had no idea why she'd reached out to him or why she'd felt the need to become his de facto tutor on the subject. Over the years, though, her insights, intel, and the questions she'd asked, had led him to be able to more than hold his own on the topic of foreign affairs.

"That's a lot of work for this Duncan Calloway to go to," she said. "You piss him off recently?"

Cal smiled. "My existence pisses him off. He's just one of those guys. You know the type."

"No, I don't know. *We* don't know," Anika said, jumping into the conversation. "All we know is that you two appear together at quite a few of the same public events."

Serena muttered something about getting drinks and Cal

swung his attention back around to the team he was relying on to clear his name.

"May I?" he asked, gesturing to a chair. Isiah was the proprietor, so it was to him that Cal looked. The SEAL didn't look convinced it was a good idea, but again, Alexis intercepted and, leaning forward, whispered something in his ear. Isiah nodded, and within seconds, everyone was seated. Beni had scooted her chair over to make room for the extra seat, but he managed to scoot over, too, so that she wasn't too far away.

A few seconds later, Serena and Huck, the other retired CIA employee who worked at The Shack, brought a tray full of drinks. The two set beers down in front of everyone except for Beni. With a very intentional look at him, Serena set down two tumblers of rum in front of Beni and ordered her to just holler if she needed more. Cal tried to glare at Serena, but she'd given him her back and walked away.

"So," Anika prompted, leaning forward in her seat and pinning him with a look. She was a stunning woman, with a little bit of a Nordic goddess look going on, and it would be easy to focus on her superficial attributes, but he wasn't about to underestimate her. Detective Anika Anderson had only recently joined the team as the official liaison for the Tildas Island Police Force, but he'd seen her record. Her test scores had been off the charts and the rate that she closed cases was the highest in her department, despite the department, as a whole, being less than hospitable to women.

Cal let his attention drift to Dominic Burel. He knew the former Air Force Pararescuer and Detective Anderson were a recent couple—Shah had told him that—but if he'd hoped to get any support from the man, the grin on Dominic's mug and the twinkle in his eye told Cal he was on his own when it came to dealing with the pint-sized woman at his side.

Cal took a sip of his beer then set the glass down. "Calloway is, and has always been, a hanger-on. In college, he had enough money to keep up with the wealthy, but never enough to live in that world. He had enough charm to be interesting for an evening or two, but never more than that. He was always not quite *enough*—not smart enough, not charming enough, not rich enough, not poor enough—just not *enough*.

"He was a senior when I was a freshman and even with the age difference, it was clear to me when I joined the same fraternity that he was just the guy that hung around. He was a brother, for sure, but was always a bit of an outsider. He may or may not have sensed it, but the more he tried to become an insider, the more he faced walls and barriers to that status.

"I'm not the only guy from the fraternity that has made a name for himself. I would bet that if you looked for pictures of Calloway at events with a few of the others, you'd find him trying to hang out with them, too. So, to answer your question, Detective Anderson, yes, we have been at several public events at the same time, but never *together*. Somehow, he always manages to hang around me long enough, or time his approach to me in such a way, that he ends up in a picture. It's probably hard to believe, given how often we end up being seen together, but he's never been in my company for more than ten minutes since he graduated. Though, I realize you have no reason, other than my reputation, to believe me about that."

Skepticism was written on the detective's face, so Cal swung his attention to Alexis. If anyone would understand the persistent irritation of hangers-on, it would be her. She'd been raised in the rarified world of the rich and famous. When he saw the look of understanding on Alexis' face, the muscles in his chest relaxed a bit. He wouldn't go so far as to say she looked like she *believed* him about his relationship—or lack thereof—with Calloway, but she did look like she recognized, and acknowledged, the existence of the type of person Calloway was.

"You said you're being framed," Rodriguez said. "Why should we just believe you?"

Cal searched the man's face, unsure how to answer. He'd already made it clear that he wasn't guilty of committing the crimes Damian referred to, but making the same assertion a second time wouldn't satisfy the team.

As he considered his answer, Cal's gaze swept around the table. When it landed on Beni, and he saw the hesitant anticipation in her eyes, he knew he needed to back up a step. The call he'd gotten from Sunita Shah earlier that morning had put a different lens on a few odd things that had happened to him recently. He'd met with her just prior to his arrival at The Shack, and they both now had a pretty clear picture of what was going on—something the team wasn't yet privy to. They might not believe him, but he'd tell them what he now knew, and they could confirm it with their director.

He took another sip of his beer and, unable to stop himself, he lifted his hand and draped it across the back of Beni's chair. He wasn't touching her like he wanted to, but he could feel the heat from her shoulders which were bare in the tank top she wore.

Cal almost smiled when, as one, everyone else's gaze went to Beni, as if to check in and ask if she was okay with his move. He liked how clear they were that their loyalties lay with her—at least in this situation—rather than with him. Beni leaned forward and picked up one of the glasses of rum as she rested an elbow on the table. Apparently, the fact that she hadn't shaken his arm off was enough of a message to the team, and their attention flickered back to him.

"Last year, Calloway approached me at a political fundraiser and mentioned a party being hosted by Peter Gregson. I know you're familiar with him," Cal said.

"Fucker deserves to die," muttered Serena from the doorway. Both she and Huck had abandoned their shift at the bar and were now leaning against either side of the doorway leading out to the veranda. It was a good thing The Shack was closed for the night and there weren't people to serve—or anyone to overhear them.

"I'm definitely not sad about what happened to him," Alexis said, echoing Serena's distaste for the human trafficker. The previous summer, Gregson, whose father was a major donor to the Democratic Party, had hosted a lavish party on Tildas that had included supplying trafficked young women to the attendees. The task force, with the assistance of Tildas Island's SWAT team, had raided the event and put an end to both Gregson's activities and that branch of the trafficking ring.

Cal lifted a shoulder. "I'm not sure anyone is. He was always a douche. Granted, I didn't know just how much of one he was, but I'd occasionally run into him at events he attended with his father and I always felt like I needed a shower after. Thankfully, I didn't see him often."

Anika had choked on her drink when he'd used the word "douche" and Dominic was patting her back. Cal probably should consider watching his words a little more; after all, he *was* the Vice President of the United States. Then again, Beni never suffered fools lightly and this team was clearly just that to her, *her team*. She trusted them and, even after all these years, he trusted her. Letting his guard down around this group of men and women felt right, it felt comfortable. And if he dug a little deeper than that, he might even admit that he wanted them to like him.

"I knew the trafficking ring was more than meets the eye," Serena said. "I said it then and I stand behind it now, that small ring had access to people it shouldn't have. It popped up overnight and that's not something that happens in that world— there are too many people out to protect their own territories to let a newbie enter the scene the way that one did."

Cal glanced at the former agent and nodded. "I don't know the specifics of how it came to be, who funded it, or even the current status—I'll leave that to you all—but I agree. Traffickers are like gangs and new factions don't just show up and get to claim power."

"So, back to the invite?" Dominic prompted.

Cal swung his attention to the man. "I declined and that was it, really. Gregson wasn't someone I wanted to spend any time with and if I was going to visit Tildas Island it certainly wasn't going to be to hang out with that crowd." He let his eyes linger on Beni as he spoke, making his implication clear. She held his gaze with a steady—and annoyingly unreadable—one of her own.

"But it was weird that he invited me at all," Cal continued, then he took another sip of his beer. After he set the glass down, he spoke again. "First, as I said, Calloway and I don't spend any time together and second, why would he think I'd be interested in attending a party hosted by Peter Gregson? Sure, his dad is a big donor, but there's nothing in either Gregson's life or mine to suggest that we'd ever be interested in spending time together."

Damian frowned. "Okay, we can accept that's weird. What else?"

"Last fall, Calloway approached me at a charity event. Again, he invited me to a club opening here on Tildas Island, one owned by DJ Kitt who was pretty popular during our college years. His music was played a lot in the fraternity house so, on one hand, I can see Calloway thinking it would be a fun thing to revisit those days, but on the other..."

"You never hung out with him back in those good ol' days, you're not likely to hit up the club scene in general, and if you were going to travel to Tildas Island it wouldn't be to go to a random club hosted by a washed-up DJ," Alexis finished, her attention darting to Beni as she spoke. For a split second, Beni's eyes narrowed at her friend, then her expression relaxed back to unreadable.

"That pretty much sums it up," Cal said. "It was weird in so many ways."

"You know what happened with that club?" Jake asked.

Cal nodded. "Shah told me just a few hours ago. I hadn't given it a thought until today, though." After his ninety minutes of enlightenment—as he was coming to think of his recent meeting with Director Shah—he'd learned that the team had stopped the development and distribution of a terrifying new drug. A drug that had been taken for test drives on unsuspecting patrons of the club in discussion. "Like I said, at the time, I just thought it was weird. Coupled with his invite to Gregson's party a few months earlier, I assumed Calloway was trying to do what he always did. I assumed he was trying to inveigle his way into my inner circle in a vain attempt to gain some sort of prestige or power. It wasn't until I spoke with Shah that I understood those two invites were more than just a power grab."

"That's not all, though, is it?" Damian asked.

Shah had told Cal that Rodriguez was good at reading people. Yes, Alexis was the psychologist, but Damian's skill was something more innate.

Cal shook his head. "It's not. Four months ago, Ronald Lawlor scheduled a meeting with me."

Surprise and recognition flashed in everyone's eyes. Lawlor was an FBI agent who Cal now knew had cropped up in a few of the team's investigations. He'd never been a person of interest, but he was a stakeholder in the holding company that owned the island where the designer drugs had been developed. And Shah definitely had no love for the man.

"It's interesting that a Special Agent in Charge openly scheduled a meeting with the Vice President of the United States," Beni said. It didn't surprise him that the first words she spoke since they'd sat down went right to the heart of the matter.

"Yes, it is," he said.

"Lawlor is high ranking, but not *that* high ranking," Damian said, picking up on Beni's train of thought.

"He wanted people to know he was meeting with you," Dominic jumped in.

"That seems the obvious motive, but what was the actual substance of the meeting?" Jake asked.

"He left the door open when we met and he said he wanted to talk to me about The Bank of DC investigation," Cal answered then smiled at the colorful epithets that filled the evening air. Seemed the team held the same opinion of SAC Ronald Lawlor that he and the director held.

"What exactly did he say about The Bank of DC investigation?" Beni demanded.

"He didn't actually say much," Cal answered. "Just that he wanted to discuss some follow up issues. He said it loud enough for the office to hear, though. I very pointedly reminded him that the investigation was closed and that I wasn't at liberty to speak on it."

Just days ago, the task force, led by Anika and Dominic, had closed a case involving several murders. Each of the three men had been killed in a murder-for-hire scenario, and each of them had, prior to the investigation, touched the accounts Cal held at the institution.

The investigation itself had grabbed the national headlines for weeks leading up to the last presidential election. Hardly a surprise when the front-running candidate for the office of the vice president banked at an institution being investigated for funneling money to terrorist organizations. It was only after the bank, and he, had been cleared of any wrongdoing, and Anne-Marie Cunningham had unequivocally stood by him, that the news furor had died down.

There was one thing he'd learned early on in his career, though, and that was that stories—especially lurid ones—never truly died. If the press picked up on the case the team had just closed, it wasn't hard to imagine a fresh set of stories suggesting that the deaths of those three men proved the original investigation had been nothing but a sham. And now that the second term election was coming up, Cal was cleaning up loose ends.

"What did he do when you refused to engage with him on the topic?" Alexis asked.

Cal thought back to that bizarre meeting, recalling how it unfolded. "He rose, shut the door, and then started talking about other things."

"Other things?" Alexis pressed.

Cal wagged his head. "He said he'd heard that the press might drag the investigation back up again and wanted to prepare me. Then he started asking if I was being briefed on the current threats being made against me—"

"Threats? What threats against you?" Beni demanded.

Cal bit back the smile that fought to emerge at the concern, and indignation, in Beni's voice. She might not know what to think about his barging back into her life, but she still cared about him. He'd take that. For now, at least.

"He's the Vice President of the United States, Beni. There are always going to be threats against him," Damian said, stating the obvious but keeping his voice empty of anything that might call attention to what she'd just revealed.

Beni sat back then quickly shifted forward when her skin came into contact with his fingertips. She closed her eyes, took a breath, then opened them and looked at him. "Did you get the sense he actually had new information or that he was just passing the time to make it look to everyone else that the two of you were having some deep conversation?" she asked.

"Definitely the latter," he said, leaning forward to grab his drink and *accidentally* letting his hand fall to the area of bare skin just above the top of Beni's tank. She stiffened at his touch but didn't move away. Gently—slowly—he started tracing the line of her spine with his fingertips.

"I'm briefed every morning and every night on my security situation," he said. "My Secret Service team handles that. If there's an actual threat, then there's even more briefings than the two. Sometimes the FBI joins in, depending on what's going on or if I'm traveling and there's something they think I should know, but there's no formal briefing structure between my office and the FBI."

"How long did he talk?" Isiah asked.

"Not more than fifteen minutes," Cal answered. "He could get away with talking about security briefings for a little bit, but any longer would have been very awkward."

Silence fell over the table as everyone seemed to mull over the information he'd just delivered. Beni picked up her second glass of rum, or was it her third? She'd had an empty glass in her hand when he'd first entered the veranda and heard her defending him. Regardless, the count didn't matter because just then, she seemed to forget that she wasn't so sure about him and leaned back in her chair. He slid his hand up and started kneading her neck as she took a sip of her drink.

A few minutes ticked by before Anika asked, "So, what brought you down here?"

He flashed her a smile and, for the first time since he'd set foot on the veranda, someone smiled back. Actually, Anika laughed as she turned to her partner. "His grin is almost as mind controlling as yours, babe," she said.

Dominic rolled his eyes. "Obviously mine is losing its power since we're not back at my place—"

Cal laughed when Anika narrowed her eyes at Dominic and the man instantly shut up.

"Dude, things not to say in public..." Jake staged whispered.

"Right," Alexis interjected with an eye roll. "Coming from the man with no filter whatsoever, that's rich."

"My filter is better than Rodriguez," Jake shot back and everyone at the table, except Cal who wasn't in on the inside jokes, snorted with laughter.

Jake feigned a hurt look. "Charlotte is always telling him to stop sharing," he pointed out. "Nia never tells me not to share."

"That's because Nia's filter is only ever so slightly better than yours," Damian pointed out. "It would take *a lot* for you to cross one of Nia's lines."

Jake seemed to consider this then nodded and turned to Cal. "It's true, I have to admit that. I'm not sure if I've ever crossed one of Nia's lines and that's saying a lot."

"I'd ask if that's saying a lot because you've never found one of her lines to cross or because you've never intentionally crossed one once you've found it, but I think I know the answer to that one," Cal said.

Jake grinned, shrugged, then took a sip of beer. "So, back to Nik's question, what brought you here? To Tildas."

"Shah," Cal answered. "She called the office early this morning and left a message saying she wanted to talk to me about Ronald Lawlor's recent visits."

"Not *that* recent if the meeting was four months ago," Beni pointed out.

Cal held her gaze as he answered, knowing that she would put two and two together in less time than it took to even say the words once he told her what he and Shah had discovered.

"She asked about his *visits*," Cal said. "According to the official records, in the past four months, Ronald Lawlor has had four meetings with me."

CHAPTER TWO

THE SHOCK of having Calvin Matthews, her childhood friend, first love, and yes, now Vice President of the United States walk into The Shack was, well, it wasn't *quite* wearing off, but his last statement had definitely distracted Beni from the weirdness.

"Four visits?" she repeated. He nodded. "I take it that none of the subsequent three actually happened?"

"You would be correct," he said, playing with the hair at the nape of her neck. She really should stop him from doing that, it was distracting. On a number of levels. After all, *she* was the one who should be trying to get back into his good graces. She was the one who'd left him without so much as a by your leave all those years ago.

But Calvin Matthews was, and had always been, an exceptional human being. Despite the fact that she *had* to have hurt him when she'd left, here he was, making his intentions toward her very clear. And overachiever that he was, not only was he putting his hurt aside and letting her know his feelings for her hadn't changed, he was also doing it at the same time he was being framed for a series of very serious crimes.

"Where are the visits logged?" Alexis asked, bringing Beni's attention back to the group. She hadn't missed the way her teammates—who were also her closest friends—had been watching her. Yeah, she was going to have a lot of explaining to do in the morning. Until Cal had walked into The Shack thirty minutes ago, she hadn't so much as hinted that she knew the man, let alone that they had, at one time, known each other *quite* well.

"Official visitor record. It's electronic," Cal answered.

"You keep a paper record of your appointments as well?" Damian asked.

"We do," Cal answered. "The meetings aren't in that book, although one of them made it onto the calendar on my computer, after the fact."

"Is the official visitor record like a sign in?" Anika asked.

"It is," Cal confirmed. "It's located at the reception and everyone visiting has to sign in and out. I can't argue that he wasn't in the building, because he did sign in. I didn't see him, though, despite the fact that he listed my office as his destination."

"You only noticed the discrepancies when Shah mentioned 'visits?'" Beni asked.

Cal nodded. "Shah isn't known for making a slip like that so, yes, when I heard the word, it definitely piqued my interest. It also made me uneasy. Uneasy enough that I decided the conversation was one she and I should have in person. It wasn't until I arrived late this afternoon that I learned of the three additional meetings and found the rogue entry on my calendar."

"I, uh, hate to ask the obvious question, but I feel like someone has to. Is there any chance you forgot you met him?" Jake asked, cringing as the words left his mouth. It *was* an obvious question, but also a fair one. Cal met dozens of people every day. Forgetting a quick fifteen-minute meeting with someone inconsequential wasn't out of the realm of possibility.

Cal chuckled and the sound rolled through her. He'd grown

as a man, of course he had. But until thirty minutes ago, it had been years since she'd seen him in any way other than on TV. And seeing him on television was a far cry from having him beside her in person. His eyes were still as blue as ever and his frame was still on the leaner side, though he'd filled out and become more solid. His voice had also deepened and gained a surety—a confidence—to it that was distracting her more than it should. And then there was the energy that had always—and apparently still—buzzed between them. All of her senses seemed heightened when he was beside her, from the light scent of his cologne that teased her nose to the heat of his fingertips against her skin.

"Fair question," Cal said. "But no. My memory is freaky good, almost eidetic." As he spoke, he ran a single finger from the base of her neck down her spine. A reminder to her of other things he remembered. A neon sign would have been more subtle, and finally, she did what she should have done several minutes ago and sat forward, severing the connection between them.

"So, someone placed the meeting on your calendar at some point after the date," Beni said. "Surely that can be traced or tracked?"

She looked at Damian as she spoke, and his gaze held hers as he slowly nodded. "I'm sure it can. Not by us, but by Naomi, Brian, and Lucy," he said.

"Lucy James?" Cal asked.

Damian drew back in surprise. "Yes," he answered, drawing the word out.

Cal grinned like the boy she'd once known. "She's amazing, isn't she? She did some work for the office right after the inauguration. Came in and set up a whole new system and security. Found a shit ton of bugs and security gaps and things that really should have been caught by the regular team. They didn't take too kindly to her pointing out the deficiencies."

Damian laughed. "I bet she didn't give two fucks what they thought."

Cal joined Damian in his laughter. "No, she did not. We've hired her a couple of times to keep an eye on our security but clearly, we need to bring her in again."

"Her husband, Brian, and her sister-in-law, Naomi are just as good. Put the three of them on the task and they'll probably have answers for us by tomorrow, day after at the latest," Damian said.

"Is that something Shah can authorize?" Cal asked. Damian nodded. "Good, you should also know whoever it was did make one mistake. The third visit in the log *looks* like a time that we could have met—I didn't have any other meetings and I was in the office that day—but I'd taken a break and gone down to the gym. I'd left my ID up in my office, so my Secret Service detail used his card to let me into the facility in the basement. Lucy and her team will see his card keying into the room about ten minutes before Lawlor's *meeting*. There aren't any security cameras in the gym itself, but all the doors have them. There will be video of me entering before Lawlor arrived and not leaving until well after he signed out."

"Which is a good sign," Beni said. Cal swung his head in her direction, and she was momentarily startled by the fact he was *here*. She blinked and, in an effort to regain some equilibrium, she picked up her drink. "If they made that mistake then it probably means that no one in your office, or at least your trusted circle, is involved. If they were, they would have known not to use that time for one of the fake meetings."

His gaze held hers and then he let out a deep breath. "I hadn't thought of it that way, and honestly, that was where my head went when I was talking with Shah. If someone wanted to schedule a fake meeting, who better positioned to do it than someone close to me? But you're right, those in my office, those in my close circle, all knew I went to the gym that day. We'd had some bad news—a record breaking violent day in Chicago—and going to the gym is sort of my way of working through things. Everyone who knows me well knows that."

Beni hadn't known that, but then again, why would she? She looked away and let her eyes settle on the darkness beyond the veranda. The moon was bright, reflecting off the sea, and a scattering of house lights could be seen twinkling through the dense foliage that hugged the hillside.

Cal must have sensed her sudden change of mood and he removed his hand from the back of her chair and picked up his beer. After taking the last sip, he glanced at the team. "So, you guys are going to take care of this?"

"Take care of what?" came Charlotte Lareaux's voice from behind them. Everyone looked toward the doorway and both Damian and Cal rose. Charlotte paused, taking in the scene, and Nia bumped into her from behind. "Cal! What are you doing here?" Charlotte asked. Beni shouldn't have been surprised that the world-renowned economist would know the vice president.

Charlotte stepped forward and behind her Nia gave a little squeak of surprise, which, in and of itself was a surprise, since Nia wasn't much of a squeaker.

"Charlotte, good to see you again," Cal said, giving her a kiss on the cheek. "I'd heard you got married and moved down here. Although why I didn't get an invite to the ceremony is something I intend to make you feel guilty about." He was clearly teasing her, and Charlotte just rolled her eyes.

"I did get married." As she spoke, she walked to Damian's side and the man wrapped his arm around her, pulling her to him as he lowered his head and kissed her. "It was a small ceremony, though. You almost made the cut, if that makes you feel any better," she said, after Damian ended the kiss.

Cal chuckled then Nia cleared her throat and they all shifted their attention back to where she stood. She was bouncing on the balls of her feet, her hands at chest height, looking like she was trying not to clap. In fact, she reminded Beni of all the old videos of the young girls at Beatles concerts who were trying to contain their adoration, but not doing a particularly good job of it.

"You must be Dr. Lewis," Cal said, holding out his hand.

Nia stared at it for a second then rushed forward. "He knows who I am," she said to no one in particular. Behind her, Beni heard Jake grumble something. "Seriously, I'm a *big* fan," Nia said, taking Cal's hand. "The work you've done on improving our environmental footprint is legendary and that Oceans Act you spearheaded last year was everything so many of us in the field needed in order to make sure our research gets heard and leveraged to protect the seas."

"The work you and your colleagues do is essential to repairing the damage—or at least some of it—that we've done over the last hundred years. We have one more bill in the works and then, if we get re-elected, a couple more lined up. Dr. Gerritson is one of my key advisors."

Nia all but swooned. "Jeanne is a goddess among scientists. You really can't go wrong listening to her."

"My thoughts exactly," Cal answered with a sincere smile.

"I'm beginning to feel a little inadequate here," Jake said, his face a picture of dramatic despondency.

Nia swung her eyes to her partner and Beni watched to see what would happen next. Jake and Nia were two of the most spontaneous and, outside of work, unpredictable people she knew. Really, Jake's comment could elicit any number of reactions from Nia.

Nia paused, then grinned. "There's nothing inadequate about you, babe." As she spoke, she walked toward Jake then launched herself into his arms. Apparently used to the move, Jake caught her with ease as her legs wrapped around his waist, and she planted several kisses on his face. "You have a good day, babe?" she asked, leaning back just enough to look Jake in the eye.

He tilted his head. "It's definitely getting better."

"It's going to get even better later. I dragged Charlotte to that oils shop, you know the one?"

Damian's eyebrows shot up and Charlotte blushed a little.

"You got more of that tingly oil?" Jake asked, his voice sounding a little strained.

Still in his arms, Nia nodded vigorously. Beni couldn't see Nia's face, but she suspected the woman was waggling her eyebrows at Jake.

"Fuck and you had to tell me *now*? We still have to eat. Actually, no, we don't need to eat, I'll call for takeout when we get home." Jake started to move away from the table, carrying Nia with him. She had other ideas, though, and unhooked her ankles and slid down his body. Jake groan. "You're going to make me wait, aren't you?"

"Delayed gratification is a sign of higher intelligence," Nia said, patting his chest before lowering herself into a seat. Jake pulled her up and over onto his lap as he retook his own. Nia glanced around, taking in the other couples—who all sat in their own chairs—then shrugged and looped an arm around Jake.

Such displays of affection weren't uncommon for the couple. They'd both grown up in pretty fucked up homes and it was a testament to their strength and character that they'd both become the people they were. It might get a little uncomfortable being around them at times, but Beni had zero interest in asking them to be anything other than who they were, since who they were, were two pretty amazing people.

"So, it looks like you all were having a pretty intense conversation when we walked in," Nia said, pointing out the obvious.

"And by the looks of it, I'd bet it's not a conversation we can join in on," Charlotte said.

Damian picked up his wife's hand as he sat back in his chair, his nearly empty pint glass hanging between the fingers of his other hand. "Let's just say that I think we," he gestured to the team with his glass, "have a lot to do tomorrow."

Charlotte glanced at Nia. As the only members of their merry band who weren't law enforcement—or a consultant, like Isiah—it was sometimes hard to keep things from the two women. Charlotte's clearance was actually higher than most of theirs, considering what she worked on for the government, but what the team was currently working on didn't meet the "need to know standard" for her, so they wouldn't share. Thankfully, both women understood the sensitivities and while it sometimes felt wrong to stop conversations when they walked in the room, neither woman seemed to mind.

"I'm sure whatever it is that brought you here, Cal, or whatever *else* brought you here," Charlotte said, her gaze flickering to Beni, "is in good hands."

Cal chuckled and draped his arm over the back of Beni's chair again. And suddenly, it was too much. All of it. The knowledge that someone really was trying to frame Cal, his presence not just on the island, but beside her, and last, but definitely not least, his physical touch.

It was all just too much.

"I'm going to head out," she said, rising. Cal jerked his arm back as her chair scraped across the floor. "As Rodriguez said, we have a lot to do tomorrow. I'm going to call it early and I'll see you all tomorrow." And what a fun tomorrow it would be. She had no doubt her team would want answers from her, and unfortunately, they knew her well enough not to be thwarted by her reluctance to share.

"You've had three rums, are you good to drive?" Cal asked.

She glanced at the three empty tumblers and damn if he wasn't right. Two drinks and she was good. She was probably fine with three, but it was pushing it and there was no cause to be stupid. Fearing Cal would offer her a ride home, she flashed a panicked look to Jake. He might have been willing to stay for dinner at Nia's request, but he'd made it clear he wouldn't mind taking Nia home and using whatever oil it was that she'd picked up. Which, as random as it was, Beni filed away as something to ask Nia about. Not that she'd be using it, she was just curious. Really.

Jake might be the most ridiculous pubescent boy in a man's body, but, as he was always telling them, he noticed things. Beni's eyes had barely landed on him, when he was rising from his seat, Nia sliding to her feet beside him.

"We'll take you home," he said. "Your place is on the way to Nia's and well, I don't think I made too big a secret of the fact that while I love you all, there are just certain things that are way more fun than sitting around drinking and eating."

Nia rolled her eyes but slipped her hand into Jake's. Beni would get a grilling from them during the ride, but she'd rather that than risk Cal offering to take her home.

"I'll ask Yael and Eric to bring your car down tomorrow," Alexis said, referring to the wife and husband team who were her head of security and her in-house chef, respectively.

Beni waved Alexis' offer off as she moved toward the bar that would lead to the exit. "I'll come up and get it tomorrow. No need to put them out."

"They're going on some sunrise run down on the other side of Havensted," Alexis said, referring to the biggest town on Tildas Island, the town where Beni lived. "It won't be a problem."

Rather than stand and argue, Beni nodded, pulled her key fob from her bag, and handed it over to Alexis. "I have an extra car key, so I can just get that one from you later. Please thank them for me," she said. Alexis nodded and set the fob on the table.

"I'll see everyone tomorrow. Cal," Beni said, facing him. She might be turning tail, but she had enough pride to not let her cowardice take over too much. "It was good to see you. For what it's worth, we'll do everything we can to sort this out. You're a good man and a good politician. I'd hate to see that taken away from you and everyone you serve."

She might have started her goodbye to him as a challenge to herself not to run away too fast, but by the time she'd finished speaking, she was speaking from the heart. He *was* a good man, and the American people were lucky to have him on their side.

And that was exactly why she'd left him all those years ago. She'd known it then, just as she knew it now—Calvin Mathews was born to be a statesman.

His eyes held hers and for a moment, she found herself lost in them. Memories of the years they'd known each other, first as friends then as more. Memories of the laughter they'd shared, of the tears they'd shed, of all the little moments that were, at the time, inconsequential, but now, sixteen years later, filtered through her mind like a home video.

Cal, who'd risen from his seat, leaned forward and brushed her cheek with his lips. "Thank you," he said. She inhaled deeply at his nearness, and instead of pulling away, he lingered. Then he drew back just far enough to look her in the eye. "I meant what I said, Benita. I'm not letting you go again."

She blinked at him as adrenaline lanced through her body. She couldn't pinpoint the source of the panic, but there were so many reasons why his words might cause that reaction that maybe she didn't need to settle on just one.

She was the first to drop her gaze and turn away. Not looking at the rest of her teammates, she glanced at Jake and Nia who were both wearing slightly worried expressions.

Beni forced a smile. "Ready?" she asked. They were standing by the door and Jake had his keys in his hand. They both nodded in answer to the stupid question.

"Great, see you all tomorrow. Except you, Cal. I'm sure we'll be in touch, but I won't see you tomorrow." She waved to everyone over her shoulder as she walked away, hoping that what she'd just said was true. Cal hadn't mentioned how long he'd be on the island, but surely he had to get back to the mainland sooner rather than later. Taking this impromptu trip to Tildas must have messed with his schedule and he'd have a lot he'd need to get back to in Washington.

The bar was eerily silent as she, Jake, and Nia left The Shack. Not even Serena popped her head out to make a snarky comment about one thing or another. Feeling more and more like a coward, which pissed her off because it was true, Beni didn't look back as she pushed through the door and stepped out into the parking lot.

Heading straight to Jake's car, she climbed into the back seat and shut the door behind her. A few seconds later, Jake and Nia joined her. Jake gave her a quick glance over his shoulder, but to her surprise, he said nothing.

And wasn't that a new kind of fresh hell. The day Jake McMullen held his tongue was one she'd never thought she'd see.

"Look, I know everyone will have a lot of questions and I'll answer them all tomorrow. For now, can you just let me be a coward, let me run away, for just a little while? I hate it, don't get me wrong. I hate that I feel this way, and," she actually cracked a smile. "let's be honest, I probably hate that I'm having *feelings* in general, let alone all the ones I'm having now. I just need some time to sort through everything. Or maybe, I don't know, just let some of the dust settle before I have the strength to bare my soul to you all. Which, let's also be honest about that —I'm not going to want to, but you all won't let me avoid it."

Jake had pulled out of the parking lot and was making his way west toward Havensted. The roads weren't the best on the island, they twisted around mountainsides, were ravaged by the weather, and rarely, if ever, were lit. But even with his attention on the road, she heard Jake let out a little snort.

"You may think you're being a coward, Beni, but you're not," he said. She nearly rolled her eyes at the placating statement... but wait, Jake didn't really do "placating." He was the man with no filter. He occasionally had tact, but no filter. Despite herself, despite being certain she'd just turned tail, she glanced at Jake's profile.

"Every now and then, we just need to take a breath and remember who we are and what we're capable of," he said. "There were times on the circuit, especially after a bad run, that I didn't get back on a board for a week." Before joining the FBI, Jake had been a professional surfer...it was definitely a weird career transition, but it had suited him. "My coach never pushed me, he never insisted I get back out there right away. One day I asked him why he let me stew, because that's what it felt like I was doing. He said that sometimes when we get hit by something unexpected, especially something threatening, whether that's a physical or a mental threat, we just need to take a breath and give ourselves a little time to adjust to that fear. Kind of like learning to live with a new roommate or something. For some people, that fear can take hold and grow, but we're not like that, Beni. None of us are. It may set us back for a moment, but if we give ourselves time to *not fight it*, if we let it settle around us, then we can start to pick apart the threads and figure out how to live with it.

"Whatever it is with Calvin Matthews that has you running, it's a big thing. You're not a runner, Beni, so if this makes you run, don't belittle it and don't add to the anxiety by berating yourself for needing a moment to catch your breath. Just let yourself feel whatever it is you're feeling, and you'll figure out how to be okay. Of course, it goes without saying that if you need help with that, we're all here for you."

Beni turned her head and stared out into the night. The street was dark but the glow of the lights of Havensted could be seen above the tree line. Sitting back and letting things settle wasn't really her style, but damn if Jake wasn't right. Maybe she just needed to let up on herself a little bit. Maybe she just needed to feel the guilt, feel the anger, feel the anxiety and let it all roll over her. Because he was also right in that she, like everyone on the team, was a survivor. She didn't wallow, she didn't play the victim, she didn't let anything beat her down. At least not for long.

She had a lifetime of evidence demonstrating to herself that she'd make it through the miasma of emotions seeing Cal again had dredged up. She needed to trust in that.

They reached the edge of town and she let out a deep breath. "I know I say this all the time so you'd think I would know better, but sometimes you really do surprise me, Jakey. You're right, I have some shit I need to sort through. I don't need to make things worse by getting my pride all mixed up in it by focusing on what a coward I feel like. I suspect it will be easier said than done, but I hear you, I just need to let that go, focus on the actual issues, and trust in myself that I'll figure this out."

Jake nodded, the light catching his profile and casting a shadow in the car. "Don't forget, you have us."

Nia twisted around in her seat and met Beni's eyes. "Yes, don't ever forget, you definitely have us."

CHAPTER THREE

BENI SAT on the couch in her living room, a glass of untasted whiskey in her hand. She'd changed into a pair of sleep shorts and a loose cotton tank top and, though the night was still warm and humid, she'd opened the sliding door to let the heavy air in. There was a time and a place for air-conditioning—and in the topics, that was most of the time—but sometimes a woman just needed a dark and sultry atmosphere.

From where she sat, she couldn't see the ocean. Hell, she could barely see the ocean when she stood on her tiptoes on her tiny balcony. But unlike Damian, who liked a more rural setting, or Jake who preferred his boat, Beni was a creature of the city. Despite its high rent and lack of view, she liked living in Havensted. She liked being able to walk places and hear the hubbub that humanity created. She liked looking out her sliding doors and staring at all the lights, reminding herself that regardless of whatever was going on with her, life still went on.

Somewhere among the lights, a family sat down for dinner. Somewhere out there, kids were complaining about doing homework. Perhaps somewhere, someone was cheating on their partner or, alternatively, celebrating an anniversary. Somewhere, someone's family member was dying and somewhere, a baby was being welcomed home for the first time.

Life just went on.

She sighed and gently swirled the liquid in her glass, the single, large ice cube clinking against the side. Cal's arrival might have sparked all sort of feelings Beni wasn't comfortable with, but there were two things she knew. First, life went on, even though, for the first time in over a decade, she felt like she was in over her head. And second, Jake was right, she needed to give herself some grace.

Finally, raising the glass, she let the drink touch her lips, then she drew in a small sip. As the liquid burned down her throat, she considered everything she'd been feeling since Cal had walked into The Shack. She'd never been great at dealing with emotions. Taking the time to understand and manage them had always seemed like a luxury she didn't have. Not when she and her mom were trying to put food on the table as she was growing up and definitely not when she was in the Army. She was a get-shit-done kind of woman and most of the time, that didn't include time, or encouragement from those around her, to examine her feelings.

But as Jake had pointed out, she had a lifetime of evidence to support the fact that she'd figure this shit out, too. Sure, it might be new territory and sure, it might not be able to be written up in an after-action report, stamped, and filed away, but she'd figure it out.

So just what was she feeling?

Guilt was the strongest emotion, which was closely followed by anger. At least she was self-aware enough, though, to know that the anger was directed at herself and more a product of the guilt than anything else. Unfortunately, the anger was what would make her defensive and she hated being on the defense. That was something she'd have to watch out for.

So back to the guilt. Maybe she should apologize for leaving

Cal all those years ago? But she wasn't really sorry she had. No, that wasn't quite right. She'd missed him horribly, especially during those first tough years in the Army. Leaving him had been the hardest thing she'd ever done—which was saying a lot —but she still couldn't bring herself to regret it. So maybe it wasn't the leaving part that made her feel guilty, but how she'd gone about it. Yeah, that felt right.

Memories of the week before she'd left filtered through her mind. She'd already signed up with the Army, she'd already known she was leaving, yet every night when she and Cal had spoken, she'd not said a word. Instead, she'd talked about her exams and about how excited her mother was for her graduation, and she'd listened as he'd talked about his lectures and a campaign he'd been getting involved with. They'd talked about family and they'd even made plans for the summer.

She winced at that particular memory. Yes, they'd even spoken about summer plans and all along, she'd known she'd never be there.

She owed him an apology for that at least. He might not accept it, and she would understand if he didn't, but she'd behaved badly and the least she could do was acknowledge and apologize for it.

She sighed in the darkness and took another sip of her drink. She was just setting the glass down on the table when someone knocked on her door. Frowning, she glanced at the clock on the wall. It wasn't that late, but she didn't usually get visitors at night unless it was her team—all of whom, except for Jake and Nia, were at The Shack. And there was no way Jake and Nia were anywhere other than at Nia's place making use of that oil.

The knock came again and with an annoyed huff, Beni rose from her seat and made her way down the short hall to the door. Peeking through the peephole, she let her forehead fall against its surface.

"I can hear you in there, Nita," Cal said, using the name he'd used all those years ago. Usually it was Benita, or occasionally Beni, but when it was just the two of them, he'd always called her Nita.

Turning the deadbolt and releasing the chain, she swung the door open. Cal strode into her small apartment and she stuck her head out the door after he'd passed.

"Where's your Secret—" She never got to finish her question, because Cal spun her around, managing to get the door shut and her pressed against the wall, before his lips descended on hers. In a flash, everything but the feel of him was forgotten. Gone was her guilt, gone was her anger, and gone was the panic she'd felt at seeing him again. Because yes, panic was one more emotion she'd felt. What did he want with her? What did she want with him?

None of that mattered as they stood in the hall kissing each other like they wanted nothing more than to be a part of the other.

Despite the heat between them, though, neither took it further. There were no wandering hands and no trailing kisses. No, as their lips, and bodies, reacquainted themselves with each other, his hands remained cupping her face while hers stayed loosely resting at his waist.

Finally, Cal pulled back and rested his forehead against hers. She dropped her gaze and stared at the column of his neck as she caught her breath. Despite how good it felt, how *right* it felt, to be with him, not much had changed in the past sixteen years. She wasn't that same young woman, and he wasn't the same young man. She was an FBI agent, and he was the Vice President of the United States—that combination was not a couple in the making.

Not to mention the fact that he might not even want that. Or, for that matter, she might not, either. The kisses definitely confused things, though.

"You have to stop doing that," Beni said, her voice quiet in the still darkened apartment.

"What, kissing you?" Cal asked, using one of his fingers to tip her head up.

She met his gaze then nodded.

The left side of his mouth tipped into a hint of a grin. He stepped back then walked toward the main part of her apartment. "That is *not* a promise I'm even going to consider, let alone make," he said over his shoulder as he entered the living room.

She frowned at his words, unsure how she felt about them. She *should* be irritated at his dismissal of her demand, but she was honest enough with herself to acknowledge that there hadn't been much conviction in it. So how *did* she feel about his statement? Standing there watching him, curiosity was the emotion she identified most quickly. What did he mean by his answer?

She wasn't about to sound like an insecure teen and ask him, though, so she did the next best thing and changed the subject.

"What are you doing here?" she asked, joining him.

He stared out her sliding doors, then spun slowly and faced her. "I'm staying here tonight."

She might have dropped into one of her upholstered chairs at his proclamation, but her heart rate spiked up so fast she could hear the blood pounding through her system.

"Uh, no, you're not. Don't you have somewhere to be tomorrow?" she managed to ask.

He grinned again and damn if Anika wasn't right about that smile because she felt herself wavering.

Thankfully, he pulled his attention from her and moved toward the couch. Taking the same seat she'd been in before his arrival, he leaned over and picked up her still mostly full glass.

"Ardbeg?" he asked after smelling it. She nodded and he took a sip. "I do have somewhere I need to be tomorrow," he answered. "My meetings start at ten and my flight from here will leave at six. We have," he glanced at the clock, "ten hours, Nita. Whatever shall we do?"

Now he was just taunting her. With something she wanted, sure, and yes, she was woman enough to admit that a roll in the sack with Cal was something she wanted. But just because she wanted it, didn't mean it would, or should, happen.

"You're not staying here," she repeated. He didn't quite lift a shoulder, but it was close. She narrowed her eyes at his refusal to argue. "It's not secure here. Surely your security detail is aware of that."

He took another sip of her drink. She should take umbrage with his consumption of her alcohol, but she'd had three rums at The Shack. Pouring herself the whiskey had really been more about the ritual of holding it as the night progressed than actually drinking it, so she said nothing.

"The thing about security is that it's most important when my presence is known. No one knows I'm here so there's really not much of a security risk," he said.

She didn't like the sound of that. "Your security knows you're here, though, right?" she asked. She may not want responsibility for him for the night, but she sure as hell didn't want him unprotected. In the four seconds it took him to answer her, about a dozen different worst-case scenarios rolled through her mind.

"They know," he answered. "They are around. Trying to be as inconspicuous as they can, but they are around."

Beni let out a quiet breath. At least that was one thing she didn't need to think about. Now she could focus on the issue at hand. "Why do you think you're staying here?"

He flashed her a smile. "Because this is where I told my security detail I was staying the night and they've made all their arrangements based on that."

She didn't bother to stop the curse that flew from her

mouth. He had her between a rock and a hard place, and he knew her well enough to know which decision she'd make—the one that respected the job the men and women of his detail were tasked to do. There was no way she would ask his team to scramble to make alternative plans just because having Cal in her space was uncomfortable for her personally.

She let out a loud huff. "Fine, you can stay. Just this once," she added. She had no idea if he was ever planning to visit the island again, but she wanted to add that last bit for good measure. "I actually just changed the sheets this morning, you can take the bed."

"I'm sleeping where you're sleeping, Nita," he shot back.

At the serious tone in his statement, her gaze jerked back to him. She studied his expression, trying to get a read on the real reason he was in her apartment. Because despite their still-existent chemistry, *she* knew Cal well enough to know that he wouldn't expect them to have sex within hours of meeting for the first time in sixteen years.

And she couldn't imagine just spending the night cuddling. She'd never been much of a cuddler anyway and she certainly wasn't going to cuddle with a man she hadn't seen since she was twenty-two.

"No," she said. "You're sleeping in my bed and I'll sleep on the couch."

He finished the whiskey and set the glass down. "If you sleep on the couch, I'm going to sleep on the floor next to you. I told you, I'm not letting you go again."

She held in an exasperated growl. "Do you even hear yourself, Cal? First, you can't come waltzing back into my life after sixteen years and expect to get what you want—whatever that is. Second, 'you're not letting me go'? That makes no sense since you just told me that you're leaving tomorrow. I can't—and won't—go with you, so by default, you will have to let me go tomorrow."

"I'm only 'waltzing back into your life' because you waltzed right out of it," he snapped back. "Well, 'waltzed right out' isn't really the right term since that implies dancing which usually takes two people," he continued. "You made the decision to leave on your own. Did you even tell your mother before you signed onto the Army?"

She blinked at his logic—or lack thereof. Waltzing in and out of someone's life was a turn of a phrase that had nothing to do with dancing, but she stopped herself from pointing that out. Snapping her mouth shut, she forced herself to take a deep breath. Guilt-fueled-defensiveness was hovering on her tongue and she needed to stuff it back down, because he had every right to be angry at her.

She took two more deep breaths then answered. "Cal, I'm truly sorry for how I left you. I really am. I don't expect you to forgive me and maybe you won't even believe me, but I am sorry."

His eyes held hers and the hurt she'd caused flashed in them, bringing back all her own pain from that time. Just because she'd been the one to leave didn't mean that it had been easy.

"Then why did you do it?" he asked, his voice quiet in the heavy night air.

"I left because we both had things we needed to do with our lives that we couldn't do if we were together." She paused, hesitating. Within the question he'd asked, there was another question. She needed to answer it, but it wasn't going to be easy. The truth often wasn't. "I didn't tell you I was leaving because I was a coward," she said softly. "I'm not proud of that, but it's the truth. It would have taken more strength than I had to tell you what I was going to do and why than it took to just leave."

His gaze never wavered from hers, but he gave no indication of what he thought of her confession. Finally, he spoke. "You said there were things we *needed* to do with our lives. What about what we *wanted* to do?"

His words lanced through her like a spear. There was so much they had *wanted* to do. They had wanted to travel and see the world. They had wanted to spend the rest of their lives together, maybe even raise a family. Perhaps those dreams were just those of young lovers, but they had been real. And she'd taken them all away when she'd left.

"We don't always get what we want," she answered, and although she tried to keep her voice steady, even she could hear the touch of sorrow in her response.

"Yeah," he said. "I learned that lesson pretty clearly sixteen years ago."

She deserved that, although she'd only let it slide once. Like she'd told him, she didn't expect his forgiveness, but neither did she need to suffer his disdain. Not that that was exactly what she heard in his voice, but he was definitely still harboring resentment. She didn't—wouldn't—blame him, but if he couldn't let it go, there was no reason either of them needed to be around the other and the constant reminder of what had once been.

"I don't want to create work for your team, but maybe you should stay somewhere else," she suggested softly.

Cal leaned back against the cushions and looked out the sliding doors, still open to the lights and sounds of Havensted. They sat that way—with her watching him and him watching the night—for nearly five minutes. Then finally, he turned to face her again.

"I'm not going to lie and tell you I forgive you or that I'm over what happened. I want to get there, though. Because I also wasn't lying when I told you I don't want to let you go again. I clearly have things I need to work through, but I'm not willing to let them get in the way of being with you again. It feels too right, Nita, and you know it. What's between us is real. It always has been. I guess the question we need to answer is whether it's worth fighting for this time."

Instinct had her opening her mouth to point out all the ways they'd *never* work. There was too much water under the bridge. His position made it difficult for him to have *any* relationships. Her position would be significantly jeopardized if she started dating Cal—the FBI preferred their agents to keep a low profile and dating the vice president was just about as *not* low profile as a person could get.

But Cal cut her off by rising from his seat and pulling out his phone. "I think that's enough for now. I'm hungry," he said. "What can we have delivered?"

CHAPTER FOUR

BENI WALKED into the office at eight the next morning to find the rest of the team in the middle of various activities. As one, though, they all looked her way.

Jake, who sat at his desk, a piece of paper in hand, flashed her a knowing smile and in his best Desi Arnaz impression said, "Beni, you have some 'splainin' to do."

There were mumbles of assent from the rest of the team, but to her surprise, it was Shah who came to the rescue. Well, not exactly rescue, but she gave Beni an out that Beni was all too quick to take her up on.

"Now that you're all here," Shah said, coming out of her office. "I think we have some things to discuss." Without another word, she walked to the larger of the conference rooms.

Beni quickly dropped her bag at her desk and grabbed a pad of paper as everyone followed Shah. As the last one in, she shut the door behind her then took a seat beside Alexis.

"I assume that Calvin Matthews found you all last night and updated you on the conversation he and I had?" Shah asked.

Beni nearly rolled her eyes when everyone, except Shah, looked to her to answer. "Seriously, guys, is this how it's going to be?" she muttered, before looking up at Shah. "Yes, he did find us and yes, we're up to date," she answered. "And you all need to grow up," she added, swinging her fingers between her teammates.

Shah didn't respond to that although Beni would swear there was a twinkle in her eye. "Rodriguez," Shah said, turning her attention to the agent. "I'm authorizing you to bring the DeMarco twins and Lucy James on board to help sort through what was, essentially, a hack into the vice president's computer and, likely, his broader network. Actually, start with Ms. James as she is already familiar with the system."

Damian nodded.

"We're going to double down on Calloway, now," Shah said. "You all have been itching to do this since we connected him to the sale of Serena's identity last summer, but I held you back because I wanted to better understand his reach before we made any moves. Through our own investigations, we know he has connections to the Democratic Party leadership, the CIA, and the mafia. Now, thanks to the information Vice President Matthews provided, I think it's safe to say that whatever Calloway is involved in, Ronald Lawlor is, too, so Calloway also has the FBI."

"If we're playing things safe," Beni interjected, "given who we know he's connected to, and the fact that Cal's network was breached, I think we should also assume Calloway has ins at every alphabet agency there is and access to some pretty heavy hitting hackers, too." Beni hoped no one noticed her familiar use of Cal's name, which had just slipped out. He'd only ever been "Cal" to her, or, in some moments, Calvin. When she looked across the table, though, and saw Damian's raised eyebrow and Dominic trying to suppress a grin, she knew her hope was in vain.

Ignoring her agent's antics, Shah nodded. "I agree with you, Beni. In addition, I think we all agree that Calloway isn't capable of being the mastermind behind all this. He's the lynchpin here and he's who can lead us to whoever is behind this, but Calloway isn't the one pulling the strings."

As one, the team nodded.

"I'll let you decide how to run with the investigation, but we want all the usuals—deep electronic survey, finances, travel, you name it, we want it," Shah continued. "Once we have the data, even if we don't find anything *in* it, we can work with Ms. James and the DeMarcos to look at it as an aggregate and see if it tells us anything."

"Director Shah?" Anika interjected. Shah nodded for her to continue. "I know we think something big is being planned that is tied to The Summit, but one of the questions that always bothered me about the recent murders was why did the perpetrators pick this island to commit their crimes on? Sure, The Summit is happening here, but that's not until next month. If the sole purpose of this series of crimes is to implicate the vice president, then none of those crimes actually *needed* to happen here, and yet they did. I'll be honest, I'm not even sure I'll know where to start, but I'd like permission to examine that line of inquiry."

The Summit of World Leaders was the original driver behind the task force. Seventeen months ago, Director Shah had brought the five agents together to prepare both the island and Hemmeleigh, the resort that would host the event, for the arrival of 150 leaders from around the world. That task alone was a significant undertaking. The conspiracy they were now working to unravel was just a little bonus they'd uncovered along the way.

Shah studied Anika, and as she did, Beni did, too. The question of "why Tildas" *had* come up in the last few weeks as they'd investigated the murders. The three men had been sent to the island under various pretenses, but in reality, they'd been brought here to be killed by a hitman hired by Calloway. They now knew, from the hitman himself, that Calloway had wanted the murders to take place in proximity to each other so that the connection to The Bank of DC would be discovered. Had all the men been killed in their respective cities—LA, New York, and DC—that connection wouldn't have been made. But nothing in the investigation had revealed the answer to the very question Anika now asked—*why* Tildas. Why not New Orleans or Austin or any other place?

After a beat, Shah nodded. "It's probably going to be a convoluted path, but it's a good one to follow. Why don't you and Dominic work on that one together." It wasn't a question, but both Anika and Dominic nodded.

"All right, everyone, you know what we need to do. As Detective Anderson pointed out, we can all agree that The Summit plays some part in this and that's less than six weeks away. We still need to uncover significant intel, but after last night, we have a better picture of the scope of the conspiracy, and I think you'll find we have more than we think we do."

Beni wasn't so sure about that, but she trusted Director Shah, so said nothing as the woman left the room, leaving Beni sitting with her teammates to come up with a battle plan. Although, judging by the way they were all looking at her, they were far more interested in hearing her explain just how she knew Calvin Matthews.

After Shah shut the door behind her, Dominic cleared his throat. "Well, let's see, Damian's best friends with the best super hackers in the world, Alexis was kidnapped as a child, Jake has ties to the mafia, Anika has an entire newly discovered family, and you, apparently know the vice president well enough to play tonsil hockey with him in public. I think I'm the only one with no secrets."

Alexis raised an eyebrow at him. "You had a life changing event four months ago when you thought your mom was dying that you didn't share with any of us until this week. I don't think you're *exactly* without secrets."

"She has a point, babe," Anika said.

Dominic mock glared at Anika. "I think the point is, while Jake's secret was rather interesting and Alexis' was horrifying, I think this one might take the cake since it actually has to do with one of *us*. Not something done to us by someone else or who our friends or families are. So, Benita, you know none of us are going anywhere until you spill."

Five sets of eyes zeroed in on her. She knew they'd demand this, and even though she wasn't looking forward to opening up this particular vein, if she was going to do it, it would only be with these people.

"We grew up together," she started. "My mom was the housekeeper for his mom. We were always friends. When I turned eighteen, it grew into something more. He was off at college already, but when he wasn't, we spent just about every waking hour together. And yes, Jake, because I know you'll want to know, it was love. We loved each other with everything we had as young adults."

She expected to see shock on the faces of at least a few of her teammates when she started to openly talk about love. She wasn't the most touchy-feely person, even on the best of days, but to her surprise, no one seemed surprised.

"I went to a local commuter college and while there, it became clearer and clearer to me that Cal was meant for bigger things than an early marriage and whatever else might come our way. He was already deeply involved in politics and so fucking smart and amazing with people. I started to feel like if we let the relationship progress, it might be amazing for *us*, but it wouldn't be great for him.

"Then once I started thinking about *that*, I started to think about my own life. Sure, I was getting an education, but I didn't know what I wanted to do with myself. Yes, I loved Cal, but did

I just want to settle down—because that's where we were headed—and not have a chance to even discover who I was? So there I was, twenty-two years old, in a relationship with a man who was the love of my life, slowly realizing that we both had a lot of growing up to do. Over time, I grew to know, with everything inside of me, that if we wanted to be the people we were meant to be, the people we each *wanted* to be, we needed to stand on our own. At least for a little while."

"Then 'a little while' turned into a few years, and so on," Alexis said, her voice soft and without judgment.

Beni nodded. "I'm not proud of how I ended things with him, but the lives we've led only reinforce that I made the right decision. I'm proud of what I've done and what I've accomplished in life. I do work that I love and with people I both like and respect and it's work that *matters*. In a very different way, Cal does, too." She paused and took a deep breath. Strange how that hadn't been as difficult as she thought it might be. Perhaps Damian-the-sharer, Jake-the-one-to-never-hide-a-feeling, and Alexis-the-shrink had rubbed off on her. That thought made her smile, mostly because it left Dominic out and he'd be annoyed to high heaven if he knew. Then again, Dominic was as steady as a rock—yes, he had a wicked sense of humor and adventure, but he was as rock solid as they came and was the one the team, often unwittingly, looked to to ground them.

"So what now? 'Cause I gotta tell you, that declaration he made was *hot*," Anika said. Dominic slid her a look, his eyes narrowed. She grinned back at him. "I'm not retracting that statement, no matter how much you glare at me."

Dominic shook his head then switched his attention back to Beni. "I know we're all on board with him being in the clear, but he's still the vice president and you're still an FBI agent working a case that involves him. I take umbrage at Anika's description of his statement, but I will agree that he did not sound like a man that was willing to walk away from you. So, what *are* you going to do?"

Beni looked out the window to avoid the question. Not because it was a surprise. Honestly, she'd thought of little else since Cal had climbed out of bed at five that morning and left her apartment. And yes, he had won the stupid argument about the sleeping arrangements, but only because he'd cheated. He'd gone to sleep in her bed, but sometime in the middle of the night, he'd come in, scooped her up off the couch, and brought her back to her bed with him. It said more than she cared to admit that his actions hadn't woken her. That, along with the fact that when his alarm had gone off, she'd been draped over half his body, were two things she didn't want to think about.

Thankfully, Alexis stepped in to save her—which again, spoke volumes about Beni's state of mind since never before had anyone felt the need to save her. "That's probably a question for another day," Alexis said. "We have a few things we need to sort out and quickly. As Shah pointed out, The Summit is less than six weeks away and if this conspiracy is as deep and as wide as we think it is, we're going to need every one of those days to figure it out."

"And stop it," Jake said then grinned at Beni. "I mean, I know we all want to stop it and prevent the downfall of our political systems and the demonization of a good man. But really, I want to stop it because I want to see what happens with Beni and Cal. I'm going to bring popcorn."

Beni rolled her eyes. "We are not a soap opera."

Jake's eyes widened. "Oh my god, that would be awesome. Was there a secret baby? Please tell me there's a secret baby somewhere. Or maybe you got brought back from dead some time when you were deployed?"

"You really can be an asshole, can't you?" Anika said as she rose from her seat. She shook her head but the smile on her face gave away her true feelings.

"I told you, but you didn't listen to me," Dominic muttered, rising and following Anika out.

"Life's more fun when I don't listen to you, Dom." Anika's words faded as the pair walked away, leaving Beni in the room with Jake, Damian, and Alexis.

"Can we just not go there?" Beni asked. Her gaze slid over her three colleagues. Alexis and Damian would respect her wishes; Jake was the unknown.

Jake looked at her then shrugged. "I don't know what you're talking about. Go where?" he said, then he rose and left the room, too.

"Is it just me or is he getting weirder and weirder?" Beni asked as she watched Jake take a seat at his desk.

"No, it's you," Damian said. Beni looked back just in time to see Alexis nodding. "He's Jake," Damian continued. "He's special. He's just never turned his special brand of special—the one that comes out when love is in the air—on you."

"Truth," Alexis agreed.

"So, I have that to look forward to until this is all over?" Beni asked, pointing to Jake through the open door.

Damian paused at the end of the table and chuckled. "Your options are to either put up with Jake or hook up with Cal. I think he'd prefer the latter, because he thinks it will make you happy, but he'd be okay with the former, too."

Alexis laughed as well. "The good news is, we only have six weeks to go."

Beni's friends left the room with those words hanging in the air. Six weeks. Six weeks of dealing with both Jake and Cal. Because yes, she agreed that Cal wasn't about to let bygones be bygones.

She closed her eyes and let her head fall to the table. It was going to be a long-ass six weeks.

CHAPTER FIVE

LATER THAT AFTERNOON, Beni was sitting at her desk, staring at her computer screen, when her phone dinged with a notification of a message from a service that wasn't one of her usual ones. Picking up the device, it took her a moment to find the icon for the app that had alerted—a texting app that time bound all messages so that they'd disappear within a certain time frame after having been read. It was the modern day—accessible to everyone—version of "this message will self-destruct."

Opening the app, a number she didn't recognize popped up, but it was associated with a name she knew well. Clicking on the message, it opened on her screen. *"Made it to my meetings, though I was sorely tempted to cancel and stay this morning. I'm not exaggerating, if you hadn't kicked me out, I would have. I'll be back next weekend. Before you say anything, you can't stop me. You can refuse to see me, but I'm coming in the hopes of convincing you otherwise."*

Beni bit back a growl of frustration. She had too much to do to deal with Cal on top of everything else. Curiosity got the better of her, though, and she pulled up a browser and queried the vice president's schedule. She *had* kicked him out that morning, but what had he been so willing to give up for just a few more hours with her?

She sucked in a quick breath when she saw who his meetings had been with, and then she laughed, drawing the attention of her team. She waved them off and returned to the article. Cal's morning meeting had been with the king of a European nation that was leading the charge on renewable energy. The king, who was probably a decent human being, was naught but a figurehead, which explained why Cal would have considered blowing him off. Had it been the politicians who drove the renewable energy strategy, or the scientists themselves, well, that would have been a different story.

"It's nice to know I rank above a king, but you can't come down here."

"You rank above everything."

That wasn't true, but she wouldn't call him on it. He could live in his little fantasy that they were magically going to start being a couple because he wanted it that way, but she knew better.

"Back to the main point. You can't come down here. Regardless of what I think or feel, whoever is behind this will start getting suspicious if suddenly you're flying down here every other week."

The messages were disappearing as soon as they were read or sent. It was weird to be staring at a blank screen, but there was no way Cal would drop the conversation and just agree to her logic.

"Have more faith in us than you did back then."

Oh, that was low. *"You are not persuading me."*

She could almost hear him chuckle. *"Fine then, practically speaking, it's easy for me to travel without everyone knowing where I am. Believe it or not, I do it all the time. Well, maybe not all the time, but I've done it several times. My team blocks my calendar, tells the press I'm having some time with my family, my mom and sister play along and lay low, and I go do what I want or need to do."*

There was so much in that message that Beni wanted to unpack. Not the least of which was to ask if he'd done this with other women before, but asking that was definitely beneath her. So, she went with the obvious.

"Not to encourage you in this delusion, but the flight?"

A few seconds passed before the little bubbles indicated he was responding. *"I have friends that can fly me when needed without all the hoopla. I still bring my detail, a smaller version of it, but I'm never completely alone."*

She chuckled at his use of the word hoopla then paused over the last sentence. What would it be like to never be alone? Sure, he was probably alone in his office or his bedroom, or at times like that. But she doubted he was ever truly *alone*. And that sounded, well, it actually sounded kind of isolating and lonely. It might be one thing if he had a family or something, but that wasn't the case.

She sighed, not wanting to feel anything *more* for Cal than she did. She might empathize with his situation, but that didn't change her position.

"I'm glad you have it all figured out, but you still can't come down here. In case you've forgotten, we're in the middle of a massive investigation into a conspiracy to topple the current administration AND we're simultaneously preparing to host 150 world leaders on this small island for a week. Even if I believed you could get down here without anyone knowing, I don't have time for anything other than work."

"Running again, Nita?"

"And that is one of the reasons why I don't have time for you, Cal. I apologized. I was wrong to have left you in the way I did. I'm not interested in having it thrown back in my face every time I tell you something you don't want to hear."

Her phone was silent for so long that she started to think he might be done with the conversation. If so, she didn't like how it had ended, but at least she had a lot of work to do and she could funnel her annoyance into something productive.

She was just about to set the phone down when it rang. The number was a different one than the one she'd been texting with, but she knew who'd be on the other side. Hitting the answer button as she rose from her seat, she put the phone to her ear.

"Yes?"

"Fuck, I'm sorry, Nita. You're right. I shouldn't have said that," Cal said as she walked to a small conference room and shut the door, giving herself some privacy.

"You won't get any argument from me on that."

"I know you're busy and I appreciate everything you and the team are doing to identify who's involved and clean up the mess they've created. All that doesn't change the fact that I want to see you. And before you say it, I know we don't always get what we want, but we're adults now, Benita, this is something we can make happen if we want to. The question is, do you *want* to make it happen?"

And wasn't that the question. What she wanted was complicated and unrealistic. She was woman enough to admit that the attraction between her and Cal, both physical and emotional, was still there. They might not know each other in the same way as they had—they might not have any clue as to the other's daily life or what their current favorite restaurant was or what they did last Christmas—but they still *knew* each other in a way that was both comforting and tempting.

But any relationship they might have would never be about just the two of them. Given both his job and hers, that fantasy was impossible. If she were being honest with herself, which she often wasn't when it came to matters of the heart, she wanted Cal, but she didn't want all the baggage that went with being with him. Which wasn't fair to either of them.

"Cal—"

A knock stopped her, and she spun around to find Damian cracking the door open. A second later, his head appeared.

"Sorry to interrupt," he said. "I'm just about to call Lucy and Brian and thought you might want to join?"

She'd been about to tell Cal not to come. It wasn't an answer to his question, but she wasn't ready to tell him what she'd only just now realized. The message was harsh and, though she knew it to be true, she found she wasn't ready to say it out loud. Maybe because some things could never be taken back. Damian's interruption gave her just the excuse she needed. And no, it did not escape her notice that once again, she wasn't exactly being brave.

She nodded at Damian and held up a finger, asking for just one minute. He nodded in response and backed out of the room, closing the door behind him.

"I have to go, Cal. We're bringing in Lucy James and Brian DeMarco to help with the technology piece and we're just about to get on a call with them."

"You didn't answer my question," Cal pointed out. She hesitated and, in that pause, he continued. "Don't answer now, then," he said. "I can wait for that, but I'm not going to wait to see you again."

"Cal," she warned. She might be a little worried about her ability to cope with having him in her space. What she was *really* worried about, though, was drawing any attention to what she and the team were investigating, which his presence on the island would most definitely do.

He let out a huff. "How about I ask Shah? If she thinks my traveling to the island will compromise your investigation, then I won't come. She's kind of a neutral third-party, don't you think? She'll be able to make the call without all the emotional baggage we're both carrying."

The way he so easily tossed out a reference to their collective emotional baggage made her a little uneasy, but he was right about Shah. Beni had her own ideas about Cal's travel but could acknowledge those were definitely clouded by self-preservation. She was a little concerned Shah would say it was fine, but she couldn't argue with Cal's reasoning without sounding petulant.

She let out her own huff, barely keeping her frustration in check. "Fine, talk to her. In the meantime, you have a job to do and so do I, so do *not* do anything that gets in the way of either of us doing what we need to."

Cal's deep chuckle rolled through her. "I think we both know what we both need, Nita. Last night was too soon, but tomorrow is another day."

She'd be lying if she said her body didn't respond to his comment. Thankfully, she was old enough now not to be (completely) governed by her hormones. "Goodbye, Cal. Go save the country or something."

His chuckle transformed into a laugh. "Bye, Nita. I'll call you soon." And with that, he hung up before she could tell him not to. Not that he would have listened.

"Everything okay?" Damian asked when she joined him in another small conference room.

Beni nodded and took a seat. Damian didn't look like he believed her, but he let the subject drop. Hitting the button on the phone and bringing it to life, he then punched in a phone number.

A man answered on the second ring. "Rodriguez, what's up?"

"Hey, Brian, thanks for talking today. This time still good?"

"Yeah, we're at Naomi and Jay's since Naomi got wind that something was going on and even if she can't do much—"

"I can, too," Naomi interrupted. What followed sounded like the rustling of a phone, the squeak of a baby, and some conversation between the twins that Beni couldn't catch. She knew Naomi DeMarco had just had her own set of twins, two girls, with her husband, the retired All-Star pitcher for the New England Rebels. But from the sound of it, Naomi and her own twin seemed to be not much more mature than babies.

"Put that phone on speaker," Naomi demanded. "You know what I'm capable of if you don't."

"With at least one kid attached to your boob at all times, it will be months before you can sneak up on me like you did last time," her brother shot back, clearly enjoying taunting his sister. Silently, Beni thought it probably wasn't a good idea to taunt a woman who was running short on sleep and high on post-pregnancy hormones and who had the skills Naomi DeMarco did, but she also thought that the DeMarco twins had a lifetime of figuring each other out.

"Children," came a new voice.

"Ah, the voice of reason," Damian said.

"Hey, Damian," Lucy James said. "Don't mind the brats and I don't mean the six-week-old ones. They are adorable."

"You're the one we really want to talk to anyway, Lucy," Damian said.

"These days, I don't blame you. Naomi and Jay are in that weird state of exhausted manic happiness and Brian is worried they aren't taking care of themselves so is picking at his sister like a little kid who is unable to deal with his emotions."

Damian laughed then grew serious. "Lucy, Beni Ricci is with me. I know you two met at the wedding. We'd like to talk to you about Cal Matthews."

"Nice to hear from you again, Beni. Hold on," Lucy said. In the background Beni heard Lucy say something to the DeMarco twins but it was muffled. Whatever it was, it must have brought some order to the chaos, because when she rejoined the call, the bickering seemed to have stopped.

"Okay, you're on speaker now and it's me, Brian, and Naomi who is holding Rowan, but since Rowan can't talk, I think we're okay discussing security issues. Jay and Niamh are napping," Lucy said, referring to Naomi's husband and other daughter. "What's up?"

Damian took a few minutes to fill the three tech geniuses in on the conversations from the past twenty-four hours, including the role they thought Calloway was playing. When he was done, silence greeted them. For about two seconds.

"I told Cal he needed to stay on top of the security," Lucy groused. "Why do they never listen to us?" Beni didn't know who that question was directed to, but Brian answered.

"Because they forget that computers aren't like books that are static things. It's also the government. They have zero appreciation for the speed at which the rest of the world, especially the tech world, moves."

Lucy grumbled something, but Beni couldn't catch it.

"So, you want us to track down who placed the faux appointment into Cal's calendar?" Naomi asked.

"If you can, yes," Beni answered.

"I know the system at Cal's office well, I can take that piece," Lucy said.

"You didn't ask, but Naomi and I can look into Calloway himself," Brian said. "And just to be clear, I think Naomi should be resting and trying to enjoy these early days with the girls. I know she won't, though, so I'd like to note that I am accepting her participation against my will but with grace."

"Gee, you're so gracious," Naomi drawled. "And just to be clear, I *am* enjoying these days and I'm not as tired as you seem to think I am. Between our parents, Jay's mom and sister, and the thousand cousins we have, I'm getting plenty of rest."

"Before we travel down that road for the hundredth time," Lucy interjected. "Let's all just agree on a plan. The hack into the system is the priority. If they know how to get in, who knows what else they might have gotten into. We need to both track the hack and shut it down. Calloway is important, but let's tackle him once we're sure the vice president's system is secure."

"We weren't going to ask you to help with Calloway," Damian said. "We're authorized to bring you on to help, but thought it might be better for us to do some leg work first so as not to waste your time."

"*Pfft*," Naomi said.

"I'm the one who offered, so I obviously agree with Nano," Brian said, referring to his sister by a nickname Beni had heard before.

"Me, three," Lucy chimed in. "It's going to be way easier to just hand that over to us. In addition to this investigation, you all still have The Summit to prepare for. There's no need for you to work yourselves through all hours of the day when you have us."

Beni looked at Damian. His lips were pressed together and there were two lines between his lowered brows. He was conflicted and she understood why.

"It doesn't feel right to dump this on you all. It's our investigation and we can't just turn it over. I mean, we could, but we don't want to," Beni said.

After a beat, Lucy spoke. "I get it. Why don't we take Calloway's phone records and you guys take everything else, from credit cards to travel and the deep background. We can probably do a deeper background check than you can, but let's start with what you guys find. That should give us a good direction so that the three of us can cast a deeper line rather than a wider net when needed."

Beni looked at Damian again and he raised a brow in question. She nodded.

"That sounds like a good plan, Luce. Thanks," he said.

"Any time," Lucy answered. "Maybe we'll even come down and see you all. Damian and Charlotte's wedding was a blast, but we didn't get to spend as much time in the area as we would have liked."

Beni smiled at Lucy's sudden excitement over the idea. It might start to get a little crowded in the office if they both showed up, but Beni wouldn't mind seeing them again.

"Yeah, aside from the human trafficking, designer drug dealers, and hitmen, it's fabulous. Really special," Beni said.

Lucy snorted a laugh. "We're hackers," she said. "You can't imagine the things we consider fun."

Beni laughed at that, then, after goodbyes all around, Damian ended the call.

"You think they'll come?" Beni asked.

Damian let out a long exhale and shook his head. "Honestly, when it comes to the three of them, you really never know."

CHAPTER SIX

"WE NEED to get close to him somehow, but the problem is, he knows all of us," Alexis said to the room. It was late afternoon, five days after Cal had left, and the team, along with Shah were in a conference room discussing their lack of progress. The deep background they'd run on Calloway had revealed nothing, his credit card and travel information showed he traveled a lot, but they couldn't link his travel to anything nefarious. Even Lucy and Brian had been unable to find anything interesting in his phone records.

The only good piece of intel they had was that Lucy and Brian had a lead on the hacker who'd inserted the faux appointment into Cal's calendar. It had taken longer than both experts had anticipated, but once they'd gone into the system, they'd found so many security gaps that they'd had to spend time closing them to ensure there was no more unauthorized access. Through this process, less than twenty-four hours ago, they'd located the gap the calendar-hacker had used. They were now actively tracking the hacker's footprint in the hopes of finding where it came from and who instigated it.

Now, because of the team's overall lack of progress on gathering useful intel, they were discussing other options. Unfortunately, there weren't a lot.

"Any chance Calloway doesn't know who we are?" Jake asked in response to Alexis' comment, though his tone of voice said he knew the answer.

"I think we're safe making the assumption he does," Shah said. "He might not have met any of you personally, but it would be basic due diligence to know who was tasked with managing security at The Summit when planning to do something potentially illegal at said Summit."

"That and the fact that we've actively investigated three of the conspiracy's criminal activities that he's spearheaded," Beni added.

"So, that rules out any undercover work unless there's someone we can pull out of the woodwork?" Damian asked as he glanced around the table. Shah had once told them all that she'd essentially picked them for the task force because none of them were considered team players. It was useful for her purposes because she wanted agents who wouldn't be talking shop with colleagues in other offices. The downside was that none of them had anyone else they could call on that they trusted enough to help them out.

A round of headshakes confirmed what Beni already knew, no, they didn't have anyone else. She looked at Shah, hoping their director would have a suggestion, only to find her staring out the window.

After a beat, Shah turned back to the team. "I might know of someone who can help. With Ronald Lawlor involved, I think we can all agree that calling on someone within the FBI that isn't on this team, isn't an option. I have a contact that I'll reach out to. There's a woman on his team who, if we can get her on board, will do nicely. Now, what else?"

"If Calloway isn't using his phone to make the plans he's

making, he must be using burners. Is there anything in his credit card statements to support that?" Dominic asked.

Beni shook her head. "Not in the statements, but every Friday he withdraws three thousand dollars in cash. That's plenty of money to buy burner phones."

"Or pay for hotels if he's traveling and wants to stay under the radar," Anika said.

"Any chance his car has a GPS that we can ask Lucy to hack into?" Alexis asked.

"He has two. One has it, but the other is an old school Suburban, made before the advent of GPS. That said, when he flies, he rents cars that probably have them. Can we ask Lucy about that?" Beni asked Damian.

He nodded. "If we get her the information on the car rental companies and dates, I'm sure she'd be happy to look into it."

Shah drummed her fingers on the table then looked at the team. "I'll reach out to my contact to see if we can manage to get someone *physically* close to Calloway, and while we continue to research on our end, Ms. James and Mr. DeMarco can follow up on the calendar hacker and, assuming they agree, the GPS of Calloway's car rentals. There are a lot of open questions, but what about the Tildas Island angle you two were looking into?" she asked, directing her question to Dominic and Anika.

"The only connection we can find between Tildas Island and the crimes we've uncovered is The Summit," Dominic said.

Beside him, Anika sighed then nodded. "The Summit is here and if we think that's going to be the location of the dénouement then there's some *logic* to the crimes taking place here, but we haven't found any real reason. We don't know why Imperium Holdings decided to invest in the region, we don't know why the victims of the hitman were all brought here, and we don't know why the sale of Serena's identity was supposed to occur here. Other than convenience to The Summit, we can't find anything."

"You don't think the convenience of The Summit is a good enough reason?" Shah asked.

Both Dominic and Anika shook their heads, but Dominic was the one who answered. "The islands aren't that easy to get to. There are only three airports with direct flights to here, four if you include Puerto Rico. Not to mention that, other than Matthews' brief visit to the area during the last campaign, and his connection to Beni, which most people probably don't know about, *he* doesn't have any ties to this area, either. If you were going to pin a bunch of crimes on a guy, wouldn't you want it to be just a little more plausible? I mean, I could see doing it in Chicago, where he's from, or maybe even in the DC area, but here?"

"Maybe we're looking at this all wrong," Anika said slowly. When everyone's attention shifted to her, she flicked her gaze to Dominic as if focusing on him would help her arrange her thoughts. "Maybe it isn't what's in his phone records or what's on the island we need to be looking at. What if what we need to be looking at is, well, not exactly the opposite, but close to? Like instead of asking 'why stage all the crimes on or around Tildas?' maybe we should be asking 'what is it about Tildas that would make this the right place for the crimes?'," she said.

The room was silent for a moment, then Jake spoke. "So, shift the focus of the question from the crimes themselves to the island? If we ask *that*, it could open up all sorts of other avenues to look into, including economics, the close proximity of so many different island countries, and I hate to say it since Anika, you're technically still part of the Tildas Island Police Force, but a traditionally sub-par law enforcement structure. If we start to look at it from that angle, there might be lots of reasons why someone would pick Tildas to commit crimes."

"They wouldn't be the first. We all know how many tax shelters there are in this region," Alexis said. "It's a good angle to take. It opens up a lot of questions that are going to be hard to answer, but shifting the focus of the question is a good idea. Especially since we were consistently coming up with the same answer to the original question that none of us liked."

"If we switch the focus of the question about Tildas," Beni said. "We should do the same for Calloway. If our investigations aren't revealing who he's working with, maybe we should come up with a list of folks who he *could* be working with and then work backward to see if we find any common denominators."

"I think those are both good options," Shah said. "Alexis, you join Dominic and Anika on the island angle and Jake, Damian, and Beni, you three start brainstorming who might have the interest, power, and money to hire Calloway. You should probably start with the shareholders of Imperium Holdings since we know several powerful people are already involved, whether they know it or not, through that company. Now the last of the big questions before us is, what are they planning for The Summit? However," she paused and took a deep breath, "I think we have enough on our plate right now and can table that question for a few days. Between what we're already looking into and the security work we're still responsible for related to The Summit, we're spread thin enough as it is. Besides, what they are planning at The Summit might become a moot question if we can get ahead of the situation."

Beni wasn't so sure they'd be able stop what was being planned for The Summit. It was possible that those dominoes had already started to fall. But even if that was the case, Shah's point still held—regardless of what might already be in motion, getting to Calloway and the people behind the conspiracy was the best way to stop, or at least minimize, the damage they planned to cause.

"All right, everyone has their marching orders," Shah continued. "Let's convene tomorrow afternoon, same time, to go over anything new. In the meantime, as always, if anything urgent comes up, we can address it as needed."

Beni was rising from her seat when Damian pulled his phone out of his pocket. When a frown appeared on his face as he appeared to be reading a message, she paused. There was no reason his actions should cause her to hesitate. There were any number of people who could be texting Damian, including his wife. Even so, the hairs on the back of her neck tingled and she waited. When he let out a low sound, the entire team, except for Shah, who was already stepping out of the room, stopped their own departures.

"Uh, Director?" Damian said, his phone still in front of him.

She stopped and turned, "Yes?"

"I think I might know what they're planning for The Summit."

CHAPTER SEVEN

EVERYONE RETURNED to their seats and Damian hit a couple buttons on his phone then set the device on the table.

"I guess I was right to reach out to you then," a woman answered without preamble.

"Hey, Jess," Damian said. "About that text. Yeah, I'm glad you reached out."

"I'm on speaker?" she asked.

"Yes, the entire team is here, including Director Shah," Damian answered.

"Oh, hey, Sunita, how's it going?"

Startled at the familiar greeting, Beni flashed a "what the hell" look at Damian who just shrugged and shook his head.

"Good, Jessica, how are you?" Director Shah asked.

"I've had better days, but why don't you introduce me to the team, and I can tell you everything I know about why I texted Damian."

Shah looked to Damian who then took the lead and introduced the rest of them to Jessica Kilkenny. Beni saw a flash of recognition in Dominic's eyes and she wondered if Jessica was the reporter that Damian had nearly lost his job over before coming to Tildas.

"So, now that you know everyone, why don't you tell us more about the text you just sent," Damian prompted.

Jessica didn't hesitate to jump right in. "Yesterday afternoon, I got a call from Howard Jacek. He's a reporter, but I'm not sure I'd go so far as to call him a colleague. He's too into gossip and rumors for me, but he is a reporter nonetheless and has broken some good stories over the years. Usually the more salacious ones.

"Anyway, he called to ask me about you all. He knows I know Damian from that thing a couple of years ago, and he wanted to know if I was hearing any rumors about the upcoming Summit. The Summit's not really my kind of thing to cover, so I said no. But because I'm, well, a reporter, I asked a couple of questions. Turns out, he had a lead on something. He said he'd heard that one of the key participants might be involved in some seriously shady shit—his words, not mine. He also mentioned applying for a press pass so he could attend. He wasn't any more forthcoming than that, though, and I don't know if that's because he didn't know more or because he was protecting his story. I should also add that while The Summit isn't my beat, it's not really his, either, unless something unsavory is going to happen."

"Did he give you any hints as to what kinds of things this participant might be rumored to be involved in?" Shah asked.

"No, he just said it was stuff that would shock the world. Given that all the attendees are political figures, his comment led me to believe it must be something along the lines of an underage sex scandal or treason of some sort."

"That's not the end of the story is it, Jess?" Damian pressed.

She paused and when she answered, her voice was more subdued. "No, it's not. Look, Howard wasn't my favorite person, but he wasn't a bad guy. I don't know how he got into what he got into, but he was found dead earlier this morning. While the authorities are calling it an accident, I have to wonder."

And judging by the sudden stillness in the room, Jessica wasn't the only one.

"How did he die?" Beni asked.

"Single car accident on a rural road in Virginia, about 30 miles south of DC."

"No witnesses?" Jake asked.

"No one has come forward," Jess answered.

Beni glanced around at her teammates as everyone seemed to consider the information Jessica had just dropped. It raised a lot of questions, but it also raised some possibilities.

"Thanks, Jessica," Shah finally spoke. "We'll send a couple of folks up to have a look around. Have you talked to anyone else about this?"

"No, I haven't, but I can't vouch for Howard. He liked to let us know he had leads, kind of a one-upmanship type of thing. That said, he only contacted me because he wanted information on you all, not to gloat."

"So, what you're saying is, it's possible he talked to others about this new, great lead, but it's also possible he didn't?" Damian clarified, a hint of teasing in his voice.

"Shut it, Rodriguez," Jess said with a laugh. "I may be good, but I can't tell you what went on in Howard's mind. Even if I could read minds, his wasn't one I'd want to be in," she added.

"Thanks, Jessica," Shah repeated. "You still in the DC area?"

"No place I'd rather be. Except maybe down in the Caribbean on a beach with a daiquiri. Except I hate daiquiris. What's the drink down there?"

"Pain Killers," the entire team, minus Shah, answered at the same time, making everyone chuckle.

"Right," Shah spoke, bringing the conversation back around to the latest bombshell. "As I said, we'll look into Howard Jacek's death from down here, but I'm going to send Rodriguez and

Ricci up to investigate a few things on the ground. I assume you'll be available—and interested—if they have any questions?"

Beni's attention snapped to the director at the pronouncement. It seemed a bit extreme to be hopping on a plane to DC because a journalist died, but Shah's gaze was fixed on the phone still sitting on the table.

"I will make myself available. Damian knows where to find me." And without so much as a goodbye, the journalist ended the call.

"I assume neither of you have a problem with that?" Shah asked, looking first to Damian then to Beni. Both shook their heads. "Great, run it like any other investigation, but more discreetly. I'll call the pilot and have him prep the plane. Alexis, I know you like to fly it, but I want you here."

Alexis nodded. The few times they'd used the private, FBI plane, Alexis had usually been the one to fly it, but it made sense that Shah would want to keep her here. In truth, Beni was surprised Shah was sending two of them to DC—they weren't exactly rolling in resources on the island and between the investigation and The Summit, pulling two agents out was going to stretch the team even further.

"The trip will be taken under the guise of reporting to the president and vice president on The Summit. That way, no one will question your presence in the capital," Shah said.

Beni opened her mouth to argue. They'd never done an in-person briefing with either the president or the vice president, and it seemed to her that doing so now might call unwanted attention to them. She started to speak, then caught Alexis giving her a subtle, but sharp, shake of her head. Beni frowned but cut off her question.

Shah turned to Jake. "I want you to look into Howard Jacek's phone records. I want to see if he called any reporters other than Jessica."

When Jake nodded, Shah rose. Everyone else followed suit

and the sound of chairs scraping across the floor momentarily filled the room. When it was once again quiet, Shah spoke. "Unfortunately, as these things tend to go, you now have even more marching orders. Rodriguez and Ricci, head home and pack. I'll have the plane ready in an hour. Safe travels and I know it goes without saying but stay in touch. We need to know everything you do." And with that last direction, Shah walked out of the room.

Beni looked to Damian who raised a brow at her as he spoke. "I have to say, when I woke up this morning, I didn't think I'd be headed to DC, but what the hell. My mother-in-law will be happy to see me. I'll stay with her tonight and if you don't want to stay at a hotel, you can stay at my place. I have a service that keeps it clean since I let friends use it all the time."

Beni nodded, hearing the words, but not really processing them as her mind was already ten steps ahead. She and Damian needed to work fast. Once in DC, there would be a lot they needed to get done, but they needed to do it quickly and efficiently since they were needed back on the island. The problem was, there was no doubt in her mind that Cal would want to see her when he learned she was coming to DC—which he would since she'd be on his calendar for the briefing. Aside from him being a distraction she couldn't afford, she wasn't sure she was ready to see him again quite yet.

She glanced up at her teammates to find them all staring at her.

"You know there's no chance in hell Calvin Matthews isn't going to try and see you," Anika pointed out, gleefully but unhelpfully.

"Maybe he's out of town," Beni said.

"Uh, I doubt it," Jake said. "No way would Shah send you up there to brief the president and vice president if one or the other wasn't in town. That would be the world's shittiest cover story otherwise."

Damn, he had a point.

Beni sighed and rose. Maybe she could just ignore Cal and he'd go away. Or maybe she could bury herself in the investigation and avoid him that way.

"Or maybe you could just spend a little time with him," Alexis said with a knowing smile.

"Stop reading minds, Alexis. No one likes a showoff," she grumbled, making her team laugh. "Now, if you don't mind, I have some packing to do."

"Maybe you should pack that dress from Puerto Rico," Alexis called after her, referring to the uber sexy dress Alexis had made her buy when they were undercover on another investigation.

"And don't forget a razor," Anika added.

"She doesn't need a razor," Jake said. "If a guy has a partner naked, I can assure you, he's not put off by a little leg hair."

"Fuck off. All of you," Beni said over her shoulder as she left the room. She needed to head home and pack—where she knew she'd spend at least five minutes debating whether to pack her razor or not.

CHAPTER EIGHT

CAL DIDN'T KNOW what he'd done to deserve it, but for some reason, Sunita Shah had taken a liking to him. When she'd given him Beni's location at The Shack, he'd suspected she wasn't averse to his attention to her agent; and the call he'd received a few hours earlier, all but gave him her blessing. Beni was on her way to DC to investigate the death of a journalist, and thanks to the notice Shah had given him, he'd had more than enough time to make a plan.

Now, as he watched her plane touch down and taxi to the private area of the airport, he smiled to himself. It was a damn good plan if he did say so himself. Beni might not think so, but he was pretty sure he could change her mind.

Sitting inside his idle car in the cold DC night air, impatience tugged at him. In an effort to take his mind off the fact that Beni was less than a hundred yards away, disembarking from her flight, he glanced around. His security detail had been cut back to the minimum and it was almost like he could pretend he was just a guy waiting for his girlfriend.

Finally, Damian and Beni emerged from the private air terminal. They paused to talk, probably making plans for the next day. He could see the fog created by their breath as they spoke, but he couldn't hear what they were saying. Then they nodded to each other and Damian climbed into a waiting cab, likely headed either to his apartment or to his mother-in-law's house.

Once Damian was on his way, Beni raised a hand and the taxi pulled up. She tossed her carry-on into the back seat, then slid in beside it as she rattled off an address in Georgetown. The taxi pulled away from the airport then, instead of turning toward the city, it headed south toward Alexandria.

"You're going the wrong way," Beni said.

"No, we're headed exactly where we're supposed to," Cal said, looking over his shoulder from where he sat behind the driver's wheel grinning at her.

He had a fleeting thought he might have gone too far when he got zero reaction from her. He'd expected something. He'd actually anticipated outrage, or at the least, disgruntlement. The complete non-reaction left him nonplussed and had him second guessing his plan.

"Shah?" she asked, her tone flat.

With his attention back on the road, he nodded. He hardly ever got to drive on his own anymore, and though the borrowed cab wasn't exactly a dream to drive, he was still going to enjoy the freedom.

Beni sighed. "Where are we going?"

"A friend's," he said.

"Cal," she warned.

He flashed her a grin in the rearview mirror, but it died when he saw she wasn't even looking at him. No, she had her head facing the window and she was staring into the darkness.

"My sister owns a house in Alexandria that she uses for business clients. It's empty for the next few days. We're going there," he answered.

"I'm tired, I'm hungry, and I'm still in the middle of an investigation that I need to focus on in order to ensure your administration doesn't implode, and now there's a potential dead body involved. We're not having sex tonight, Cal."

Knowing she wasn't watching him, he smiled at her line of logic. Eventually those excuses would go away. And she hadn't said they couldn't *sleep* together. Or that they weren't *ever* going to have sex. Just not tonight. He was fine with that. Well, mostly fine with that. He'd make himself be fine with that.

"Dare I even ask where your security detail is? You really must be a menace for them to manage," she said.

"Two in front, a couple following us. If it makes you feel any better, I never do anything they strongly caution against," he answered.

She snorted a laugh at that. "Why do I find that hard to believe?"

"It wasn't until you that I started pushing the boundaries a little. Before you get worked up about that statement, though, no, I'm not placing the blame at your feet. My decision to push the boundaries is my decision. You just happen to be the reason I'm pushing them."

Beni muttered something that sounded like "lucky me."

"I can't help you with the investigation, but I can help with the other things," he said. "The beds, and yes there are more than one, are extremely comfortable at the house, and about ten minutes after we arrive, I'll have your favorite pizza ready. Not from the place in Chicago we used to go to, but the owner gave my chef the recipe when I took office and he makes it for me now…not quite the same as eating it at the restaurant, but it will do when you're craving the Chicago style pizza."

"The only real pizza there is," Beni said. He smiled to himself. She may not be happy with him, but she was thawing with the possibility of pizza.

Ten minutes later, they pulled into a garage and shut the door behind them before climbing out. A member of his security detail opened the door that led from the garage to the house and gave them both a nod. Cal grabbed Beni's bag and, without giving her an option, took it upstairs and deposited it next to his small overnight bag in the master suite.

When he came back downstairs, he found Beni in the kitchen with a beer in hand leaning over and looking through the glass window of the oven. Inside, the crust of a deep-dish pizza was turning a golden brown and the sauce was bubbling at the edges.

"I can't believe you got Marco to give you his recipe," she said. Her eyes remained on the pizza, but she gestured to an open bottle of beer on the counter.

"Yeah, well, it turns out having your pizza recipe being used in the White House is kind of a big deal, so we came to an agreement."

Beni straightened, gave him a funny look, then shook her head. "You're not in the White House. Yet," she pointed out as she leaned against the counter beside the oven.

Cal set his beer down and took the four steps needed to bring him within six inches of her. Her shoulders tensed, but she didn't back down or look away. "Anne-Marie likes pizza. I'm not allowed to share the recipe with the White House chef, but my chef goes over and makes it. It's a pretty common staple for all the late nights we put in."

Again, she gave him a funny look.

"What?" he asked, placing his hands on the counter on either side her. She didn't appear excited about the development, but he was under no illusions that if she really didn't want him in her space, she'd let him know and he'd be lucky to have his balls intact at the end of it.

"I gotta admit, it wasn't like I didn't know you were the VP— I even voted for you—but it's weird to hear the boy I used to know talk about having pizza at the White House with the President of the United States like you're talking about a buddy."

"Anne-Marie is cool. You'll like her." He could tell from the expression on Beni's face that she thought befriending Anne-Marie Cunningham was as likely as seeing a pig fly by the window.

"Is there a reason you're in my space, Cal?" she asked instead, gesturing to the now only four inches that separated them.

"I thought you'd never ask," he said, then lowered his head and kissed her. Unlike last time, this was a slow burn kiss. He could feel Beni's restraint, as if she was testing whether she wanted to be doing this or not. That could have been a bad sign, but he decided it was just the opposite—if she was slowing things down that meant she was actually thinking about them. She wasn't caught by surprise, she wasn't swept up in hormones, no, she was considering the kiss, which meant she was considering him.

Deciding not to push things too far, he pulled back and returned to the other side of the kitchen. Picking up his beer bottle, he asked, "Want salad with that? There's one in the fridge."

She shook her head as the timer dinged and, after grabbing a couple of potholders, she pulled the pizza out of the oven and set it on the stove. "Oh my god, this smells good. Do you know how long it's been since I've had one of Marco's pizzas?"

"Actually, I don't," he said, rummaging in one of the drawers and pulling out a pizza cutter. He handed it over then started looking for plates. "How long has it been since you've been back to Chicago?"

"Not since I left," she said, keeping her attention on the pizza. "As you know, my mom remarried and moved to Boston. Once I was out of the Army and in the FBI, I worked out of the Boston office so I could be close to her." She pulled two pieces out and slid them onto the plate he held then did the same with the second plate.

Not bothering with utensils, they each grabbed their drinks then took a seat at the small table in the breakfast nook.

"Our family was sorry we couldn't make the wedding," Cal said.

"We understood, Cal. Really we did," Beni said, her voice gentle.

Four months before Beni's mom had remarried, his sister, Stella, had been kidnapped and held for ransom. He and his mom had gone to great lengths to keep it quiet, but Beni and her mother were like family to the Matthews clan. Beni had been out of the country on a deployment, but her mother, Maria, had been told everything.

Stella had been home and safe for nearly two months when Maria remarried. The kidnappers hadn't been kind, though, and his sister had been a long way from okay.

"How is Stella?" Beni asked.

Cal took a sip of his drink wishing it could wash away the memories. Those two months were a time none of them would ever forget, but every day that Stella thrived, it got a little easier. "She's doing great, actually. Really great. I'm sure your mom told you she got married, but what most people don't know is that the man she married, Hunter Zatoro, was one of the guys on the kidnap and rescue team. Now they run a small, but very well-respected security company."

Beni smiled at that. "Stella was always a hellion. I can't imagine what she went through during both her captivity and her recovery, but it wouldn't surprise me at all to hear she channeled some of her pain into learning how to kick ass and take names. All while not breaking a nail, of course," Beni added, making Cal laugh. Stella had *always* had a thing for her nails.

"You'd be right about all of that. Hunter, and some of the guys on his team, trained her. She's now the primary hand-to-hand combat trainer for their company. She's scary good."

Beni smiled. "I'm surprised you don't have her on your team."

"She'd love bossing me around, but we can't afford her," he answered, still smiling. "What about you? I know you were a medic and I know you were deployed more than your mom wanted, but are you..." He wasn't quite sure what he was asking. She had a career in the FBI and was well respected, so he knew she was *fine,* but being fine and being really fine were two different things.

Beni finished off her first slice of pizza and picked up the second. She pondered the food for a beat, then answered. "I'm fine in that I discharged without any significant mental health issues so long as you don't count the huge chip on my shoulder from always having to be one of the only women medics. Or from always having certain people ordering me around when I knew they didn't know shit. Don't get me wrong, there were a lot of good officers and leaders in the Army. Some of the best people I ever had the honor of knowing or working with. There were also enough dumbasses that came through the academy or officer training that didn't have a lick of combat experience and still expected everyone to ask 'how high' when they said jump. We lost more people than we should have because of people like that. I wasn't always the most diplomatic when that happened."

Cal grinned. "Yeah, I can only imagine." He took a bite of his pizza then, once he'd swallowed, asked the question he wasn't sure he wanted to know the answer to. "Were you ever hurt?"

Beni studied him as she finished her own bite, then, after taking a sip of beer, she nodded. "I have shrapnel scars on my left side from a suicide bomber, my leg got broken when a piece of car fell on it after the car drove over an IED, and last but not least, I was shot in the arm. It was a through shot, though, so I was lucky as far as those things go."

He'd known it was more likely than not that she'd been injured at least once. In the ten years she'd been in the Army, she'd been deployed a lot. More than the average medic. But even knowing she'd been in the line of fire more than the usual, her matter-of-fact recitation of her injuries made his stomach churn. It also enraged him, but he knew better than to let that particular beast out.

"Any lasting effects?" he managed to ask.

She shook her head. "Nothing major. Sometimes my arm aches if I've had a hard workout, or my leg if I've gone for a long run, but nothing more than that. I saw enough while serving to know how lucky I am."

He knew that statement to be both true and false—she was lucky she hadn't been more seriously injured or even killed, but there were also thousands of soldiers who were never physically injured at all. He wished Beni had been one of them, but he couldn't go back and change the past.

He cleared his throat and picked up his empty beer bottle, silently asking her if she wanted another. She shook her head.

"So, I saw that I have a briefing with you and Damian tomorrow, but I know that's not the real reason you're here," he said, changing the subject to something a little less gut wrenching, at least for him.

As they each helped themselves to one more slice of pizza, she told him about the death of the reporter, Howard Jacek, and the investigation she and Damian would kick off tomorrow—albeit a very under-the-radar investigation. There were a few gaps in the plan she laid out for him, but he got the sense they were gaps she'd intentionally left open. He didn't like not knowing what she and Damian were going to do the next day, but he understood that he was probably better off not knowing everything. Just as there were things he wouldn't be able to tell her about his job, he needed to respect when she felt the need to hold something back as well.

When they were done eating, they cleaned up the kitchen and headed upstairs. He wasn't interested in fighting about whether or not they were going to sleep together so he showed her the master suite and told her he had a little bit of work to do. When he came back upstairs an hour later, she was out cold. Telling himself that he'd never promised her he'd sleep elsewhere, he very quietly got ready for bed, then slid between the sheets. He waited until his body warmed up, then he inched closer to Beni and gently tucked her to his side. She murmured something in her sleep, then flung an arm over his torso and burrowed in next to him, a bare leg sliding over his.

He smiled into the darkness. Awake-Beni might not be so ready to jump on the bandwagon with him, but asleep-Beni didn't seem to have any of the same qualms. Now he just had to figure out how to combine the two.

CHAPTER NINE

AT EIGHT THE NEXT MORNING, Beni and Damian were escorted into the Oval Office. Not once in her thirty-eight years had Beni ever contemplated seeing the Oval Office, let alone having a meeting in it. President Cunningham was leaning against the edge of her desk with the windows at her back, and Cal was sitting on one of the couches. Both were dressed in suits, but the glint in Cal's eye, and the little wave he gave her, told her he hadn't forgotten where those fingers had been, or what they'd been doing, less than two hours ago. She tried to send him a quelling look, but it was really hard when she also couldn't forget where his fingers had been. Or the orgasm she'd had thanks to those very talented fingers.

The hint of a grin he wore transformed into a smile as he rose and introduced the president. It was a little surreal that other than his one quiet question seeking her consent for his morning activity, the first words he said to her that day were to introduce her to the president. She wondered, fleetingly, if she would ever get used to the fact that Cal was the vice president. And, all things going the way many anticipated, would likely be the president after the end of Cunningham's second term. But that was a thought for another day.

To her surprise, Beni found herself liking President Cunningham. Not just as a president, but as a person. She was sharp, asked thoughtful questions as they walked her through the program and security measures in place, and was gracious to the staff that wandered in and out of her office during their meeting, including thanking the woman who had brought them coffee and inquiring after her newborn granddaughter.

They covered a lot of ground in the thirty minutes allotted to them, and five minutes after the meeting ended she and Damian found themselves being escorted out by her chief of staff who chatted with them about the history of the White House and the changes made by the various administrations. As they were handing in their visitor badges, he also expressed his hope that when he accompanied the president down to Tildas for the opening of The Summit, that they'd give him some insider knowledge on local eats. Apparently, there was nothing President Cunningham liked more while traveling than to explore local foods.

After giving the man their contact information, and readily agreeing to help out with foodie recommendations, they made their way off the White House grounds. They were silent as they left, but as soon as they hit the sidewalk, which was filled with tourists, they paused and looked at each other.

Damian grinned. "You ever think you'd meet the President of the United States?"

Beni laughed. "No, I can tell you straight up, that was most definitely not on the list of things I ever thought would happen to me."

"She seems pretty cool, though," Damian said, hailing a cab. "I mean, I like her as the president, but she seemed like a good person, too." As he spoke, a taxi pulled over and Damian opened the door.

"I agree," Beni said, lowering herself into the cab then sliding over to make room for Damian. "So where are we going now?" she asked once he'd taken a seat beside her and closed the door. They'd sketched out a rough plan for the day, which included visiting Howard Jacek's home as well as the police who had conducted the initial investigation, but they hadn't talked specifics. "Maybe a car rental agency?" she suggested. Riding around in taxis or even a car service wasn't really a great option.

Damian rattled off an address to the driver, then grinned at her. "I have a car we can take. And while we're out and about, you can tell me all about just where you were last night, young lady. Because I know you didn't stay at my apartment."

"Police department first or Howard Jacek's apartment?" Beni asked once they were seated in Damian's muscle car. It was a far cry from the beat-up vehicles they drove on Tildas where the weather and the roads made it hard—or not worth it—to have anything nicer.

"His apartment's in Reston. Let's hit that first then the investigating department. Did the warrant come through?" he replied.

Beni nodded. "Jake did his thing, we're all set. There's a manager at the complex who can let us in."

"Good, now, with nothing to do other than drive, want to fill me in on last night?"

Beni slid him a look, debating whether to tell him the bare minimum or nothing at all. In the end, and despite Damian's persistence, she just said that she'd ended up in Alexandria. Well, she might have also mentioned the pizza, but she didn't once discuss Cal or the sleeping arrangements.

"That looks like a happy place," Damian said, sarcasm heavy in his voice, as he pulled into a parking spot at Jacek's complex.

There were some nice places in Reston, but Jacek's wasn't one of them. Paint was peeling off the gutters and window trim, the metal railing that ran along the stairs leading up to, and along, the second floor was warped, and the stucco was chipped in a number of places. Most windows had curtains hanging in them and, with one exception, all seemed to be the same dingy white.

"I don't know a lot of journalists, but maybe he's not particularly good? Or maybe the salacious market isn't what it used to be?" she suggested.

Damian shrugged. "Want to go find the manager? Maybe take a few bets on how much info he tries to pump us for?"

Beni chuckled as she opened the door and slid from her seat. "My guess is that in a place like this, the only thing he'll care about is when he can rent the apartment again."

In the end, they were both wrong. The manager was a woman in her mid-forties who was both efficient and helpful. She also let them know that she'd just inherited the building from her uncle and was trying to make some changes. She didn't owe them an explanation, but it was nice to hear that she was going to keep it as a business.

They stepped into the small, one-bedroom apartment that looked as good on the inside as it did on the outside. That is to say, not well kept. The off-white wall-to-wall carpet was stained, and a brown sofa dominated the living room. Across from where they entered was a dining area that held a table for two, and beside that was a kitchen that was even smaller than hers back on Tildas. Following a short hallway off the kitchen, they found the bedroom and bathroom.

Beni poked her head into the bathroom and scanned the area. Personal hygiene products were scattered across the counter, including an ungodly number of hair products, and one towel hung on a bar while another was in a heap on the floor. There was dried toothpaste in the sink.

Retreating from the bathroom, she joined Damian in the

bedroom, which looked in much the same state as the rest of the house. A dresser sat on the wall opposite from the bed and three of the six drawers were partway open. The bed was not only unmade but looked like someone had just thrown a set of sheets and a blanket on top—sometime in the last century.

"Smells as good as it looks, doesn't it?" Damian asked. The air was musty, dusty, and stale.

"I'll flip a coin with you for the bedroom. Loser gets the bathroom," she said.

"I'll take the bathroom if you take everything else," he countered.

She narrowed her eyes at him in suspicion. The rest of the apartment wasn't *that* big, nor was it on the same gross-scale as the bathroom. Finally, knowing Damian would pitch in if he finished before her, she nodded in agreement. Moments later, wearing gloves from the evidence kits they'd brought, they got to work.

Damian made a few disgusted noises as he went about his search of the bathroom, but for the most part, she ignored him as she started in on the bedroom. Twenty minutes later, with nothing to show, she moved onto the kitchen.

And realized why Damian had made the deal he had.

Dirty plates were piled in the sink, food scraps were left out on the counters, and when she opened the fridge, her gag reflex almost had her vomiting all over the floor.

"Fuck you, Rodriguez," she shouted to him, still in the bathroom. His laughter floated down the hall. Taking a step back, she took in the room as a whole as she decided where to start. The counters, though filthy, were actually free of anything she'd consider potential evidence or places to hide evidence. Same with the sink.

Opting to take her chances with the cabinets, she started with the one closest to the refrigerator. The top shelves were empty, but the bottom two were filled with cans of soup.

Moving on, she discovered one filled with plates—marveling that he even had more given the number in his sink—one with glasses, and one with a few mixing bowls. In the lower cabinets, she found more pots and, surprisingly, one with a plethora of baking sheets and muffin tins.

"Find anything?" Damian asked from the edge of the room.

"Nothing yet, you?"

"I've got his medications, but other than that nothing." As he spoke, he held up three evidence bags, each with a prescription pill bottle inside. "What's left in here?" he asked, tucking the medicines back into his evidence kit.

"Just the fridge and it might kill you when you open it, so how about opening some windows or maybe giving me some of the Vicks I know you carry in your bag?"

Damian grinned at her. The jerk had known exactly what she'd find in the kitchen of a sloppy bachelor when he'd made his trade. "Here you go," he said, tossing her the small jar of the scented cream. "I'll go check out the living room."

The next time Damian made his presence known, she'd just finished with the fridge—only gagging six times as she'd searched it—and was closing the freezer. Once the door was shut tight, she leaned against the counter. "I got nothing," she said. "You?"

"He has lots of books, but I went through most and didn't find anything. I also didn't find any laptop or other device, but he may have had them with him in the car. We should be sure to ask the police when we meet with them. There's really nothing here?"

Beni shook her head. She hadn't expected to find a smoking gun. Sure, it would have been nice to walk in and find his laptop opened to an email that contained the lead he'd told Jessica Kilkenny about. But if wishes were...what was that saying? She turned to ask Damian the inconsequential question only to find him staring at the counter.

"What?" she asked.

"Something's missing," he said.

She spun back around and took another look. After a beat, it hit her. "I know it's a cliché, but how many reporters do you know who don't drink coffee?"

"There's no coffeemaker," Damian said.

"More to the point, if there's no coffeemaker, why does he have this," she said, opening the freezer and pulling out a can of a generic coffee brand from the local chain grocery store.

Damian took the can from her and pulled off the plastic top. Inside, the canister was three-quarters filled with coffee grounds. Passing it back to her, she took it then gave it a little shake. Sure enough, the corner of what looked like a piece of paper peeked out from the top of the grounds.

With gloved fingers, she gently pulled the discovery out only to find that it wasn't a piece of paper, but rather a folded business-size envelope. After giving the canister one more shake and rotation to make sure they hadn't missed anything, she set it down and turned her attention to the envelope.

It was addressed to Howard Jacek's home address in plain typeface, stamped with an American flag stamp, and postmarked from DC. Turning it over, she gently flattened it, opened the flap, and pulled a single sheet of paper out.

She handed the envelope to Damian, who slipped it into an evidence bag, then began to unfold the tri-folded paper. With Damian looking over her shoulder, they both scanned the contents.

"Ask RLB Construction about the World Bank bid and look into the death of Jason Grant."

For a moment, the two agents were silent, then Beni raised her gaze and looked at her colleague. "It's interesting that the letter alludes to two of the five incidents we've investigated, but not the sale of Serena's identity, the trafficking ring, or the drug lab," Beni said, as she guided the note into another evidence bag.

Damian was silent, his eyes still lingering on the paper now sealed in the bag. Then he raised his phone and gestured for her to hold the note up so he could take a picture of the message. "Of all the things that we've investigated," he said, "the two that were mentioned are the ones that are most easily tied—even if falsely—to Vice President Matthews. *We* know Calloway was trying to get Matthews down to the island to visit the club where the drugs were being tested and also for the party where we busted the trafficking ring. Those stories would be hard for a reporter to connect to Matthews without more information, though."

"Whereas looking into Grant's death and finding the connection to The Bank of DC would be pretty easy," Beni said. "And if RLB Construction didn't know about the connection between Matthews and Calloway, who was running the World Bank project at the time, they'd have no reason to suspect that the request they received to submit a bid wasn't legit."

"And no reason to hide the fact that they'd been asked," Damian added. RLB Construction was a company owned and operated by Cal's ex-wife and her current husband. But the marriage had been a short one—only two years—and early enough in Cal's career that it was unlikely Roberta, the ex, knew about Calloway's connection to Cal.

"So just as Jessica said, there's enough to whet his appetite and point him in a direction, but not enough to give anything away."

Damian held up the evidence bag with the envelope in it and looked at the back. "Dated seven days ago. Just enough time for him to do some digging, discover the link to Matthews, and get killed."

"If he was killed," Beni said.

Damian grinned. "I like how you said that as if it were a possibility he wasn't."

"A woman can but dream," Beni said as Damian stored both

evidence bags in his kit. "So down to the accident scene or to the police first?" she asked.

"It's been ages since I've driven a real car on a decent road. The accident site is farther away. Let's head there first, then to the station."

Beni nodded and they made a final round of the apartment to make sure all the lights were off before leaving. Satisfied that everything was as it should be, they stepped outside and, after closing and locking the door behind them, they paused to look out onto the parking lot below. A woman was getting out of her car with a basket full of laundry and a dog was skulking around the corner of the building. Despite the building's obvious need for, at the least, cosmetic repairs, Beni hoped it wouldn't become like the thousands of other apartment buildings in the area that cost too much for anyone living on a minimum wage job to afford. Those who worked in the service industry needed affordable places to live near the jobs they worked, and year after year, those places were becoming fewer and farther between.

"Pain Killer for your thoughts," Damian prompted from where he stood beside her.

She smiled. "Pain Killer?"

"I figured your thoughts were probably worth more than a penny, or even a dollar. And I have to admit, I think I've gotten used to the weather on Tildas and these freezing temps made me want to be back on island. With a Pain Killer."

She laughed at his logic that, in a bizarre way, made sense. She was just about to take him up on the offer when something caught her eye. She stilled for a moment, keeping her face forward but her attention on the man she'd spotted in her periphery.

"What?" Damian asked. Smart agent that he was, he kept his body language casual even as his tone indicated he'd recognized something was going on.

She shifted her body slightly to face him. "See that dark green SUV parked at the end behind me?" Damian nodded. "There's a man inside, or at least someone built like a man, and I would swear he was just watching us with binoculars. Or a scope," she added, hoping it was the former. "I caught a flash of reflection."

Damian casually leaned against the railing, or at least gave the illusion of leaning against the railing. *She* wouldn't put any outward-pushing weight on the metal, and she was a good fifty pounds lighter than her colleague.

"You think they knew we were coming or that they've been waiting to see who dropped by?" he asked, his expression still light and easy going. He even had a smile on his face.

"I kind of like the idea of whoever it is sitting on their ass in the cold DC weather having to wait to see who shows up. But given what we know these people are capable of, I suspect someone tipped them off that we're in town. You get the license plate?" she asked.

"I can see the first three numbers, but not the rest. We need to stop by the manager's office and drop the key. That will take us out of his line of sight. Why don't you go to the car and I'll take the key back? If you can keep him distracted, I can circle around behind him, get the number, then join you at the car."

Beni nodded. "Sounds like a plan."

As one, they moved toward the stairs and started down. When they reached the parking lot, Damian handed Beni his car keys and evidence kit then made a show of holding the apartment key up so it would look like they were discussing returning it. After a beat, he left and started toward the management office. She made a show of juggling the two evidence kits —hers and his—and jangling the car keys as she headed toward where they'd parked.

Opening the trunk of Damian's muscle car the old fashion way—with the key—she dumped the two kits in the back, then pulled her phone out and took a seat on the bumper. Pretending to text, she managed to snap a few pictures of the SUV. She was far enough away, though, that she didn't hold much hope that they'd get anything off them.

She was just about to slide her phone into her back pocket when it rang, the screen flashing a number she didn't recognize.

"Hello?" she answered.

"It's me," came the response.

"How many burner phones do you have?" she asked Cal, not bothering to hide the irritation in her voice. Although why she was irritated she couldn't say.

"Caught you by surprise, didn't I? You never did like surprises."

Oh, yeah, that was probably why she was irritated.

She sighed. "What do you want?"

"Is that a specific question or a more philosophical one?"

"Cal."

He chuckled. "Just wanted to hear your voice. Are you leaving tonight? Or do I get one more night?"

Beni glanced around, making sure Damian wasn't approaching from a direction where he could overhear. "You have a country to help run and, if I heard your chief of staff correctly when we were leaving this morning, you have some dinner you need to attend. It doesn't matter whether I stay or not, you have other things to do."

"Other things to do than you? No, I do not."

"Cal," she said again, trying to chastise him but knowing he would hear the smile in her voice.

"Just answer the question, Benita. Are you here tonight again or not? Don't recite my schedule or responsibilities to me. It's a simple yes or no question."

She exhaled. "It's actually not that simple. I don't know. If things keep going like they're going, we'll probably head back tonight. If something comes up, then we'll stay. It's the nature of the job. You work with enough law enforcement and intelligence folks to know that."

He was silent for a moment and when he answered, all teasing was gone from his tone. "I do, you're right. How is it going?"

Knowing Damian would show up any minute, she gave him a quick summary of what they'd found in the apartment. She conveniently left out the part about being watched, knowing he might have a reaction to that that she didn't want—or have the time—to deal with.

Just as she finished, she heard footsteps behind her. Turning, she saw Damian approaching along the walkway that ran between the two buildings.

"It's funny how I never doubted that what we discussed was happening, but is it weird that every now and then, it really hits me?" Cal asked, bringing her attention back to the conversation. "It's like every now and then, the air just gets sucked from my lungs knowing that there are people who hate this administration so much that they'd do the things they've done—the things they *are* doing—just to foster divisiveness, fear, and hatred for the sole purpose of making money."

Damian shot her a questioning look, and she tossed him his keys before holding up a finger to ask for a moment. He nodded and took a seat behind the wheel, leaving her to somehow come up with a quick response to Cal's heavy question.

Then, standing in the parking lot, with the late winter chill seeping through her jacket, and Cal sharing his worries, she realized she didn't really need to answer. At least not right now. Right now, she could offer him something else. "We're going to figure this out, Cal," she said. "It's fucked up, you'll get no argument from me, more than fucked up, actually. But right now, let's focus on stopping them, because we will stop them. You and President Cunningham have the will of the people behind you for good reason, you're doing good things for the country.

Me and the team aren't going to let anyone ruin that. There's too much at stake, and I don't just mean your career. I know that's a big promise, but it's one I'm confident I, and my friends, can deliver on."

"Don't take that on, Nita," he said quietly. "You don't know what's going to happen or what these people are capable of."

The caution in his voice only made her resolve stronger. "I don't," she agreed. "But there are a lot of things I do know, like how capable my team is, especially with Director Shah at the helm. In order to keep my promise, though, I need to do my job. Right now, that means I need to end this call and head down south to check out where Howard Jacek was killed before talking to the officers who investigated the accident."

"A lesser man would think you're trying to blow me off," he said, some of his earlier playfulness coming through again.

"There would be no *trying*, Cal. If I really wanted to blow you off, I would." The words were true, but the second she said them she doubted whether she should have. Especially because Cal picked up on exactly what she hadn't wanted him to.

"So, let me get this straight. Despite your reluctance and generally unwelcoming behavior toward me, you're not blowing me off?"

"I need to go, Cal. You know, things to do, your job to save."

"Benita."

She sighed. "I don't know, Cal," she said, feeling more exposed than ever before. "There are a hundred and one reasons why it would never work, but before you go disputing each and every one of them, you should know that I acknowledge there are a few pretty good reasons why I'm at least thinking about how it might work. I need space to do that, though, and if you push, I'll push right back. Even if I don't really want to. Now, seriously, I have to go. I'm not used to this cold and I'm standing outside freezing my ass off while Damian is waiting for me in the car."

Cal didn't speak right away, but when he did, he surprised her by letting her off the hook. Sort of. "Fine. Go do your job and be safe, please. I've lived for sixteen years not knowing exactly what you were doing, and I don't know if that was worse than knowing what you *are* doing. Regardless, that's my shit to deal with. Will you call me, though, once you know about tonight?"

She pushed off the bumper of the car, her ass frozen after being pressed against the cold metal. "I'll call if I can. If I can't, I'll text," she said, shutting the trunk and heading to the passenger door.

"Call, Benita," he insisted.

"You used to be such a nice boy," she muttered, her hand on the door handle.

"I'm still nice, but there's nothing boyish about me. Now, promise you'll call."

On principle, as stupid as it was, she didn't want to make the promise. "Don't push, Matthews. Like I said, I'll push back, and you won't like it. I will let you know my plan. That's all I'll promise. Now, go save the country or something," she said, then hung up before he could answer.

Looking forward to the warmth of the car, she opened the door and lowered herself onto the seat. "Please god, turn the heater on," she said, shutting the door.

"Sure thing," Damian said as he turned the key in the ignition and the car roared to life. He fiddled with the heater while she twisted in her seat to get her coat off. Once the heat was on, her jacket off, and her seatbelt secured, she leaned back into her seat and closed her eyes.

"You get the license plate?" she asked.

"I did. Already texted it to Alexis," Damian said.

The engine rumbled underneath her as the air started to heat and warm the car. Less than a minute later, Damian backed out of the spot and headed toward the exit. Beni opened her eyes, wanting to see if the SUV would follow them. She was staring intently out the side mirror when Damian finally spoke, asking the question she knew he'd been dying to ask since he'd returned to the car.

"So," he drawled, "how's your boyfriend?"

She rolled her head to find him grinning at her. The only answer he got was a one finger salute.

CHAPTER TEN

As THEY DROVE SOUTH, she managed to keep Damian focused on the investigation rather than on the situation with Cal. They were passing through a rural area on the way to the accident scene when a thought occurred to her.

"There are any number of ways to cause an accident," she said. Damian glanced at her.

"There are," he agreed, his eyes back on the road. "What are you thinking?"

"I think we need to see the car before we see the accident scene," she answered. It was a little bit of the chicken and egg—did they see the site first then look at the damage to the car or did they examine the damage to the car so that when they saw the site, they might be better able to identify any inconsistencies? Given that they were nearly certain the accident wasn't an accident, she was leaning toward the latter and having a look at the car first.

"Car then police then the site?" Damian asked without hesitation.

She shook her head. "Let's get the report from the police, then the car, then the site."

Damian gave a sharp nod. "You got it."

A few miles later, he turned left onto the county road that would take them into town and to the joint police and sheriff's department. It wasn't long before they hit the edge of Main Street and, after driving a single block lined with high-end boutiques and restaurants, Damian pulled over and parked in front of a federal style building that housed the police department as well as city hall and the municipal courthouse.

"How very quaint," Beni said, as she and Damian stood on the sidewalk assessing the building and town.

"I wonder what he was doing down here?" Damian pondered.

"You think our friend would know?" Beni asked with a slight incline of her head toward the street. The same SUV from the parking lot drove by then turned left at the next road.

Damian chuckled. "Whoever he is, he's not very good and I doubt he'd know much of anything other than whatever his current orders are."

Beni concurred with Damian's assessment, but still, she wondered. "Alexis have any luck tracing the plates?"

Damian pulled out his phone. After reading something, he frowned and handed it to her.

"So maybe not entirely inept," Beni said, handing the device back. Whoever was following them had at least switched license plates. The ones currently on the SUV belonged to a Honda hatchback owned by a college student at American University.

"Maybe we can catch a glimpse of him at some point, but in the meantime, let's go grab the accident report and find out where the car was towed," Damian said.

Together, they walked into the building and, after a stop at the directory, headed to the third floor.

"Good morning," a cheery receptionist said as they walked into the police department portion of the third floor. "How can I help you?"

A smile flitted across Damian's face at the chipper greeting and he pulled out his badge as he introduced both of them. While he told her the reason for their visit, the woman's eyes widened in surprise then quickly clouded with empathy.

"Such a terrible accident," she said. "We have a few of those a year. Usually teenagers making bad decisions, but this was the first time in several years that we've had an adult die in a single car accident. Anyway," she said, shaking herself out of her melancholy, "let me get Officer Carter for you. He was the responding officer and lead on the investigation."

She picked up the phone and dialed an extension. A few seconds—and a quiet conversation—later, the receptionist put the phone down then gestured them toward the seats in the lobby.

"Officer Carter will be right out," she said.

They moved toward the seats, but neither took one. Instead, they removed their coats, hung them on the coat tree, then stood side-by-side and looked out the window which faced the road they'd driven in on. Damian's car was visible, as was the street the SUV had turned onto and Beni's gaze lingered on the corner.

There were just enough buildings lining the side street that she couldn't see if the vehicle had parked. She assumed it had, and idly wondered if the person driving would try to follow them in. She doubted it, but one could always hope.

"Agents Rodriguez and Ricci," a voice behind her said.

Beni turned to see a wiry man, about two inches shorter and twenty years older than she was, standing near the reception desk.

"Officer Carter," Damian responded, stepping forward to shake the man's hand. After Beni did the same, Carter ushered them back to an office.

"There's not much here," he said, gesturing to the file that sat on the desk. "Single car accident, no signs of anything or anyone else involved. Most likely a deer jumped out, scared the driver, and he swerved into the tree."

Beni picked up the file and started to go through it.

"Any drugs or alcohol involved?" Damian asked.

"No drugs, his blood alcohol content was .01, well below intoxication. He might have had a drink several hours before or, hell, even some cough syrup, at that level."

"Was he conscious when you arrived at the scene?" Damian asked.

"No, ME ruled dead on impact. Not a surprise if you see the car. It was older, no air bag and none of the fancy crumple zones that most cars have these days. Still, he must have been going pretty fast for the car to have sustained the damage it did."

Beni pulled out a picture of the accident scene and had to agree with Carter. The front of the 1984 Ford pickup was, quite literally, wrapped around the tree, with the corners of the bumper nearly touching each other on the other side of the trunk.

"So, there's no reason to think it was anything other than an accident?" Damian asked.

Beni closed the file and looked up to find Carter eyeing the two of them.

"The only reason I have to think it might be something other than an accident is the fact that you two are here asking about it," Carter answered. "Was it something other than an accident?"

Damian lifted a shoulder. "Howard Jacek's name came up in another investigation and we just need to be sure."

Carter eyed them, then shook his head. "You'll want to see the truck. The address for the yard we had it towed to is in the file. We did a cursory look and didn't find any obvious interference with the vehicle."

"Thank you, Officer Carter," Beni said, moving toward the door. There were questions in the officer's eyes that neither she nor Damian could—or would—answer, and she didn't want to linger long enough for him to ask.

After a beat, he nodded. "As I'm sure you know, that's a copy," he said, nodding to the file she held. "It's yours to take. If you can let me know if you come to a different conclusion, I'd appreciate it. This is a quiet area, but if it was something other than an accident, I don't want it to appear that we're trying to hide anything."

Beni nodded at his request for the professional courtesy. If Jacek had been caught up in Calloway's conspiracy, they probably wouldn't be able to tell Carter the whole story, but they could at least let him know if they determined the man had been murdered.

"I'll show you out then," Carter said with a wave toward the door.

Beni led them out and Damian and Officer Carter followed behind, chatting about the area and its history. The two men paused to look at an old photo hanging in the hall, but Beni continued on to the reception area. With a nod to the receptionist, Beni headed toward the chairs by the window. Setting the file down on one, she grabbed her jacket.

And startled at what she saw outside.

Tugging her jacket on, she quickly pulled out her phone and snapped a couple of pictures through the window. The distance made it hard to get a clear shot, but there was no question in her mind about who she'd just spotted. Carl Westoff, a man who'd been heavily involved in the drug lab, and one they suspected of being Calloway's muscle, was lingering on the street corner in this small Virginia town.

She shifted her attention away from the window when Damian and Carter joined her in the reception area, but she caught Damian's eye and gave a subtle gesture of her head. Without question, he strolled over and casually glanced out as he, too, pulled his coat on.

After a beat, he swung back around and they both thanked Carter before exiting the office.

"That puts a new spin on things," Damian said as they started down the stairs to the ground floor.

"I let everyone know," she said, having sent a quick text and one of the images to the rest of the task force before she'd put her phone away. "So, now the question is, do we keep to our plan or do we go after Westoff?"

Damian didn't answer as they jogged down the rest of the stairs. When they were outside, they paused a few feet from the door and looked around. Westoff was nowhere in sight, likely having slipped back around the corner while they'd been making their way down from the third floor.

"I'm thinking we stick to the original plan," Damian said. "I think it will be more interesting to see what he does next. I'll send Lucy and Brian a quick text, too. It's amazing what they can track with satellites."

Beni stared at Damian as he shot off the text. "They have access to satellite tracking?" she asked when he returned his phone back to his pocket. She had to admit, she didn't know anyone outside of the military or intelligence communities who had access to the kind of satellite tracking Damian was referring to.

Damian chuckled. "You have no idea the kinds of things they have access to. *I* have no idea the full extent of what they have access to, but yes, if we give them enough information, they should be able to track Westoff. Or at least his car."

She pondered this as they walked to the car then climbed in. "So basically, we're really, really glad they are on our side."

Damian laughed outright at that. "Other than Charlotte, there is very little I give thanks for every day, but that is often one of them."

They pulled up to the junkyard thirty minutes later and Officer Carter must have given the owner a heads up that they were coming because an older man, dressed in overalls and a flannel jacket, was standing out front waiting for them.

Damian pulled into a parking spot and the two made their way to where the man stood.

"George Lester," he said with a nod.

"Agents Rodriguez and Ricci," Damian said, introducing them by pointing first to himself then to her.

"You want to see the Jacek truck? It's through here," Lester said, walking them toward a gate. "It's in the far southwest corner. My grandson comes here with his dad sometimes and I didn't want him to see all the blood."

Beni nodded her thank you as he opened a gate and they walked through. "There's a dog," Lester said. "He looks foul, but he's not bad. Won't hurt a fly unless I tell him to."

"Thanks for the warning," Beni said, tucking her hands into her pockets. It wasn't *that* cold, not like Boston, but she really had gotten used to Tildas. Lester gave a sharp nod, then pointed toward the southwest corner.

"Just watch your step," Lester added, before walking back into what Beni assumed was his office.

In silence, she and Damian made their way to the back corner, slopping through the late winter/early spring mud. The yard was bigger than she'd anticipated, and it took them a little over five minutes to finally spot the truck they sought.

The first thing that came into view was the tailgate with the iconic name painted across it. They could see no damage to the back which, though expected, sent a shiver up Beni's spine—it was disconcerting to see something so unaffected while knowing that just a few feet away a man had died, crushed to death by the metal of the same vehicle.

"I'll take the driver's side," she said, moving off to her left. Damian nodded and moved to the right. They both paused a few feet away then, on their own time, started to investigate the damage.

The first sign of impact on the driver's side came about halfway up the truck bed. There, the metal started to buckle, getting progressively worse as she worked her way to the front of the vehicle. Intentionally, she kept her eyes, and her camera, focused on the details, looking for any sign of damage that wasn't aligned with a head-on collision with a tree.

When she reached the front, she inched around to look at the truck from the point of impact. The front bumper had been bent back a bit in order to pull the truck from the tree, but it still formed a weird sort of three-quarter circle, like it was reaching around for a hug.

The point of impact was slightly offset and closer to the driver's side than to the passenger's. Fleetingly, Beni contemplated if the impact had been the other way—just a hair toward the passenger side—if Howard Jacek would have lived. Then she took a step back and looked at the entire front and all such questions fled. There was no way anyone could have survived the impact—not with half the engine block busted through the cab and pressed back against the bench seat.

Beni had seen a lot of shit in her time as a medic, but looking at the destruction, she hoped like hell Jacek really had died on impact. Otherwise, any pain he might have felt would have been beyond excruciating.

Damian joined her at the front and together they stood in silent contemplation.

"I can see why Mr. Lester wanted to keep this away from his grandson," Damian said.

Yeah, she could, too. Jacek hadn't gone through the windshield, his seatbelt and the engine block had likely held him in, but there was a massive spider web of cracks and breaks where his head must have collided with the glass. There were also blood stains all over the interior.

"There's probably more on the inside, too," Beni said. Together, they moved to the driver's side. It looked like the Jaws of Life had been used in order to extricate the body and the door hung precariously from a single hinge.

Pulling it open, they were greeted with the sight they'd anticipated, although that didn't lessen the shock. Blood stains covered the back of the seat, oozing over the sides. The dashboard—what was left of it—looked tacky, and bits of detritus were stuck on it. Everything had turned brown in the few days since the accident, but there was no mistaking what they were looking at.

"Fuck," Damian muttered.

"Yeah," Beni concurred quietly.

They both stared for a beat longer, then got to work comparing what they saw in person with the photos in the file Officer Carter had given them. They also took their own fair share of pictures. When they were done, Damian gently closed the door, lifting it into place more than latching it.

"You find anything inconsistent with the report?" Damian asked as they made their way toward the back of the truck.

Beni started to shake her head, then stopped as the afternoon sun hit the back panel and a shadow fell along the otherwise smooth metal.

"What's this?" she asked, moving to the spot where she'd seen the shadow. Kneeling to get a better look, at first glance, there wasn't much to see, and the side panel looked barely disturbed. But as she ran her fingers along it, she was able to trace a small indentation—the edge of which was what had cast the shadow.

Stepping back, she gestured for Damian to do the same. When his fingers traced the same area as hers, he leaned in.

"I was going to say that this could have happened at any time —especially given the age of the truck—but there's a scratch here, and it looks new," he said.

Careful to keep her knees out of the mud, Beni crouched down again and looked at the area where Damian was pointing. Sure enough, there it was. A single, four-inch-long scratch in the paint, a scratch deep enough and new enough that the bright metal underneath still showed.

After taking a few more pictures, she rose. "Might not have happened in the accident, but it doesn't line up with all the other damage."

Damian inclined his head. "We'll note it. We have the pictures. If it's nothing, it's nothing. Ready to go to the site?"

"Yes. I'm also ready for that heater in your car. It's freezing out here," she muttered.

Damian chuckled and started to lead the way out. Beni paused one last time and glanced back at the truck. Had Howard Jacek figured out he was little more than a pawn in a game he had no idea how to play?

Knowing no answer would come, she spun back around only to see a hound from hell barreling toward them. Lester had said the dog looked foul and he hadn't been exaggerating. The fur was a mottled gray-brown and the face looked a mash-up of mastiff, pit bull, and pug. The beast's body was the size of a St. Bernard with a large, deep-barrel chest, but its legs were spindly, more like those of a greyhound. As if sensing he had their attention, the dog started barking and drool flew from his mouth as he galloped toward them, his large teeth showing beneath his lips.

Both she and Damian reached for their weapons. With the speed at which the dog was traveling and the relatively minor distance he had to cover before reaching them, they'd never have them drawn in time, but instinct had taken over.

Beni's heart pounded as she touched the leather of her holster. Releasing the catch holding her gun in place, she reminded herself that Lester had said the dog was harmless unless he told it otherwise. Then again, had he told it otherwise? Had they walked into a trap?

The animal was less than fifteen feet away when she got her grip on her weapon, but just as she started to pull it out, the dog seemed to shift its tactics and it slowed its movements. Or at least it tried to. It took one more galloping stride, bringing it to within seven feet of Beni, then it stumbled a few small steps, before it started sliding in the mud. Straight into her.

The dog hit her with all the force of a hundred-and-twenty-pound canine traveling at close to top speed and sent her flying backward. Her head snapped back and hit the truck. Or perhaps it was the tailgate, or maybe the bumper.

Although why she was contemplating such a question as she slid down into the mud and into unconsciousness, she hadn't a clue.

CHAPTER ELEVEN

THE FIRST THING Beni became aware of when she started to regain consciousness was the cold. She'd been cold before, but now, now something was different, and she was freezing. And wet?

"Beni?" Damian's voice. "Open your eyes, Beni."

She almost snapped at him not to tell her what to do, but instead, she forced her eyelids up. Nausea swirled in her stomach as the light hit her eyes. "Oh my god, I'm going to be sick," she said, struggling to rise, or at least shift to her side.

Damian wrapped an arm behind her back and pulled her into a sitting position. Being upright helped a little and she closed her eyes and took a few deep breaths in an attempt to settle her stomach. As soon as she was confident that she wasn't going to vomit on her friend, she opened her eyes again.

"What the hell?" she asked.

"He tried to stop but couldn't in the mud," Damian said, gesturing to the dog who now lay on the ground watching them, his head resting on his paws. "He hit you at close to full speed and you hit your head on the trailer hitch. I think we need to get you to the ER for some X-rays. You definitely have a concussion and I just want to be sure there's not anything more serious than that."

Beni slid her gaze back to the dog. Felled by a fucking puppy. Okay, he wasn't exactly a puppy, and he was actually kind of cute in an ugly way, but still...

"I'm fine," she said.

Damian looked ready to argue with her, but thankfully, he thought better of it. Rising from where he'd knelt beside her, he held out a hand to help her up. Bracing herself, she reached for him and let him tug her up.

Two seconds later, she grabbed the back of the truck for support, leaned to the side, and vomited. So much for being okay.

"You're such an asshole," she said once she'd caught her breath. Damian handed her a clean tissue, and she wiped her mouth.

"I figured that letting you figure out yourself that you weren't fine would be a lot faster than trying to argue with you about it."

She tried to glare at him, but her stomach somersaulted again. She gripped his arm to steady herself as she closed her eyes and took a few more breaths. "Okay, I'm not fine. I probably—"

Damian snorted.

"Fine, I *have* a concussion," she conceded. "The doctors won't be able to do anything about it, though." As she spoke, she reached behind her and gingerly felt her head where it had connected with the trailer hitch. She winced at the pain and her fingers came away with blood. Not a lot, but enough to give her pause.

"You ready to give in yet?"

She stared at her fingertips for a moment more. She knew the blood came from her own head, but she was having trouble fully processing that. Finally, she nodded. She was tough, but she was also smart. She'd seen enough head injuries in her time to know that it would be safer to get checked out than not.

"Why don't you take me to the nearest clinic and leave me there while you go check out the accident site?" she suggested.

"Right, 'cause I'm going to leave my friend at the hospital on her own with a head injury," he said, wrapping an arm around her for support as they started back to the parking lot. The dog rose and walked alongside them, nudging his nose under her free hand every few steps.

"It will save us time, Damian," Beni said. "If we want to fly out tonight, then we don't have time for you to wait around the hospital."

"I got news for you, Ricci. The chances of us flying anywhere tonight are slim to none. I can all but guarantee you that the doctors aren't going to clear you to fly until tomorrow at the earliest."

She knew he was right. She didn't *want* him to be right, but just because she didn't want him to be right didn't mean he wasn't. But if they didn't leave for Tildas tonight, then she'd have to tell Cal she was staying in town, which also meant she'd probably have to tell him about her run in with the trailer hitch. While the idea of one more night with Cal was becoming less unappealing, having to deal with his reaction to her injury wasn't something she was looking forward to.

Unwilling to linger on that reality, she decided to focus on her feet and moving forward one step at a time. Thankfully, being covered in mud from her heels to the back of her head, and her pounding headache and lingering nausea, provided a lot of distraction from thoughts of what she might need to tell Cal.

"Everything all right?" Mr. Lester asked, emerging from his office as they approached the main gate.

Damian gave the man an abbreviated version of the chain of events and after waving off his profuse apologies and offers of giving them his business insurance information, they managed to get the address of the closest hospital. Mr. Lester's daughter-in-law worked there, and he promised to call her and let her know they were on their way in.

True to his word, Dr. Allison Lester met them at the door of the urgent care department and ushered them in. When she led them into a private room, Beni protested—she didn't want to usurp other waiting patients. Dr. Lester waved off her concern, though, assuring her they had plenty of resources to handle their current intake.

Beni handed Damian her phone and badge—the only things she'd had in her pocket—then he helped her remove her holster. After placing her scant possessions inside a bag, he removed himself from the room, telling her he'd be in the lobby. A few minutes later, she was out of her wet clothes, into a hospital gown, and was having her head examined.

She knew the drill well enough and she answered all the questions truthfully and simply—the best way of ensuring that Dr. Lester could do the job she needed to do. Not surprisingly, the doctor gave a diagnosis of a mid-grade concussion and ordered X-rays to see if there'd been any damage to the skull. She also ordered an MRI to check on any potential internal bleeding.

Beni's hair had been mostly cleaned, thanks to the efficient nurses, and she was drifting in and out of sleep under layers of warmed blankets, when Damian walked in.

"How are you feeling?" he asked.

"Warm and dry now. Tired," she admitted.

"Since you gave Dr. Lester permission to update me and you were sleeping, she and I just had a little chat. There is a significant bone bruise at the base of your skull, but no bleeding and, so long as you don't go banging it around anymore, it should heal just fine."

Beni blinked at him. "I seriously almost cracked my skull

open because an overgrown ball of fluff ran into me?" It wasn't really a question, but Damian nodded.

"So, what does that mean in terms of us getting back to Tildas?" she asked on a long exhale.

"It means that I managed to convince the doctor to release you tonight on the proviso that you be well taken care of. She said if there are no changes over night, we can fly tomorrow afternoon so long as you check in with a doctor when you land."

As Damian spoke, Beni started to think it might be easier to just stay the night in the hospital. The nurses were better positioned than Damian to keep an eye on her. She didn't love the idea, but it was practical, and she suggested as much to Damian.

He was shaking his head before she even finished. "I had your phone and a certain someone started texting you while I was waiting. I let him know what was going on and he, and his physician, will be waiting for you in Alexandria. I've already asked Dr. Lester to transfer your records over to the other doctor."

She groaned. Not that she didn't think Cal deserved to know, she just didn't want to deal with his anxiety while she was also trying her damnedest not to throw up. There was also the not-so-small issue of Westoff, too.

"You can't take me there," she said. "Westoff was following us and we can't lead him there."

Damian grinned. "We aren't. I'm going to go to the accident site and then head back to Georgetown to have dinner with my mother-in-law. He's sending someone to pick you up. Several *someones* would be my guess, but they'll be discreet. He knows what's at stake here, Beni. Give him some credit."

She closed her eyes and let the fatigue take away some of her own anxiety. "I know he does, but you have to admit, he's not exactly acting rationally when it comes to me. First, he visits The Shack unannounced, then decides to stay the night at my place despite it being less than secure. Then he dresses up as a taxi driver so he can all but kidnap me and take me to Alexandria. I'm not sure where things will go with us, Damian, but regardless, I don't want him doing stupid things. His job puts him at risk enough as it is."

A long silent moment passed and when Damian still didn't speak, Beni opened her eyes to find him staring at her, arms crossed, and head cocked to the side. "You didn't tell us he came to stay with you after he left The Shack."

"I tell you all that, and *that's* what you take away?"

Damian bobbed his head. "You have to admit, that was a pretty big piece of information you left out."

She glared at him. Or at least tried to. When she narrowed her eyes, the nausea kicked back up.

"Seriously, Beni, he's got this under control. You need to trust him. If it makes you feel any better, I agree with you. He may be engaging in activities that past vice presidents haven't, but he's doing it because he wants to be with you. And if there is any chance at all of succeeding in that—which I think there is because you haven't kicked his ass to the curb yet—then he's not going to do anything that might truly jeopardize his chances. Including putting himself in unnecessary danger."

Beni studied Damian's expression and though she didn't doubt he spoke from the heart, his words also gave her a different perspective. When Charlotte had first come back into Damian's life, he'd been in much the same situation as Cal. Charlotte and Damian didn't have the complications she and Cal had with respect to their jobs, but, like Cal, Damian had never stopped loving Charlotte. He knew what it was like to have a second chance with the woman he loved. And he knew what it was like to protect that chance with everything he had.

She wasn't sure if Cal loved her the way Damian loved Charlotte—there were so many years between who they were now and who they'd been when they'd last loved each other—but she couldn't discount what Damian was telling her. If Cal really did want them to have another chance to at least see where this thing between them might go, then he wouldn't do anything to jeopardize that.

"You're right," she said on an exhale. "I still think it's crazy, but you're right. He probably has way more security in place than he's shared with me. Enough security to protect the both of us." She glanced out the window as she spoke and noted the fading light. "Why don't you head on out to the site? I'll be fine here."

Damian studied her then nodded and handed over her bag of belongings. "He said he'd call when your ride was fifteen minutes out."

"Thanks, Damian," she said, taking her things. "You're a good friend."

He grinned. "I am, you're right. But you make it pretty easy. Now just relax and do what the doctor says. I'll update the team on my way to the site and we can touch base tomorrow." He leaned down and brushed a kiss on her cheek. "And be nice to him when you see him. It's not every day that someone you love nearly cracks their skull open."

She tried to roll her eyes and once again, the nausea told her that maybe she should just chill with the exaggerated eye movements. "Let me know if you find anything," she said.

"I will," he agreed. "You'll let me know when you get to wherever it is you're going in Alexandria?"

She nodded and a few seconds later, she was left alone in her room pondering just how Cal and his team were going to get her out of the hospital without Carl Westoff any the wiser. Not that she knew for certain if he'd followed them to the hospital, but it was safe to assume he had. Then again, when Damian left without her, it would leave him in a quandary—follow Damian or stay and keep an eye on the hospital.

Dashing off a quick text to Damian to ask him to let her know if he spotted Westoff, Beni then set the phone down and tried to convince herself to wait patiently for her get-out-of-jail card—or, as the case may be, hospital card.

A text from Cal came one hour and forty-seven minutes later...not that she was keeping track. But really, what else was there to do in the hospital when her teammates weren't responding to her texts, other than to tell her to rest, and there was only so much solitaire—or screen time—a woman with a concussion could take.

"Agent Ricci," Dr. Lester said, stepping into the room a few minutes later. "I believe your ride has arrived. I've already sent your records over to Dr. Kaplan, as your colleague requested. He should have everything he needs to treat you. He's an excellent physician and will take good care of you. That said, if you have any questions, you can always give me a call."

As Beni listened to Dr. Lester, two men who looked nothing like she'd expected stepped into the room. She wasn't quite sure why, but she'd anticipated the Secret Service type—men sporting earpieces and wearing black suits and non-descript ties. Who actually stepped into the room were two men in jeans, sneakers, and hoodies. The sweatshirts were zipped up just enough to hide the shoulder holsters they both wore. They might not have been what she'd expected, but she knew the type.

After signing a few documents Dr. Lester handed her, and getting her discharge instructions, Beni was left alone with the two men.

"Private security?" she asked. "Let me guess, former military? You look like a SEAL," she said to the lankier of the two. "And you look like a Ranger," she said to the other. Both men grinned at her.

"Stella said you'd spot us straight off," said the former SEAL. "I'm Tompkins and this is Ballinger. We'll be escorting you to the house in Alexandria. Before we leave, though, how are you feeling, Agent Ricci?"

"Call me Beni," she said, swinging her legs over the side of the bed. She was kind of surprised a nurse hadn't come in to help her get dressed, but maybe Tompkins and Ballinger had made it clear she was in their charge now. "As long as I'm mostly still, I don't feel like I'm going to get sick all over everything."

"You need a hand getting dressed?" Ballinger asked with a ghost of a smile.

Beni considered it. She wasn't particularly modest—the military made sure of that—but the thought of one of Stella's security guys, someone hired by Cal, helping her dress, didn't sit well. Thankfully, a nurse bustled in just then. She drew up short as she took in the two men, then focused her attention on Beni.

"Let me help you. These two gentlemen can wait outside while we get you dressed. The other agent who was here earlier dropped this off before he left," she said, holding up Beni's overnight bag. "I meant to bring it earlier, but we had a family with both the flu and pneumonia come in as well as a car accident."

Beni glanced at Ballinger and Tompkins. It was possible that their orders were as strict as to never let her out of their sight, but to her relief, they both nodded and moved toward the door.

"We'll be right outside," Tompkins said.

Ten minutes later, she was dressed in a pair of jeans and a loose sweater and was being wheeled out the back entrance of the hospital by Ballinger. Just as they reached the sidewalk, two black SUVs pulled up, one closer than the other. Without a word, she let Ballinger—whose first name was James—help her from her chair and into the back seat of the car. The whole process was embarrassing, but she tolerated the overabundance of caution and security because she knew it was just as much for Cal as it was for her.

The three men in her car were as professional as they came —not that Beni would have expected anything less from people employed by Stella Matthews—and they spoke very little as they made their way north to Alexandria.

At one point, James asked her how she was doing and then, as they merged onto the highway, she mentioned the SUV that had been following her and Damian earlier. The chances of it following their cavalcade were low—especially since Damian had texted her to let her know he'd spotted Westoff—but she thought they should know just in case.

Thirty minutes later, the car she rode in pulled into the same garage that the cab had parked in the night before. She looked up and, standing in the door, wearing jeans and a long-sleeved t-shirt, with his arms crossed across his chest, was Cal. The taut lines of his body told her he wanted to rush out and be the one to help her. The presence of his Secret Service detail making it equally as clear that he was not to step out of the house.

James held out his arm to help steady her and Beni gingerly stepped out of the SUV. As soon as she was within arms' reach of Cal, he gently tugged her close and wrapped his arms around her, tucking her up against his chest.

His heart beat rapidly beneath her ear and his breath whispered across the top of her head.

"I'm fine, Cal," she said, her voice muffled against the cotton of his shirt.

He didn't say anything for a moment, just held her. Then, releasing her, he lowered one of his hands and twined their fingers together.

"Thanks, guys," he said to Stella's crew. Beni turned around and gave a wave of thanks, too, but they were already climbing back into the car. "I have some tea," Cal said, pulling her into the house and toward the kitchen. Out of the corner of her eye, she saw someone bring her bag in from the garage and carry it upstairs. Bed sounded better than tea, but she wanted to stay awake long enough to hear from Damian.

"I'd give you a whiskey, but even though my doctor took a

look at your files and decided he didn't need to see you in person tonight, I think he'd disapprove," Cal said, flashing a grin at her over his shoulder as he set the kettle on the stove. She settled herself on a bar stool at the kitchen island and made a face.

"A fucking dog, Cal. Not even an attack one at that. Just a clumsy one." He chuckled at her comment, and just like that, she was laughing, too. She hadn't realized how much tension she'd been holding since just this moment. She hated being a patient. She'd also been worried about the case *and* about having to deal with a worried Cal. And he *was* worried, although he was doing his best to not add any more stress to the situation. Which, in turn, allowed her to let much of her own stress slip away. The case was still foremost in her mind, but Damian was taking over the last piece the two of them had planned and he was more than capable.

"How are you, really?" he asked, setting a mug in front of her. She smelled jasmine and something sweet.

"Annoyed that I got taken out by a dog, my head hurts, and I'm feeling a little nauseous and tired. But I'll be fine. I'll get as much sleep tonight as the doctor recommends then hopefully head back to Tildas tomorrow."

Disappointment flashed in Cal's eyes, but he didn't say anything about her leaving. "You want to go lay down on the couch? We can watch a movie or something until Damian calls. I have some lasagna in the fridge that will take about forty-five minutes to heat up, so let me know when you're starting to get hungry."

At the mention of food, Beni was suddenly starving. Any food she'd eaten that day, she'd vomited up and she hadn't felt like putting anything more into her stomach. Until now.

"Any chance you have something small to eat? Not ready for dinner yet but wouldn't mind some bread or crackers or something."

In response, he started opening a few cupboards and at the third one, he hit pay dirt. "How about some good old-fashioned saltines to go with your tea?" he asked, holding the box up.

She couldn't help the smile. "That would be perfect. Not sure I'm up for watching TV, but let's turn it on and see how things go."

Together they made their way to the living room. It sat at the front of the house, but the curtains were drawn so no one walking along outside would be able to see in. Given that this was one of Stella's safe houses, Beni suspected the windows were all bulletproof anyway. Craving just a little bit of *normal*, though, she opted not to ask.

"If you have work to do, I can do the same," she offered, holding up her phone as she sat on one end of the couch.

Cal glanced over his shoulder toward the door they'd just come through. Maybe he had a work bag somewhere or maybe one of the Secret Service detail inside the house had caught his attention. She didn't know what he was looking at or for, but when he looked back, he was all focus. On her.

"Here," he said, patting his lap. There was no way she was going to sit in his lap, and the look she shot him must have done an adequate job of communicating that because he barked out a laugh. "Your feet, Nita. Lift your feet up here. I know how much you like having your feet rubbed."

The wisdom of allowing this man to rub her feet was questionable. A woman didn't just let any man rub her feet—for as innocent as it was, it was an oddly intimate act. But Cal wasn't wrong. Between having her head rubbed and her feet massaged, it was a toss-up as to which was her favorite. But the thought of getting her head rubbed right now made her eyes water and she caved, swinging her feet up. She had to turn on her side a bit, so the back of her head wasn't resting on the arm of the couch, but she watched Cal as he unzipped and removed her boots then pulled her socks off. Tugging a throw blanket from the back of the couch, he tossed it over her, making sure to cover her toes, then, with one hand wrapped around the sole of her left foot, he picked up a remote. Expecting the TV to come on, she was pleasantly surprised when the gas fireplace burst to life.

"I usually get my news fix as I'm getting ready in the morning, or from my advisors. Other than that, I don't really have a lot of time for TV," Cal said, as he started to dig his fingers into her feet.

She watched the flames dancing behind the glass as she and Cal alternated between a comfortable silence and comfortable conversation. She managed to get a few crackers into her stomach and a few awkward sips of tea, too, though it wasn't so easy to drink while lying on her side. As the minutes ticked by, Beni realized that if she gave it much thought, it might freak her out just how easy it was to be with Cal again. But at the moment, she was battling keeping her eyes open and her food down while still enjoying the feel of his hands on her feet.

She must have drifted off at some point because she started with a jerk when her phone rang. Her mug of tea was sitting on the floor and, while Cal's hands were still wrapped around her feet, he'd stopped massaging them and was just gazing at the flames.

Reaching for her phone, she saw Damian's name on the screen, along with a couple of missed text messages from Jake and Alexis.

"Find anything?" she asked by way of answering.

"Actually, I did," Damian said. "Take a look at your texts."

As he spoke, a new text came in and in it was an image of a studio-style light—not a can light, but the almost cone-shaped ones with a metal casing and a bulbous glass front. Something niggled in her mind as she studied it.

"Where'd you find it?" she asked.

"About thirty feet from the accident site. In the bushes."

"Any chance you can bring it over?" The question was

directed at both Damian and Cal. Cal had been watching her and slowly he nodded his agreement then picked up his phone, presumably to let his security know.

"Yeah, I can come by. I don't want to head over in my car as our friend was hanging around today, though. My mother-in-law is hosting an event tonight; I'll head there, then sneak out with the caterers," he answered.

"Sounds good, we'll let them know you'll be here. Are you eating at that event, or do you want to eat here?" she asked, again looking to Cal who nodded in response to her unasked question as to whether they had enough food.

"Haven't eaten since the vending machine trail mix at the hospital. Some food wouldn't be unwelcome."

She smiled. She'd seen Damian eat and she hoped Cal wasn't counting on any leftovers. "Great, just text when you get close," she said, then, after rattling off the address, they ended the call.

"Everything all set?" she asked, rolling to her back as much as possible.

"All set," Cal responded, sliding out from under her feet. "I'm going to go throw the lasagna in the oven. Need a refill on the tea? Or maybe some water?"

She eyed him. "You're going to have wine, aren't you?"

He grinned. "I love you, but I'm not giving it up in solidarity. If anything, I suspect I'm going to need it tonight more than ever."

She questioned why tonight would be different and just what it was he thought Damian would tell them. Then her mind processed the fact that he'd just told her he loved her, and she couldn't help it, she gaped. Like an out of body experience, she felt her mouth open, then close, then open again, like a fish. There was no way he could have meant it.

"I meant it," he said.

He didn't mean it, it was just a saying ... how many times had she and the team said something like that to each other?

"You know I love you but..." It meant, well, not nothing, but not *that*.

"It wasn't just a saying," Cal said, smiling at her.

It had only been less than two weeks since he'd waltzed back into her life. A person didn't know such a thing in such a short time.

"It's been over twenty years that we've known each other, Nita," he said, bending over her and brushing his lips across hers. "I *know*."

Then leaving her to process that pronouncement, he walked out of the room.

"Stop reading my mind," she called after him.

All she heard was him chuckling.

CHAPTER TWELVE

AN HOUR LATER, an hour in which Benita refused to acknowledge what he'd told her, Cal opened the door to find not just Damian but Jessica Kilkenny as well.

"Damian," Cal said, shaking the man's hand after he'd stepped inside and set a small duffel bag down in the entry. "Jess." He leaned forward and brushed a kiss along her cheek. He had no idea what the journalist was doing at the house—or how she got past his security—but if Damian felt the need to bring one, Jessica was a good choice. She didn't write gossip or speculation and, for the most part, didn't even cover politics. She was—hands down—the best at what she did write about, though—injustice. Which often involved politics.

He led the two into the kitchen where Beni was standing at the table tossing a salad. "One more person for dinner, honey," Cal said, keeping his voice light and teasing.

Beni looked up, her gaze landing on the woman before it traveled to Damian for an explanation.

"Beni, this is Jessica Kilkenny, the reporter who put us onto Howard Jacek. Jess, this is Benita Ricci, one of my colleagues on the task force," Damian said.

Beni's expression didn't change, but Cal could feel the questions—and the tension—flowing off her. It was all directed at Damian, though, so Cal didn't mind so much. But he *was* interested to see how long it would be before Damian caught on that Beni Was Not Pleased that he'd brought a journalist over. No matter how trustworthy Jess might be.

Damian's gaze held Beni's, then his eyes narrowed. "Knock it off, Beni. I wouldn't have brought her if I thought it was an issue. She has some information on Jacek she wanted to share."

The integrity of the investigation wouldn't be the only thing Beni would be worried about, and Cal watched the by-play between the two agents as he cut the lasagna. Cal almost felt bad for Damian when it became obvious that he wasn't picking up on what Beni was trying to communicate. Then finally, Jess stepped in.

"I'm not interested in what's going on here," Jess said, wagging a finger between Beni and Cal. "That's not my beat and, quite frankly, it's not that interesting. I'm here because Jacek was a loose-lipped douchey kind of guy who I'm pretty sure was targeted for those exact reasons. And while I wouldn't wish anyone dead, not even Jacek, I especially don't like it when the bad guys start coming after journalists."

Beni eyed Jess, then flicked her gaze to Damian, before letting out an exhale. "If Rodriguez vouches for you and Cal doesn't seem to mind, I guess I don't have too much room to complain, though I won't apologize for being skeptical."

Jess chuckled as she removed her cashmere coat. Handing it over to Damian, she ran her hands over her strawberry blond hair then straightened her skirt. "You are a woman after my doubting heart, Agent Ricci. Now, I hear there's dinner?"

Cal brought another plate over and a few minutes later, the four of them were seated around the table digging into one of his favorite comfort foods.

"So, what updates do you have on Jacek?" Beni asked Jess before taking a bite.

"Before we go there, let's talk about what I found at the accident site," Damian said. Rising from his seat, he went to the duffel he'd set down in the entryway and extracted an evidence bag. Inside was the light Cal had seen in the image Damian had texted Beni earlier.

Cal reached for it and, holding it in both hands, judged its weight to be more than a couple of pounds. Beyond that, he didn't have much more insight, so he handed it over to Beni.

Without so much as looking at the light itself, Beni rotated it in order to examine the back. Something caught her attention, and she flattened the plastic of the bag over it to get a better look. Cal glanced at Damian, but the agent looked just as curious as Cal and didn't seem to know what Beni was examining.

She rubbed her finger along a piece of the metal, paused, then brought it closer to her face. Finally, she spoke. "There," she said, holding her finger on a specific spot and handing the light back to Damian.

He took it from her and dutifully looked where she wanted him to. "What am I looking at?"

"I've seen this before. In Afghanistan," she said.

"You were deployed in Afghanistan?" Cal asked, startled at the thought. Although why he should be surprised, he didn't know. It wasn't like he didn't *know* Beni had been deployed. But as she casually tossed out the fact that she'd been deployed to Afghanistan, he realized that while he was happy she'd found work she loved, he'd intentionally been putting his head in the sand about what that work meant. She was a medic in the Army, of course she'd been deployed to Afghanistan.

She shot him a funny look. "Yes. I was in Afghanistan six times, actually."

He reached for his wine and took a sip. A big sip. "Do I want to know where else you've been?"

Her brow furrowed, as if confused as to why he'd be asking. She might have a point. Maybe he shouldn't be, at least not now. But the question was out there...

"All the usual places," she answered. "North Africa, the Middle East. I did have a deployment for specialized medical training in Germany. That was a nice one."

His gaze darted to Jess who was looking amused by his line of questioning—and, no doubt, the sudden pallor of his skin at the thought of Beni in all those places. He shifted his attention to Damian who was still examining whatever it was Beni had pointed out, oblivious to the fact that his teammate had just told them that she'd been in some of the most dangerous places in the world. Then again, Damian had been an Army Ranger and had probably been to those same places.

He took another sip of wine then cleared his throat. "Right. So, about the light...?"

"As I said, I saw this in Afghanistan," Beni continued. "There was a group of locals living in the mountains. They were—are—good people, who were trying to keep the warlords and various factions out of their village. Only they were trying to do it without drawing attention to themselves and making themselves targets. What they came up with was kind of ingenious."

"In what way?" Damian asked, setting the light down and focusing on his colleague.

"There was only one road in and one road out of their village; and calling it a road is a bit of an exaggeration. It was maybe the width of one-and-half cars, packed dirt, and cut into the side of a cliff. It was a bit of a hair-raising ride, but it worked to their advantage." Beni grinned at the memory before continuing.

"They rigged up a truck to have a sort of metal arm extend off the front bumper and then, on that arm, they attached two lights. Two lights similar, but a bit more dated, than that one," she said, gesturing with her head to the one on the table. "They'd then park the truck around a bend and against the mountain so that the arm extended toward the cliff."

She paused and in that pause, Damian chuckled. "Then when the warlords came around the corner in their car, they turned the lights on so that it appeared that there were two cars coming at them, and they'd instinctively swerve to miss it," Damian said.

"Sending them plummeting over the cliff in what would appear, to most, to be a simple accident and therefore, no one to blame," Jess finished.

Beni's grin morphed into a smile. "Amazingly effective," she said. "Brutal, too, but needs must when you're trying to protect your village from warlords and terrorists."

"Out of curiosity, how many did they get?" Damian asked, rising and taking the light with him.

"That I know of? Six," Beni answered. "They did it at different places along the road so that it was never one location. They didn't have any other way to protect themselves," she added.

"That's what you think that light was?" Jess asked, waving to the bag Damian had just placed the light back into.

"It has a mechanism on the back that would have allowed it to be attached to an arm," Beni said. "I wasn't there, so can't say for certain, but I suspect Howard Jacek was barreling along the country road, someone had a similar set up to what I just described, and when Jacek swerved, the back of his vehicle made contact with the arm."

"Scratching the back of the truck and knocking the light off and into the bushes," Damian finished.

They were all silent for a moment, then Jess picked up her wine glass, speaking as she raised it up for a sip. "That is some fucked up shit, but I could see it happening."

Damian inclined his head. Cal had seen a lot of nasty things in politics and he was well-briefed on the atrocities happening in conflicts around the world—as well as those in their own country—but the thought of such violence being used specifically to bring him and Anne-Marie down turned his stomach.

With a shake of his head, he spoke. "I know the desire for power can be one of the most corrupting forces, so I shouldn't be surprised. Yet, I am. Not so much that there are people out there who hate this administration, but that there are people out there who hate it so much that they are willing to sacrifice, to kill, innocent people to destroy it."

In a surprise gesture, Beni reached over and covered his hand with hers. "I know you're not a naïve man, but *knowing* the kinds of things people do to each other and seeing it firsthand, like Damian and I have, are two different things. Frankly, I'm glad you're surprised. I'm glad that that level of perversion isn't normal to you."

He held her gaze then turned his hand palm up to twine their fingers. She offered him a small smile and he gave her hand a little squeeze. Then releasing him, she leaned back in her chair and eyed Jess.

"So, back to my original question. What updates do you have on Howard Jacek?"

Jess set her glass down. "Remember when we first talked a few days ago and I didn't know if he'd spoken to any other colleagues or if he'd just reached out to me because of my connection to him?" she prompted with a gesture of her head toward Damian. Beni nodded. "Turns out it wasn't just me. I had a couple of colleagues call me today who had also heard from Jacek. Three of them, to be precise. None of them took Jacek's original call because they're respected journalists who wouldn't be interested in anything Jacek was selling. Then, when news of his death got out and you guys arrived to investigate, well, let's just say that the messages Jacek had left them took on a new meaning."

Cal took another bite of his food. He wasn't short on brain cells and had had plenty of strategy and intelligence conversations in his life, but the one happening between the three other people at the table didn't need his input or opinion, so he took advantage of the luxury afforded him to be just an observer.

"You think that's why Westoff was following us?" Beni asked Damian. "Not to do anything to stop us, but just to make sure he could tip off some of these journalists?"

Damian finished a sip of wine and set the glass down. "How did the journalists know we were here? Were they tipped off?" he asked Jess.

She nodded. "They all got emails. All from the same address. So did I," she answered, pulling out her phone and hitting a few buttons. After a few seconds, she put the device on the table and slid it over to rest between Damian and Beni. Both agents dipped their heads to read.

"Interesting," Beni said, then, surprisingly, she picked up the phone and handed it to him. Cal took the device and read the short note.

"The file on Howard Jacek's accident was requested by two FBI agents earlier today just before both agents inspected the vehicle Jacek had been driving."

And that was it. Beni hadn't told him that she and Damian had been followed, but he had received a text from Stella letting him know that Beni had mentioned it to the men who'd been sent to pick her up. He'd been a little disgruntled at her omission, but at least she hadn't kept the information from the people who actually needed to know, the ones who were tasked with protecting her.

"Can you send that to me?" Damian asked.

"Or I can just send it to Brian and Lucy, since I'm assuming that's who you'll send it on to?" Jessica countered.

"You know Lucy and Brian?" Beni asked.

Jess chuckled. "That's actually how I met Damian. I worked in the same field as them for several years before becoming a journalist."

Beni glanced at Cal silently asking if he'd known this. He nodded. He'd known Jessica ever since she'd broken her first story years ago. It had been a tragic one, involving police and judicial corruption that had resulted in the death of her closest friend. Her research and her writing had been extraordinarily detailed. So much so, that none of the people involved had ever actually tried to dispute it.

"So, what do you think the angle is?" Jess asked before taking a sip of her wine. Beni cast a longing look at the deep red liquid and Cal slid his hand onto her thigh and gave a squeeze. Her head jerked around, and he gave a little shake of his head. She narrowed her eyes at him—and actually succeeded this time, which meant she was probably starting to heal already—but then reached for the water he'd poured for her.

"What better way to foster the seeds of a conspiracy than to kill those trying to uncover it," Cal said. Everyone at the table looked at him. "I'm just saying that it's almost a cliché. Pick up any middle grade adventure book that involves a conspiracy and somehow, somewhere along the way, the person trying to uncover it gets silenced. Maybe not killed, in a middle grade book, but you know what I mean."

Damian leaned back in his chair while Jess twirled her wine glass. Beni chewed a bite of her lasagna as she studied him. "You're right," she said after she'd swallowed. "We don't know what they are planning for The Summit, but we do know that they've committed—or tried to commit—several crimes that they are going to attempt to link back to you."

Damian nodded and took up the thread. "So, if they are going to go down the route of trying to make you look guilty of *something*, what better way to help cement that perspective than to kill a journalist who appeared to be investigating your activities in the Caribbean. Because, as you say, as cliché as it is, it will look like you had him silenced to stop his investigation."

Jess snorted, drawing everyone's attention. "You're right, I'm not saying you aren't. It's just that anyone who knew Howard Jacek knew that *investigating* wasn't his strong point. Although, that flaw actually makes him a perfect target for a plan like that."

At Damian's questioning look, she held up a finger. "Stick with me on this, big guy," she said, eliciting an eye roll from the former Ranger. "First, Jacek was as lazy as they come, and there was no chance he would ever *actually* investigate anything. Whoever tipped him off wouldn't have to worry about him uncovering anything other than what they fed him. And second, most people don't know that fact about Jacek and all they'd see is a dead journalist who died while investigating the vice president."

"They picked him well, then," Cal said. "Who would know him well enough to know that about him?"

"Other journalists who worked with him," Jess answered, picking up her glass and leaning back in her seat. "I don't mean to imply that anyone worked *with* him, in the sense of being part of a team. Jacek was strictly a solo act. Mostly because he was so stupid and had no integrity."

"Tell us how you really feel, Jess," Cal said on a chuckle.

She gave him the side eye, but grinned then continued. "Jacek's been around for the last ten or twelve years. So, even though he was a shitty journalist, he would have crossed paths with other journalists enough times in the past decade to form at least an acquaintanceship with a few. Hell, even *I* knew him. But I guess, in a way, that answers your questions. He sold complete stories and didn't pitch ideas that would require he follow-up. So, really, the only people who would know that his investigative skills rivaled a two-year-old's would probably just be other journalists."

Damian and Beni shared a look.

"What?" Jess demanded. When neither answered right away, she set her glass on the table and intentionally filled it almost to the top. It was a crime against wine to pour that much at once, but Jess was making a point. "I'm not going anywhere, Rodriguez," she said. "You may as well tell me what that look was all about and, more to the point, what the hell is actually going on. I've gone easy on you so far, figuring you'll tell me what you can, but I think the time has come to press my point."

As strange as it sounded to trust a journalist, Cal trusted Jess. He glanced at Damian and Beni and raised a shoulder, making it clear it was their call. Then on a sigh, Damian answered.

"I actually wouldn't mind picking your devious mind on what's going on," he said. "Let's tidy up and maybe go sit by the fire?"

Beni was the first to rise and she started to reach for everyone's plates. Cal made a point of taking them from her hands and gesturing to the living room with his head. She may be feeling better, but that didn't mean her body didn't need more rest.

"Why don't you get the fire started?" he asked.

Beni paused then shook her head as she accepted defeat. "Because it's so hard to push the remote button," she muttered as she walked away.

Jess waggled her eyebrows at Cal then followed Beni out of the room, saying over her shoulder, "I think the ladies shall retire to the sitting room. Once you gentlemen are done communing with the dishwasher, you may join us."

Cal shook his head at his friend and continued to stack the dishes while Damian started putting the food away. By the time they joined Jess and Beni in the living room, the gas fireplace was throwing out heat. Jess was curled up in an upholstered chair, having kicked her heels off, and Beni was back on the couch she'd fallen asleep on earlier, with the blanket tucked around her. Cal took the same spot he'd been in earlier, too, placing Beni's feet across his lap, while Damian took a seat to the left of the fireplace.

"So," Jess started, "let's start with that look you two shared. What do journalists have to do with whatever really brought you up here?"

"Damian?" Beni asked, urging her colleague to take the lead. Now that she'd eaten and was lying down in a warm room, she was starting to look tired. Damian must have noticed, too, because he started talking without hesitation.

"There is a cadre of people who are intent on framing Matthews for several crimes in, what we think, is an effort to dismantle the current administration and make the next election one to be decided strictly along party lines. We don't know everyone involved, and we don't know who is leading it, but we do have several people we suspect of being involved and many, if not all, are either very wealthy or very influential and often both."

"And who better to help influence than a journalist," Jess finished.

"It would be a nice role to round out the cast of characters," Damian agreed.

"Fuckers," Jess muttered then took a big sip of her wine. When she set the glass down, her eyes flitted to Beni who was gazing at the fire, barely keeping her eyes open. Jess's attention shifted to Cal and he could see the question in her eyes, but he gave a small shake of his head. She let out a little huff. "Okay, Rodriguez, I have a nearly full—and I do mean full—glass of wine. Think of it like an hourglass, you have this much time," she said, holding the glass up, "to tell me everything I need to know."

Damian stared at her for a beat, then huffed out a laugh. "As you wish, my lady."

For the next forty-five minutes, Beni drifted in and out of

sleep as Damian relayed the whole sordid story—or what they knew of it—to Jess. As Cal listened, for the second time, a mix of thoughts and emotions swirled inside him. He'd been a politician long enough to know there was always someone out to get you. And he and Anne-Marie had had a number of very long conversations about what it would be like to run on a bi-partisan ticket, essentially alienating themselves from their own parties. Not only did they have enemies from the other side of the aisle, but they had them from within their own house, as well. So, the idea that someone was orchestrating something so catastrophic to the administration didn't seem so surprising. What did surprise him, though, was his ambivalence around the whole thing on a personal level.

Oh, he was angry at what was happening, and devastated by the loss of innocent lives. Yet, when it came to feeling anything more than that—any fear about losing his job or being painted as a bad guy (a *really* bad guy)? Well, he felt oddly detached from it all. Either of those outcomes would be inconvenient, but neither bothered him all that much. What did matter, though, were the number of people who had put their faith in him and Anne-Marie—and in the election process—who would be impacted, in a bad way, by a return to acrimonious bi-partisan politics. People the administration had managed to help in the past three years. People they'd hoped to have another four years working for.

Hopefully, they'd get those four more years, but looking at Beni, who was now soundly asleep, he realized that so long as the work he and Anne-Marie had started could go on, it wouldn't be the worst thing in the world if he wasn't a part of it. He had a responsibility to his office, and it was a responsibility he'd willingly taken on and would continue to fulfill. But he had no illusions that the fact he was the vice president factored into Beni's reluctance to explore rekindling what they'd lost. He didn't want to lose his job or be painted the bad guy, but if it meant there was one less obstacle between him and Beni, well, he wouldn't cry over spilled milk. Especially because he knew, in the end, he'd be vindicated—maybe not in time for the election in the fall, but eventually.

"So, that's where we stand," Damian said, obviously wrapping up the summary of the investigation.

"Perfect timing," Jess said, holding up her empty glass. "Then again, after what you just told me, I could probably use another."

"Which you're not going to get because you drove me over here and not only do I want to go home now, I also do not want you to drive under the influence," Damian said as Beni stirred under her blankets. "We also need to get out of here because Beni needs to go to bed," he added.

"I don't, I'm fine," Beni mumbled, making Cal laugh. Her eyes popped open then she blinked, as if she'd forgotten where she was and who she was with.

"I need to go to bed," she said, repeating what Damian had just said. She'd fillet him alive if she knew that he was thinking she looked pretty adorable all sleepy.

"I'll help you up," Cal said, swinging her feet off his lap and setting them on the ground.

"No, you stay and see everyone out. No need to leave your own party. It's only eight, anyway." She didn't wait for him to say anything, just walked out of the room and headed upstairs.

When he was sure she made it to the second floor, he switched his attention back to the room to see Jess staring at him with that same questioning look.

"Don't, Jess," he warned.

She rolled her blue eyes at him. "*Pfft,*" she said with a wave. "I don't print gossip or love lives or any infotainment, you know that, and if you don't apologize for not remembering, I will make you regret it."

Cal studied her, then nodded. "You're right. I know you

don't and I'm sorry I implied otherwise. It's just that she's the one that got away and she's skittish enough as it is that if there's one whiff of this in the media," he said, gesturing between himself and the upstairs where Beni was, "it will send her running."

Jess let out a deep breath. "Unlike most hetero women or gay men in this country, I would be *incredibly* happy to see you find someone with whom you can share your life, Cal. But you have to know that, even with the history that goes along with being the one that got away, you're a threat to her in so many ways."

He startled at that. "How so?" He was almost afraid to ask, but he forced himself.

"I did my research on everyone on that task force," she started. "Benita Ricci made a name for herself as a no-nonsense medic who was never afraid to enter the fray. Do you know how many soldiers owe their life to her? She deployed more than the average medic, she worked more hours when on tour, and has been recognized by more than one general for her dedication. *And then*, she joins the FBI and distinguishes herself enough to come to the attention of Sunita Shah who I think we both know is, well, something of an enigma in the intelligence and law enforcement worlds. What I'm trying to say is that her *life* has been defined by her work, Cal and, like you, she's damn good at it. Pursuing this thing with you puts all of that at risk... after all, how many partners of the president or vice president do you know who actually still *work* when their partners are in office, let alone work in law enforcement? I'm not even sure the FBI would let her do that since she'd be too big a target."

Cal looked down, wishing he had a glass of whiskey even knowing he probably didn't need it. Not with the way his stomach was churning. "I have to admit, I knew my job would be a big hurdle for her, but I hadn't really thought about just how high she might see it."

Jess shot him a look of disappointment as she rose from her

chair and slipped her heels on. "I would love to see you happy with someone, Cal, but you damn well better think of what it will cost her, because I can assure you, she's definitely thinking about it."

Jess held his gaze until he nodded, then, apparently done with the conversation, she looked to Damian. "I think I may head down to Tildas in the next few weeks," she said with a suspicious grin.

Damian tried to hide his deer-in-headlights look, but Jess just laughed. "Don't worry, I won't call attention to myself. Or at least not much."

And with barely a pause for Damian to follow her, she was gone.

CHAPTER THIRTEEN

"How was DC?" Jake all but shouted as Beni and Damian walked into the office two days after her injury. Beni had tried to convince Shah to let them come home the day before, but the director had insisted on twenty-four more hours of rest—and one more MRI—before allowing them to hop on a flight home. Beni had mostly followed the orders to rest, but she and Damian had spent some time working with Brian and Lucy on back tracing the email sent to Jess and the other journalists.

"I like how you ask that as if we haven't been in touch every few hours since we left," Damian answered.

"Hearing your voice is one thing, seeing your expressions as you talk is another. Now how was it? And Beni...in case you're missing your snuggle partner, Nia and I got you this." Reaching beneath his desk, Jake pulled out a large plush toy—in the shape of a giant mastiff—and handed it to her.

"You are such an asshole," she muttered, but she took the dog from him, nonetheless. It would be better for her if she kept it in her possession, because god only knew what Jake would do with it if she refused to accept the *gift*.

"See, I knew you missed me," Jake said with a grin.

"So, what's going on around here?" Damian asked, setting his computer bag down on his desk.

"What's going on is that we need to convene in the conference room. There have been some developments," Shah said, walking out of her office.

Beni glanced at Damian and he shook his head in response to her silent question as to whether he knew what Shah was referring to. While the two of them had been providing updates to the team on the DC aspect of the investigation, she didn't know what her colleagues might have uncovered in the few days they'd been gone.

Like little ducklings, they all followed Shah into the conference room. Once everyone was seated, Shah looked to Beni and Damian.

"Welcome back, and Agent Ricci, I'm glad you're feeling better. Now, I received a call from Lucy James this morning and they've discovered that Anthony Connaught and Lawrence Egerton have been making phone calls to the same phone. Or rather, phones. Several unregistered burner phones," she said.

"Uh, who are Anthony Connaught and Lawrence Egerton?" Beni asked. Brian and Lucy had mentioned a few leads but hadn't gone into any detail.

"The chairs of the Democratic and Republican parties, respectively," Alexis answered.

"I see," Beni said. And she was starting to. "Let me guess, while the phones are unregistered, Lucy and Brian could trace their use to a general location, or locations, and those locations happen to coincide with Duncan Calloway's travel plans."

"Bingo," Jake said.

"So, we think the chairs of the two parties are working together?" Damian asked, though it wasn't really a question.

"True bi-partisanship at its finest," Dominic said, eliciting a chuckle from the room.

"We've known all along that someone was pulling Calloway's strings. At least we have a solid lead now," Beni said.

"We do," Shah agreed. "We also have an opportunity to make contact with at least one of them." Shah gestured to Alexis, who pulled a small card out from a file.

"In two nights, Anthony Connaught is having a fundraiser at his house on Nassau, in the Bahamas. My parents are big donors to the party and were invited. They happen to be taking a little vacation on the boat before making their way down here to visit after The Summit and were planning to attend. Isiah and I will be going with them."

Beni almost smiled at Alexis' statement. Calling her parent's yacht a "boat" was like calling Windsor Castle a summer cottage. She'd seen pictures of it, and it was a three-hundred-and-twenty-two-foot vessel with six bedrooms, a media room, game room, bar, and dance floor. You could also land a helicopter on it if you were so inclined.

"To what end?" Damian asked.

"Connaught's computer networks are all connected. I'm going to try to get into his systems," Alexis answered. "I spoke with Lucy and Brian while you both were in flight and they have a device they are overnighting to me that they think can help. Essentially, from what I could glean from the tech talk, it's a small device that simply needs to be set next to the computer and it can wirelessly hack into the system and copy files."

"Like those charging pads that you can just set your phone on to charge without plugging it in?" Beni asked.

Alexis smiled. "I think it's a little more complicated than that in its capabilities, but from what I could tell, from an operations perspective, yes, it's similar."

"That sounds both extraordinarily cool and very dangerous," Anika said. Beni had to agree. Such a device could be an amazing asset to their intelligence community, but only if it stayed in their hands.

"It's a prototype and while Lucy and Brian are 99% sure it will work, there's a possibility it won't. But we don't have anything to lose in trying, so we figured we'd at least give this a shot. If it doesn't work, we're no worse off than we would be otherwise."

"Wouldn't it just be easier for the dynamic duo to hack into Connaught's network?" Damian asked. "Or Egerton's for that matter? I also feel obligated to ask about the legalities of hacking into either man's computer."

"I've taken care of your latter concern—everything is above board, though, for obvious reasons, the warrants have been sealed. As to your second question, they will be working on Egerton's," Shah responded. "But the device is one Brian and Lucy have been wanting to test, and I felt obliged to agree that this was a good opportunity. They will continue to follow the leads they are already working on and, by sending Alexis, we'll also have the unique opportunity to observe Connaught first-hand."

The logic was sound, and Beni nodded.

"Now, before we get to what Dominic and Anika have been looking into, why don't you tell us about your conversation with Jessica," Shah asked. Damian had told her that the journalist had joined them for dinner and he'd even given her a cursory overview of their discussion, but they hadn't talked details.

Beni looked to Damian and he started to relay to the group the theory they'd all discussed about Jacek being used as a pawn to pique the interest of other journalists. Damian went into detail about Jacek's death, the subsequent emails to other journalists regarding the FBI's interest in the man, and their belief that the intent behind bringing Jacek into the picture was solely to create the illusion that he had been silenced—a situation sure to at least lure one or two journalists to look into the story.

"Essentially they want to get the journalists digging so that by the time The Summit rolls around, and whatever dénouement they are planning takes place, those *respected* journalists will have, if not all, most of the details of the other crimes," Anika said. "It's clever. Kind of like orchestrating a movie with all the clues leading to a big reveal, but without the benefit of being able to completely direct the cast."

"Jess agrees with that and is going to reach out to her colleagues who received the same message and see what they're looking into," Damian said.

"She also said that, to the extent she can without tipping our hand, she'd try to steer them a bit, or at least plant some seeds of doubt," Beni added. Jess had come back to the house in Alexandria the day after their dinner and Beni had developed a begrudging respect for the journalist. It didn't hurt that Jess didn't once ask anything about Beni's relationship with Cal and had stayed almost maniacally focused on how to keep her peers from being used as pawns.

"So, that's what we have," Damian said. "Jacek was almost certainly murdered, and we think we know why, but we're not any closer to figuring out how everything is supposed to come together at The Summit."

"That's where we might be able to come in," Anika said then gestured to Dominic to proceed.

"After you guys left for DC, Anika and I got to talking about the four incidents that seem to be the focal point of this conspiracy: nepotism as it relates to the World Bank, selling Serena's identity, development and distribution of drugs, and organized crime," he said.

"Don't forget the trafficking," Beni said.

Dominic grinned. "See, that's where you're wrong. We never intentionally investigated the trafficking ring. We stumbled across it when Alexis and Jake went to Honduras to find and warn Serena, and then Serena happened to stumble across it again when she was here on the island. *Our* primary focus during that time was protecting Serena and stopping the sale of her identity."

"The trafficking was just incidental to all that," Anika said.

Normally, Beni was pretty quick on the uptake, but at the moment, her mind felt like it was wading through sludge. Maybe the concussion was slowing her down, or maybe it was because what Anika and Dominic were proposing was a very different take on the events that took place the prior summer. Whatever the reason, the concept of what her colleagues were suggesting was only slowly coalescing in her mind.

"Think about it," Anika continued. "What are the major, unforgivable crimes that a politician could commit? Nepotism —although, let's be honest, that happens all the time, so on its own, probably isn't unforgiveable. Treason—which selling out our intelligence community is. Drug trafficking—not only does it kill people, but everyone knows that drug trafficking doesn't happen in a vacuum, so any such involvement would irrevocably tie the politician to unsavory characters around the globe. Then last, organized crime. These days, most people tend to think organized crime is all about cyber-crime. But when you bring in a hitman, it conjures up the era of Capone and John Gotti and no one wants to openly support a politician with those kinds of connections. It doesn't help that, in our case, it was more than just a connection and the hitman actually killed three innocent people that we can tie him to."

"After treason, drugs, nepotism, and organized crime, what's left?" Dominic posed.

"Trafficking," Beni answered, now understanding their logic. "You think that the trafficking ring Serena brought to our attention is the final straw. That somehow, likely during The Summit, Cal will be implicated in the trafficking ring?"

"We're not focusing on it exclusively, but we think there's a pretty good chance that's how it's going to shake out," Dominic said.

"I want to take a step back for a minute," Beni said. "I hear what you're saying and, based on what we've seen since we arrived on the island seventeen months ago, I think you're probably right. But is there any chance that Patrick Dearil's capture might be causing them to change their plans?"

Patrick Dearil had been the hitman who carried out the murders of the three young men on Tildas Island. All on Calloway's orders and all solely because they each had the misfortune to be connected to the investigation into The Bank of DC four years earlier.

Beni's gaze swept around the table to find her colleagues contemplating her question. "We know that this whole conspiracy doesn't *require* that Cal be incontrovertibly linked to the crimes—that just the possibility that he might be is enough to accomplish their goal," Beni pressed on. "But they tried to kill Dearil to silence him and they failed. Is there any concern that with Dearil still alive and potentially able to provide information implicating Calloway, that they will change their tactic?"

"Dearil and Calloway are definitely the two loose ends," Jake said.

"We have Calloway covered," Shah replied. "I called in some outside help and we don't have to worry about his security. As for Dearil, as far as most people are concerned, he's in federal prison awaiting a trial date."

Beni's gaze snapped up at that. Patrick Dearil had signed a plea deal, there would be no trial. Thankfully, her mind seemed to be waking up and she instantly saw the benefit of Shah's plan. Even if she had no idea how the director had implemented it.

"So, according to general knowledge, he hasn't ratted anyone out," Alexis said.

Shah nodded.

"Let me guess," Dominic said. "He'll either commit suicide or be killed in some event while awaiting trial? Or it will appear that way, anyway."

Shah smiled. "Nothing as drastic as that. He'll develop an infection and succumb to that. After all, his injuries from the blast that nearly killed him *were* quite severe."

Across the table, Anika's eyes narrowed. "This better not be a way for him to get out of serving time," she said. Anika had been the one who'd figured out that Dearil's kills, which were staged to look like either accidents or suicides, were in fact murder. Her insistence had nearly cost her her job, and she was personally vested in Dearil serving time for killing the three men on her island. Not that Beni could blame her.

Shah shook her head. "He'll be getting a new identity and serving time under that name."

Anika studied the director, then nodded, apparently appeased by the answer.

"So, back to my question," Beni said. "Is the idea that if they continue to believe Dearil didn't talk before he *dies*, then they will feel comfortable progressing with their plan?"

Shah inclined her head. "It's hard to know for certain what criminals will do or believe, but Connaught and Egerton are limited by experience and ego. It's likely they'll believe they are in the clear and will progress with their original plan."

Beni didn't like the potential margin of error, but she also knew that despite Shah's apparent confidence in her own logic, they'd be keeping a close eye on both Connaught and Egerton. No one wanted anything—or anyone—to slip through the cracks and threaten the investigation.

"We're going to bring Serena in to help look into the trafficking angle," Anika said, bringing the conversation back to their tasks at hand. "I know you all have a lot on your plates with The Summit rapidly approaching, so she and I can take the lead on that."

"I'll work with Lucy and Brian on following the Connaught and Egerton lead," Damian said.

"We need to catch up with our Summit tasks," Beni said with

a pointed look at Damian. Despite wanting to focus one hundred percent on protecting Cal and stopping whatever it was that was being planned, they couldn't lose sight of the fact that 150 leaders from all over the world would be descending on Tildas Island in less than four weeks.

"I can do both," Damian said. "And I'd recommend you pick Cal's brain a little more on his relationship with Calloway."

"Since when did you start calling the vice president 'Cal'?" Jake teased.

Damian flashed a smile back. "Since he started sleeping with one of my friends."

The speed at which five heads swiveled in her direction could have caused a hurricane. "I will fucking kill you, Rodriguez," Beni said, closing her eyes at the sudden attention.

"On that note," Shah said as she rose from her chair. "I will leave you all to it. Let's all reconvene tomorrow for a general update and to go over the device being sent to Alexis."

Beni tried to rise, too, but Jake, who sat beside her, slapped his hand down on her arm, staying her. She thought about teaching him some manners, but in the end, she realized that the sooner she got this all over with, the better.

The door closed behind Shah and Beni raised a hand, staving off any questions. "I will say this only once. Cal and I are not sleeping together. Well, we're not having sex," she clarified since they *had* shared a bed. Then the memory of waking to Cal's hand sliding over her skin and under the waistband of her pajamas rushed to the forefront of her mind and she reconsidered her clarification. Then she decided that that particular event had been one-sided, so didn't qualify as her and Cal "having sex together." Technically, she hadn't lied to her friends.

"But you're sharing a bed?" Anika asked, her head cocked ever so slightly.

"He lives in DC, I live here. We are not sharing a bed," Beni answered.

Damian cleared his throat and Beni shot him a nasty look. He grinned.

She sighed. "We slept in the same bed for the three nights I was in DC. It was a safe house in Alexandria owned by his sister's security firm. There was no sex." Why she felt compelled to add that last bit, she didn't know.

All five sets of eyes remained fixed on her. She stared back. Despite knowing that they wanted all the details, she didn't intend to say any more.

Finally, Alexis looked away. "Since Beni was the only one who minded their own business when we were all meeting—or finally getting together with—our significant others, I think we should all just back off."

Jake opened his mouth, but Alexis cut him off with a look. When he'd snapped his mouth shut, Alexis fixed Beni with a look. "For now," she added.

Beni was under no illusion that the team would let it go altogether. Over the months they'd worked together, they'd become more than colleagues...more than friends, even. In some ways, she considered the four agents sitting around the room, as well as Anika, Isiah, and Nia, as her family. Kind of a weird, extended family, but family, nonetheless.

Rising from her seat, Beni gave her friends one last pointed look. "Thank you, Alexis. We have more important things to think about than my sex—or lack thereof—life. And on that note, I'm going to head out to Hemmeleigh and run some security checks."

"I'll come with you," Alexis said, also rising. The rest of the room chuckled, but Beni groaned. It seemed her reprieve was short lived because everyone knew Alexis wasn't just coming along with her to keep her company. At least she'd only be interrogated by one person and not the entire group.

With a sigh, Beni gave a dramatic wave to the door. "By all

means, Alexis, join me. I'm sure, at the very least, it will be entertaining. For you."

Alexis flashed her a smile as she passed by. "Oh, it will definitely be entertaining for me. I'm going to make you talk about feelings."

"No, you're not," Beni shot back, following her out the door.

"I am, and you know it," Alexis retorted, not at all put off by Beni's refusal.

"She is," Jake called from somewhere behind her.

"Oh, she definitely is," Dominic weighed.

"No doubt about it," Damian added.

In response, Beni raised a middle finger over her shoulder and walked out of the office.

CHAPTER FOURTEEN

CAL WAS ALONE in his bed at Number One Observatory Circle, his residence since taking office just over three years ago. The bed was comfortable, but empty and the cool of the sheets had him lying awake and staring at the ceiling.

His day had been like so many others. He'd met with a few key groups that he wanted to bring into discussions about the provision of health care in rural and inner-city areas. He'd had his security briefings then met with Anne-Marie and reviewed the current slate of proposed bills. He'd been on the go since leaving the Alexandria house—and Beni—at six that morning and it was inching close to midnight now.

And still, he couldn't sleep.

Rising from his bed, he pulled on a robe and wandered over to the window. It was mid-April in DC and the world around him was shifting from the hibernation of winter to the reawakening of spring. The cold weather snap that had hit this week had kept the trees from unfurling their leaves but shoots of green grass were making their way through the spring mud.

He glanced back at his bed and, not for the first time, wished Beni were with him. Although, after Jess' pointed warning, he had a new appreciation for what it would take to win her over. Truth be told, he didn't have much to offer her other than himself—for many, that would be enough, and it might be enough for Beni, too, but he doubted it. She'd want, and she deserved, a partner. She deserved someone who could and would support her own goals and dreams. Which was exactly where he fell short.

It wasn't that he didn't support them—Beni was a remarkable woman, and the world was a better place because of her commitment to the life she'd chosen. The catch was, he wouldn't always be in a position where he *could* support her. Jess had been right about that. If being with him meant an increased risk to either of them, then the decision would be out of his hands and his security team would take over. Even if that meant denying her a position in the FBI.

Walking to the sideboard, he poured himself a finger of whiskey and switched on the gas fireplace. Taking a seat in a wingback chair in front of the flames, he let his mind contemplate the possibility of not running for a second term. It was a drastic decision, but in some ways, it was the decision he felt he had before him—he could either have Beni or he could have a second term.

That was assuming she wanted him. He smiled at the presumption. He was fairly sure Beni felt something for him. Something more than just what they'd *had*. Something based on the people they were now. But she'd never been one to be swept away by feelings. She had them and, contrary to what many people thought, he knew she felt things deeply. She just kept a tight control on any outward display of them.

He took a sip of his drink, the amber liquid reflecting the flames as he lifted the glass. The whiskey burned a trail down his throat and as it did, he let his thoughts drift to Duncan Calloway. He'd never liked the guy but had always remained mostly polite to him. In retrospect, Cal wasn't sure why. He didn't owe Calloway anything other than basic courtesy. The man had been riding other people's coat tails for decades.

And because of that, there were an infinite number of people to whom he might owe favors. An infinite number of people who could be pulling the man's strings, so to speak.

Cal's mind caught on that thought. There were an infinite number who *could* pull his strings, but who *would*? Who would most benefit from the administration falling apart? He agreed with Beni and her colleagues that the wealthy who preyed on the middle class would benefit most. But they were an amorphous bunch and he just didn't see that class of people able to come together in the way they'd need to in order to execute the kinds of activities that had taken place.

He took another sip of his drink and pondered that question. The very wealthy might not be able to organize themselves into a conspiracy, but lobbyists could. Although, lobbyists' interests were so varying, yet specific, that he had a hard time seeing them working together on any sort of joint effort. Even if that effort was focused on breaking up the administration that had interfered with their efficacy.

A thought floated into his mind and sensing it was important, though not fully formed, Cal stilled. Whoever was organizing these events had to be at the top of some food chain. A food chain that had influence with, or at least the support of, the uber wealthy. Cal straightened in his seat as the thought coalesced. He knew who had to be behind the conspiracy.

Rising and walking to his desk, he grabbed his phone, then retook his seat. Pulling up his emails, he found the one he was looking for and forwarded it to his chief of staff. When that was done, he sent a quick text to Beni asking her to call him when she woke. The text had barely sent when his phone rang.

"I'm awake, we can talk now if you have the time?" she asked.

"I think Anthony Connaught and likely Lawrence Egerton could be behind everything," he said. "They are the only people I can think of with access to the kind of money needed to pull this off and the connections to do it."

"Do they have any connections to Calloway that you know of?" she asked, sounding not at all surprised by his deduction.

"You already figured that out, didn't you?" he asked.

She let out a small huff of a laugh. "Just today, so don't feel like you're too far behind the eight ball. If it makes you feel any better, you were only about twelve hours behind us and we've been able to focus all our time on the question, while you've been otherwise occupied with helping to run the country."

He smiled. "You're stroking my ego."

At that she did laugh. "You sounded so crushed at not having delivered the critical piece of the puzzle that the very least I could do was tell you the truth. It might have been a little assuaging of the ego, but not stroking of it."

All this talk of stroking had a predictable effect on his body, but Cal ignored the reaction. "Anthony Connaught is having a fundraiser in the Bahamas the night after tomorrow. I hadn't planned to go, but I've changed my mind."

Beni sucked in a quick breath. "Cal, don't. We already have people scheduled to be there. Agents who are trained in this kind of thing. You shouldn't go."

His gaze stayed fixed on the flames as he considered Beni's statement. "You said 'agents,' are you going to be there?"

"No, Alexis and Isiah are going. Alexis' parents are big donors to the party and were already planning to attend. It's the best cover we had to get an agent in. Everyone will know she's FBI, but it won't appear too out of the ordinary for her to visit her parents in the Bahamas when she's stationed in the Caribbean."

"Will Calloway be there?"

"We don't know. We're in the process of obtaining the guest list."

Alexis might be able to do her super-agent thing, but no one would be able to handle Calloway like he could. Maybe he could even kill two birds with one stone, if he planned things right.

"I'm going," he said. "I already sent a note to my chief of staff asking him to make it happen."

"Cal," Beni warned.

"If Calloway is there then he'll do anything to appear in my good graces because that will give him more power with Connaught."

"Cal, you can't go involving yourself in the investigation."

He felt a little bad about the anxiety he heard in Beni's voice, but in some twisted sort of way, he also liked it. She had to care about him just a little bit.

"I'm not, I'm just going to talk to an old friend. If you want, I'll even introduce him to Alexis."

"Seriously, Cal. We don't even know if he's going to be there."

"I bet if he hears I'm going, he'll show."

Beni sighed. "All the evidence we have is so tenuous already that your presence could upset the balance. Not to mention the fact that Connaught and his people want you alive but only because they need you to go down in disgrace. If they remotely suspect you might be aware of their plan, there's no telling what they might do. Up to, and including, eliminating you." Her voice caught on that last sentence, conveying the depth of her concern for him in a way she would never say.

"Then come with me," he said, softly.

The seconds ticked by on the baroque clock sitting on the mantel. Finally, Beni spoke. "You planned that, didn't you?"

He couldn't quite get a read on her tone, it sounded part surprised, part curious, and part disappointed. He opted not to think about the latter, because yes, he had just manipulated her into spending more time with him. In public. Which was pushing her in a way that not forty minutes ago he'd promised himself he wouldn't. God, this woman had him turned around—wouldn't the American people get a kick out of him now.

"Fuck, I'm sorry, Nita," he said, rubbing his eyes that were dry with fatigue. "Yes, I did, and it wasn't fair. I'll text my chief of staff and tell him to ignore the email."

"You will really cancel the trip?" she asked.

"Yes." He didn't want to, but he would.

"And are you?"

"Am I what?"

"Sorry for pushing?"

"Yes," he said without hesitation. "I'm not blind to what it will cost you if we go public with what's between us. There is very little *I* want more in life than to be public with how I feel about you *and* what I want from you, but that's not fair to you. It would be so much easier if we could make this situation just about you and me. We both know that's not a reality, though. I might have chosen this life, but you didn't."

She let out a long sigh, then spoke. "Alexis cornered me today, in my car of all places, and made me talk about my feelings," she said. "Not much has changed in the past sixteen years and it's still not my favorite activity, but she did make me realize that ignoring what I'm feeling, *how* I'm feeling about you, probably isn't the healthiest thing. Actually, she pointed out it was pretty much the opposite of healthy, but that's Alexis for you. She looks all glamorous and gorgeous all the time, but she packs a mean emotional punch, when needed. She took great pleasure in pointing out that if I genuinely wanted to figure out if this thing between us could work, that the problem isn't just your job or mine or where you live versus where I live. How we feel about each other matters, too. It *really* matters. And if I don't let myself think about that, I'm not going to be making very good decisions."

His heart caught on a beat. "Have you thought about it then?"

Another several seconds ticked by. When had that clock become so damn loud?

"I'm working on it, Cal. It's hard, really hard to reconcile everything. When I think about the practicalities of your life and mine, everything in me says no."

His heart started thudding heavily.

"Then I think about just you and me, and shut out everything else, and everything in me says yes," she said.

Relief poured through him at hearing those words and he closed his eyes and gave thanks to whatever gods or goddesses might be listening. They could fix the first problem, but if she didn't feel the same about him as he felt about her, there was nothing he could do about that.

"I don't know what to do about all this, but I appreciate you not pushing me on it," she said.

It was ironic that the thing she was thanking him for not doing was exactly what he wanted to do most in that moment. Not that he wanted to push her, but he did wish he could touch her, hold her, pull her to him, and just *be* with her. They were over 1,500 miles apart, though, and it wasn't possible, but god did he want it.

"Can I come down and see you, Nita? Discreetly and privately. No one but my security team needs to know."

She hesitated, then surprised him. "It's tempting, Cal. It really is. But now isn't a good time. I just got back after being away for a few days and I'm still recovering from a concussion. Can we revisit that once I feel like I have a bit more control of things here?"

"Of course," he replied quickly. He was all behind anything that might leave the door open for the two of them to see each other again. "Will you let me know how things go with Alexis and Isiah?"

He could hear the smile in her voice. "It *is* your career at stake, not to mention the will of the people who love you and President Cunningham. Yes, we'll keep you updated."

"And the other thing? Your reconciliation process," he clarified. "You'll let me know if there's anything we can or should talk through together?"

She chuckled. "There's probably a lot we need to talk through, but I'm not there yet. I will let you know, though, when I am. It took a lot of courage to walk right back into my life with no subterfuge about how you felt about me. I owe you—and me—the same."

"You are a remarkable woman, Benita Ricci."

"Not so much, but you can go ahead and think so."

He smiled at that. "I do and I will. Now go get some sleep and remember what I told you when you were here. I love you."

"Cal." The softness of her tone undermined the reproach.

"I just want you to know, that's all."

She paused, then spoke. "I do know. Thank you and I'll call you tomorrow."

She didn't wait for him to say goodbye before ending the call, and in the silence that followed, he stared at the flames. And contemplated just how he might find a way to make his love for her enough.

CHAPTER FIFTEEN

"Are you sure you want to do this?" Alexis asked.

Beni glared at her. "You, literally, spent the last ten minutes telling me that searching Anthony Connaught's house would be easier if Cal *were* there because he'd be a distraction. I'm just about to text him and tell him not to cancel, and *now* you're second guessing?" She loved Alexis, she really did, but sometimes her psychology thing was too much to deal with. Now that Beni had agreed to go along with the plan, she was sure Alexis was trying some reverse psychology shit, or something like that, on her.

Alexis wagged her head but grinned. "It's not so much that I'm second guessing having him attend the fundraiser, but now that we've covered—and agree on—the practical reasons, I think we need to talk about the less practical ones."

Beni narrowed her eyes. "Do not make me talk about feelings, Alexis Emelia Wright. We already did that yesterday."

Alexis said nothing but smiled.

"I'm not interested in doing that right now. Or again. Not when we have a conspiracy to foil."

"I'd like to point out that the two aren't mutually exclusive."

They weren't. Beni just didn't want to talk about it. And though Alexis was stubborn, Beni knew she'd have her beat.

They were still staring at each other when Dominic and Anika walked in. At least Jake and Damian were at Hemmeleigh, so they wouldn't have too big an audience.

"What's going on here?" Dominic asked as he took a seat at his desk.

"A show down of some sort," Anika guessed. "Probably about Cal, if I were to place a bet."

At that, Beni swung her gaze around to the detective. "What would make you say that?" she demanded.

Anika grinned. "What else would you dig your heels in about? Certainly not anything work related."

Beni glared at Anika then returned her attention to her phone. "You're annoying, you know that? You look all cute and tiny, like you should be out cheering for the hometown football team, but you're annoyingly blunt."

Anika laughed. "It's the product of having four older brothers and being a detective. And do not," she said, pointing a finger at Dominic, "say *anything* about seeing me in a cheer-leading uniform. It wasn't my scene in high school and it's certainly not going to be my scene in my thirties."

Dominic winked. "You'd wear it well."

"Did I not just tell you not to say anything?" Anika said as she glared at her partner who grinned back. Then abruptly, she switched her attention to Beni. "Now, what's up with Cal?"

Beni summarized her and Alexis' conversation as she sent a quick text to Cal telling him he should go. She didn't like the idea of him being there, of him being in the middle of their investigation, but Alexis had a point. If he showed up at the event, most of the attention would be on him, which would, hopefully, make it easier for Alexis to do what she needed to do.

"Did you just text him?" Anika asked.

"Are we in high school?" Beni countered. "Seriously, we

sound like a bunch of gossipy teenagers."

Anika rolled her eyes. "Whatever, Beni. It's interesting that that's what you read into my question, rather than just taking it for the question it was. I just wanted to know if you texted him, because if he's going, we need to let Shah know so that she can get a message to the contact who's shadowing Calloway."

At Anika's point, Beni felt a little chagrinned—both at her reaction and at what she and Alexis had unilaterally decided. Earlier that morning, they'd confirmed that Calloway was on the attendee list and she and Alexis probably shouldn't have made the call about Cal's attendance without running it by Shah. Not to mention that professional courtesy should have had them at least discussing the situation with the contact shadowing Calloway. Whoever she was, she might have wanted to weigh in on the pros and cons of Cal's presence. At the very least, she deserved a heads up.

"Good point, Anderson," Beni said. "I'll let her know as soon as she finishes her call." All four of them looked over at the director's office to see her standing with her back to the office, facing the window, a phone in her hand. "In the meantime, have you guys found anything on the trafficking lead?"

"Don't think Alexis is going to let go of the bone she has, but I'll answer anyway," Anika said. "We're just here to print a few documents and files and then we're headed to The Shack to talk to Serena. She wants to be involved—and we want her involved —but she doesn't want to come into the office, so we have to go to her." As Anika spoke, she pointed toward the entrance of the office and to where the CCTV cameras were. They didn't have any cameras in the office itself, but there were enough in the area that for someone like Serena, someone wanting to live off the grid, it didn't surprise Beni that the former CIA operative would want to stay away.

"So, what are you printing?" Alexis asked.

"This," Dominic said, taking the papers from the tray and

handing them to Alexis. "It's a list of names that we've picked up through various official and unofficial sources of chatter, including from Lucy and Brian. Actually, given that Ronald Lawlor has compromised the FBI and the CIA is suspect, too, the list from Brian and Lucy is probably the one I'd trust the most."

"What's the chatter about?" Beni asked.

"The men and women who are linked to Abdul Aziz—the man we think started the ring," Anika answered.

"Aziz had help from one of Lawlor's informants, right?" Beni asked.

Dominic nodded. "We're tracing that informant's movements. At the moment, though, we think he was more or less just a courier for Lawlor."

"Uh oh," Alexis said, drawing their attention. Her eyes were still on the paper she held in her hand. "Um, we may have a problem."

"What's the problem?" Shah asked, stepping out of her office and startling the four of them.

Alexis' eyes bounced to Beni then to their director. Whatever it was Alexis was about to say, Beni knew she wasn't going to like it.

"So, Vice President Matthews suggested he attend the fundraiser Connaught is holding in the Bahamas," Alexis started.

Shah nodded. "Not a bad idea. His attendance will make it easier for your activities to go unnoticed, though, I will need to let my contact know."

"Yeah, well, there's someone else attending that your contact should know about. Two people actually," Alexis said, holding up one of the printouts. "Andrew Smythe and Fredrick Towers."

"Who are they?" Anika asked.

Alexis shook her head. "I don't know, but they are on the guest list for the fundraiser *and* your list of potential people involved in the trafficking ring. I haven't had time to do the background checks on all the attendees, but I do have their names and these two are on it."

Everyone was silent as they digested the information. For her part, Beni's mind was spinning. The first thing she considered was that if Connaught was a part of framing Cal, then throwing Cal into a room—or party, as the case may be—with two people tied to a trafficking ring would be a good way to lay the groundwork for that. But as soon as the thought formed, she dismissed it—Cal hadn't decided to attend until last night. If Alexis knew Smythe and Tower's names, then they'd accepted the invite long before Cal had and Connaught couldn't have planned to use the situation to his advantage. Still…

"I don't think they are planning anything during the event, but I don't like Vice President Matthews being there with them. It creates too much of an opportunity for Connaught and his cronies. An opportunity they might not be able to pass up," Shah said.

"Want me to text Cal and tell him to cancel?" Beni asked, hoping Shah would say yes. She understood how his attendance could help Alexis, and she even agreed with the reasoning. But she wasn't going to lie to herself and pretend she wouldn't feel better if he stayed in DC.

"That or we send someone else to keep him from harm's way," Dominic said. Beni whipped her head around so fast that the lingering effects of her concussion made themselves known. She eyed her friend as the subtle woozy feeling subsided. It was a reasonable suggestion, but she was pretty sure Dom had made it for reasons other than just for protecting Cal.

Shah seemed to consider the idea. "If we send someone else, we could move forward with the original plan while still keeping an eye on the vice president. We might even be able to draw something out of Smythe and Towers."

Beni's heart sank at the director's train of thought. A beat passed when no one said anything. Then Shah's gaze landed on her. "I think we need to have a private chat in my office, Agent Ricci," she said. There was a hint of compassion in the director's voice that Beni hadn't expected yet didn't come as a complete surprise. Shah might be tough as nails, but one of the things that made her so good wasn't so much her ability to read people and situations in ways that the average—or even above average—agent couldn't, but what she did with that information.

Without saying anything, Beni rose.

"Agent Burel and Detective Anderson, you two carry on with your plans and let's touch base after you meet with Serena. If needed, we can all meet offsite somewhere later tonight," Shah said before flicking a glance at Beni then walking to her office.

Beni cast one last glance at her friends then followed the director into her office and closed the door behind her.

"We need someone there with Vice President Matthews and I'm well aware that if I ask you to go, you will, but there will be consequences," Shah said as soon as the door closed.

Shah could send any of the other agents on the team, hell, she could even send Anika, but they both knew those options weren't really viable. None of the other agents, or Anika, had any history with Cal and if he just showed up at an event with one of them, it would raise all sorts of red flags. It was possible he could get away with it if Anika attended and posed as his girlfriend. But even then, questions would arise as to just how the vice president who, on record, hadn't visited Tildas Island in more than three years, happened to hook up with a local detective. No, having Beni go was the only option if they wanted a story that would stick. The only problem—the big problem—was that that story would need to be the one she wasn't ready to go public with...that *story* would need to be the truth. That she was the "one that got away" and that, after sixteen years, she and Cal had finally reconnected. Casting her as Cal's girlfriend was the only realistic option if they wanted to both have Cal at the event *and* have someone close to him if Smythe or Towers tried anything.

It wouldn't be hard to spin the story—she and Cal had reconnected through her work on The Summit. They'd started dating again and kept it on the down low until now. It would be supported by both facts and, if someone were *that* interested in digging into the story, by confirmation from people who'd known them as a couple sixteen years ago. It was a built-in—true—cover story.

But Shah was right. *If* she attended the party, she'd be subjected to the limelight regardless of whether she and Cal confirmed or denied any relationship. Just the mere fact that he'd attended an event with a woman from his past would be enough to throw her onto the front pages of, well, if not the most respected papers, then certainly the gossipy ones. And being on the front page of any newssheet, or website, didn't exactly bode well for her career.

"After The Summit, if you still aren't sure, we can put out a story that it was all for show. I'm sure Jessica could help us with that," Shah said gently.

What Shah said was true, but in her heart, which she tried not to listen to too often because it was a confusing organism, Beni knew it wouldn't be that easy. It wouldn't be that easy because she wasn't the only one that "got away." Cal was the one that, had she ever allowed herself to think about him, which she hadn't until he'd walked back into her life, she'd always regret. *He* was the one that got away, too.

She could change that now, though. She could actually give her and Cal a chance. She could give herself the chance to not have any regrets. But that chance came with a price she wasn't sure she wanted to pay. Whether or not she and Cal *did* work out was almost irrelevant because, either way, she'd probably lose her career. At least her career as an FBI field agent.

"May I have some time to think about it?" she asked. "I know we don't have much time, especially since I already told Cal to accept the invitation, but maybe just a little bit?"

Shah held her gaze, then nodded. "I wish I could give you more than a few hours, Beni," she said softly. "I know the decision ahead of you isn't one to take lightly, and I want you to know that I will always do everything in my power to ensure that you are in a position to do the job you want to do. I also know that, as humbling as it is, while my powers may extend far, they don't extend as far as to be able to guarantee you will always have a position in the FBI."

Without actually saying it, Shah had voiced Beni's biggest concern. Going public with Cal could cost her her job. And if she didn't have her job, if she didn't have the FBI, what would she have?

"Thank you," she said. "I just need a little time to myself to work things through in my head. Can I let you know in two hours?"

Shah nodded. "Why don't you head out for those two hours? Go for a walk on the beach or a hike or something where you're not distracted. I'm not going to pretend it's not a big decision, because it is, and if you're going to make the best decision you can with the information—and feelings—you have now, you need the space to consider them all."

Beni wasn't quite sure how to respond to Shah's statement, as true as it was, so she just nodded. "I'll be back by noon and will let you know then."

Shah nodded again, and Beni exited her office then headed for her desk where her bag was. Alexis watched her but didn't say anything as Beni pulled the strap of her bag over her shoulder and headed out. She had no idea where she was going to go, but Shah was right, she needed to be somewhere where her mind could quiet itself and sift through all the thoughts—and yes, the emotions, too—that she needed to as both an agent and a woman.

CHAPTER SIXTEEN

CAL GLANCED down at his phone as it vibrated on the table. *"You have a minute?"* the message said. The number wasn't programmed into his phone, because he didn't want to take the chance of someone seeing the name, but he knew who it was.

He glanced up at the senator who was droning on about the need for tighter immigration controls. The man had made his point fifteen minutes ago but loved the sound of his own voice. It was too bad because while he made a few good points, he lost any chance of swaying people to his side of the issue the more he droned on. And on. No one wanted to be associated with a windbag prat.

"Talk or text?" As much as he'd love to walk out of the meeting, it wasn't possible. Well, actually it was possible, but if he did, it would be noted and then the press, who waited outside, would start to speculate on things like whether or not he had to leave because the country was going to war or some such nonsense. It would never dawn on them that he just wanted to take a call. A personal call.

"Prefer call, but can text," Beni responded.

"I would too, but text is all I can do right now, if that works?"

There was a long pause before he saw the bubbles indicating she was typing again. When the message finally came through, he understood her hesitation, but he had to restrain himself from standing up and shouting for joy. Because he wanted to, he really, really did.

"I'll be joining you in Nassau. Long story that I can tell you about later, but I hope you don't have any qualms about going public with me, because that's the story we need to go with."

"There is no story, whatever the press will say about you arriving with me, will be the truth," he wrote back. He could all but see the news articles speculating about who she was and *what* she was to him. He had zero doubt that they'd come to the right conclusion.

"We can rescind it later if we need to," she wrote.

"I can understand why you said that, but I have no intention of rescinding anything that the press might speculate."

A long moment passed as he watched the bubbles appear, then disappear, then reappear. *"We can cross that bridge when we come to it,"* was all she said.

He had no intention of coming to that bridge, so her answer was fine with him. But as the senator continued to complain about the bureaucracy of immigration, the full impact of what Nita was telling him settled on his shoulders. He might be feeling jubilant and hopeful, but if Jessica was right—which he knew she was—Beni would be feeling anything but.

"We can talk later about what brought this on. I recognize that it's probably not what I hope brought it on, that there's probably a reason other than you deciding to take a chance on me, and I won't hold you to anything."

A few moments passed before her response came in. *"Thank you."*

He smiled at that. It was a simple Beni statement but said what it needed to. Even so, even though he had every intention of respecting her decisions, he couldn't help but add, *"I'm still going to enjoy seeing you dressed up and having you by my side."*

He had no idea how she'd respond to the provocation, but even so, her response surprised a laugh out of him, drawing the attention of everyone else in the room.

"You might be singing a different tune when you see me, big guy. I plan to let Alexis dress me and the last time she did, I looked like this." And she'd attached a smoking hot picture of herself in a dark emerald green dress that had a deep V in front and fell to mid-thigh. The color played off her hazel eyes and though Beni had always been beautiful to him, seeing her not as a girl, or young woman, but as a woman with confidence, a woman with experience, and a woman of courage, set his heart beating to a new rhythm. There were books and songs and poems with people talking about being drawn to their partners for unknown reasons—maybe chemistry, maybe something else. It wasn't like that for him, though. If asked to put his reasons as to why he was drawn to Beni into words, he probably wouldn't be very eloquent, but he could give a hundred and one of them without even touching on the chemistry they shared. He might have given her an out, but being the eternal optimist that he was, he couldn't help but believe that they were finally on the path he'd hoped they'd be on when he'd first decided to set foot on Tildas Island two weeks ago.

"So, what do we know about Smythe and Towers?" Isiah asked as they started their descent into Nassau. They were in Alexis' private plane and though Beni felt a little uncomfortable traveling in that style, it fit the image they needed to project—that Alexis was there to meet her parents and bringing along the girlfriend of the vice president. Of course they'd come in Alexis' private plane.

They hadn't expressly mentioned to anyone that she was Cal's "girlfriend," but he had told Connaught he was bringing a plus-one and alluded to their history. They'd also all agreed that if anyone asked about who she was, they would just make vague references to their shared past, but no comments on the present or future that used words like "girlfriend" or "boyfriend." The decision was a strategic one, speculation would draw enough attention without turning the fundraiser into a gossip field day. It also suited Beni just fine. Regardless of what she and Cal were, she'd always hated the boyfriend/girlfriend titles for anyone over the age of twenty-two, anyway. Why twenty-two seemed to be the cut off, she didn't know, but it just was and had been since she'd hit that milestone.

"Smythe is British. He's a music producer," Alexis said. "Should be easy enough for me to strike up a conversation with him." Alexis' father was a god among musicians and one of the world's most revered R&B artists.

"Does he actually produce music or is it a job like Calloway's where he tells people it's what he does, but no one can really confirm it?" Isiah asked.

Alexis let out a dry laugh. "Let's just say he's been loosely connected to a couple of mildly successful acts out of Europe. Enough to give him some names to drop, but not enough to open any real doors in the industry."

"What about Towers?" Isiah asked. Beni had already studied the profiles of both men and knew what Alexis would say.

"Classic rich kid who treats spending his parents' money as his job. He travels the world, posts a lot of social media, goes to all the right parties. That kind of thing."

"Isn't he in his thirties?" Isiah asked, not bothering to hide his feelings on the described behavior.

"He's forty," Beni said. "Cal's age."

At that, Isiah snorted. "If anyone ever wanted to illustrate a juxtaposition it sounds like Towers and Matthews would be it.

Same age, same background, and though it sounds like Towers has more money than Matthews, they went to the same elite schools. And while one parties his life away and possibly gets involved in human trafficking, the other dedicates his life to trying to make his country better."

"To each their own, I suppose," Alexis said as the plane dipped for the final descent. "Although, Towers seems like a pretty big prick to me. Believe me, growing up, I met more of his type than I ever care to remember. You doing okay?" Alexis asked her suddenly.

Beni kept her gaze fixed out the window. She could see Nassau, though they were still over the water. "I'm fine," she said, as the dark waters of the deep slowly changed to the iconic aquas of the tropics the closer they got to the island.

"Beni," Alexis started, but Beni raised her hand to stave off whatever she'd been about to say.

"I'll admit to having misgivings about this, but they are personal and it's too late to change things now. I'm not 100% comfortable with what we're doing, but you know me well enough to know that I wouldn't have agreed if I wasn't committed to going through with it."

"It's not too late," Alexis said.

"You could develop the flu or something," Isiah offered, making Beni smile.

"Thank you, both of you, but I'm fine. One thing I learned in the Army is that just because I'm not comfortable with something, or just because I have misgivings or doubts, it doesn't necessarily mean it's the wrong thing. It just means I don't know—I don't know how things will turn out, I don't know what might happen—and not knowing isn't comfortable, but it's not always bad."

Neither of her companions spoke for a moment and the cabin filled with the sounds of the landing gear coming down and the wing flaps adjusting. They were over land now and Beni was struck by how much more compact Nassau was than Tildas.

"Those were very wise words," Alexis finally said.

Beni flashed her a smile just as they touched down. "Yeah, well, I have this friend who's kind of annoying about making me turn a mirror on myself. I usually figure out a way to get around it, but sometimes it's impossible to escape learning a thing or two about myself."

Alexis snorted a laugh as the jets reversed to slow them down. "I guess I don't need to remind you what's going to happen next?"

Beni shook her head. Cal's plane was scheduled to land ten minutes before theirs and they'd made plans to meet at the terminal for private flights to kick off their not-so-fake-subterfuge.

"Although, I will say that if, at any time, you feel the need to come down with the flu, I'll have your back," Isiah said, rising as the plane pulled into the hanger.

Beni laughed as she, too, rose from her seat. "Thanks, Isiah. Always good to know even if I don't plan to take advantage of it."

She grabbed her computer bag knowing Alexis' staff would get the rest of their baggage and bring it to the Wright's yacht where they planned to stay for the night. As she scooted into the aisle, Isiah placed a hand on her arm. "All joking aside, Beni. I know that what you're about to do has implications beyond the investigation. You're also dipping your toes into a whole new world. Maybe you have more experience with it than I ever did before meeting Alexis, but if you find yourself needing a break —not from the investigation, but from everything else—come find me and we'll go grab a beer somewhere or something."

Beni's gaze flitted to Alexis, who was standing behind Isiah, before returning her attention to Isiah. It was true that she was here for a job and yes, that job had a personal twist to it that made it unusual. But what Isiah had said was also true and not something she'd spent much time considering—she was about to step into the world of not just the rich and famous, but the ultra-rich. People who owned private islands and chateaux, people who didn't just have one plane, but several. It was a world that was so far from her life as an only child of a house-keeper, an Army soldier, and an FBI agent that it was hard to even think about.

And so she hadn't. She hadn't thought about the world Alexis had been born into and the one Cal currently inhabited. She'd focused on the job, thinking of it as just another under-cover operation. The thing was, *this particular* night might serve a specific purpose, but the world she was stepping into was one that Cal lived in all the time—it wasn't a one-time thing he had to fake his way through. And if they were going to become something together, then the next time she attended an event like the one they'd be attending in a few hours, she wouldn't be there as an operative, she'd be there because of her role in Cal's life.

She met Isiah's gaze and nodded. "Thank you. I will keep that in mind. Sometimes even knowing there's an escape is enough to ease some of the pressure, even if I never use it."

He smiled. "Yeah, that's what I think, too." Just then, one of Alexis' staff let the stairs down and warm air flooded the cabin. "Ready?" Isiah asked, then wiggled his eyebrows at her.

She laughed and gave a shake of her head. "Yeah, I'm ready."

She let Alexis and Isiah exit the plane first and when she stepped off the stairs onto the tarmac, Cal was leaning down to give Alexis a kiss on the cheek. His eyes flitted to hers and lingered, but he pulled them away long enough to shake Isiah's hand before walking over to her.

"Hello, stranger," he said with a smile.

"It's been three days," she said, tilting her head up. He slid a hand around her waist then lowered his lips to hers. With Cal's fingers curled around her and the heat of his body sinking through her silk halter top, she wasn't even going to pretend that the kiss was just for show in case someone was watching them. The restraint she felt in Cal's hold on her, as well as her own desire to sink her hands into his hair and hold him against her, was far too real to be anything but true.

"Thank you," he said, leaning his forehead against hers. His blue eyes never wavered from hers, and in that moment, something righted itself inside her. Cal knew *everything* being with him would cost her and in his eyes, she saw gratitude, love, and most importantly, an unspoken promise to her, to them. They'd figure things out—what that would look like, she hadn't a clue, but they were two smart people, and they'd figure it out.

She smiled. "I'm not sure this is the time or place to tell you, but I'm starting to actually be glad you walked back into my life."

He blinked then took a step away. Not far, but just enough to put a little distance between them. "Fuck," he said, his hand still curled around her waist. "When do we have to be at the party?"

"Times a-wasting," Alexis called as the cavalcade pulled up. "Beni, my mom, and I have an appointment with a stylist in thirty minutes," she announced, pointing to a non-existent watch on her wrist.

Cal's eyebrows went up. "A stylist?" he asked as his hand slid from her waist to intertwine with hers.

"I told you I was going to let Alexis have her way with me. This is the second time in nearly eighteen months and she's taking full advantage. You should have seen what she made me do yesterday," Beni muttered, still a little peeved at the amount of hot wax that had been used on parts of her body that should never have seen hot wax.

Cal chuckled as they walked to the cars. Isiah was holding the door open for Alexis to climb into one of them, but she and Cal headed for the second. "I love you the way you are, but I'm not going to lie and say I'm not looking forward to exploring all the things Alexis made you do."

Beni let out a husky laugh because she was kind of looking forward to the same thing. "Yeah, well, first you get to meet Vera and Jasper, then we have a party to go to, then we have some computer files to download on the downlow, and *then* you may explore." She paused at the door of the car Cal had opened for her and faced him. "Have you ever met Alexis' parents?"

Cal shook his head.

Beni laughed at the response because she knew what was coming and Cal didn't seem to have a clue. Alexis may be fairly self-contained, her life experience and her job led her to be that way, but Jasper and Vera Wright were anything but.

"Jasper will keep your mind off of me," she said, climbing into the car.

Cal's hand released hers but skated down her back and over her backside as she took her seat. When she reached for her seatbelt, Cal captured her lips in another kiss. This one, out of sight of her friends and the Secret Service—with the exception of the two in the front seat of the car—was far more than a friendly hello.

"Chop chop, let's go!" Alexis yelled out her window. Cal pulled back and Beni laughed as Isiah's rumbling voice drifted out the same window. Beni didn't know precisely what the man was saying to Alexis, but she had a pretty good idea.

"Guess we better go?" Cal asked.

Beni nodded.

"Just so you know," he said, "I doubt there is anything anyone can do that will distract me from thoughts of you." And with that, he closed the door, rounded to his side, and slid into his own seat. After shutting the door behind him, he slipped his sunglasses on and reached for her hand.

"Sir?" one of the agents in the front seat asked.

"We're ready to go, Tom," he said, sounding every bit the leader he was.

As the car started rolling toward the marina where the Wright's yacht was docked, he caught her eye. Quirking a grin, he waggled his eyebrows so they danced up over the rims of his sunglasses.

She smiled and shook her head at his antics. He may be the vice president, but somewhere, not so deep inside him, was the boy she'd once loved and a man who could very likely steal her heart again.

CHAPTER SEVENTEEN

"I'D LIKE you to meet my friend, Benita Ricci," Cal said, introducing Beni to Anthony Connaught. Not for the first time that night was Cal grateful for his years of politicking. Yes, he was the youngest VP in history, but he'd more or less been in politics since he started working his first campaign at the age of fifteen. He knew his way around a handshake and a smile, even as he fought the urge to wash his hand right after.

"Benita, this is Anthony Connaught, chair of the national party," Cal continued, placing a hand on Beni's lower back as he introduced the two. It was a possessive move and meant to convey to Connaught that despite the introduction, Beni was definitely more than a friend. It also gave him the opportunity to touch her, something that was increasingly difficult not to do since things had changed between them. Yes, it had only been a couple of hours since whatever that moment was in the hanger, but there had been a subtle shift between them and for the first time in what felt like years, a cloak of contentment was wrapped around him.

"Nice to meet you, Mr. Connaught," Beni said, holding out her hand.

"You as well, Ms. Ricci. We were surprised when Cal said he was bringing an old friend. Pleased, but surprised. Tell me, how did the two of you meet?"

Connaught looked to Cal to answer, but Beni was the one who spoke. "We've known each other for years. Dated when we were kids. We reconnected when my office started giving briefs to the White House about the upcoming Summit of World Leaders that's happening on Tildas Island in a few weeks. I'm sure you're familiar with it?"

Connaught's eyes flickered to Cal, but he smiled at Beni and nodded. "I hear President Cunningham is opening the event, but Calvin is attending as part of the US delegation."

"I've not been involved in the substance of The Summit, but based on what I know about the schedule, it looks to be a remarkable affair and I'm sure Cal will represent us well," she said.

Cal smiled and traced a little circle along Beni's back. The material of her off-white dress was shot through with gold, highlighting her hazel eyes and sun kissed coloring. It was also delicate and barely whispered over her skin, allowing him to feel the shift of her muscles and the heat of her body as his fingers skimmed over her.

"I've been getting briefed by some remarkable folks," Cal said. "I'm looking forward to being on the island for a full week and getting to enjoy The Summit without having to jet off to some other meeting."

Connaught smiled. "Hopefully, Cunningham can keep things under control on the home front and other parts of the world don't spiral into despair. Not that The Summit is going to be a vacation, but it should give you some downtime. It's been a while since you've taken any time to yourself."

Cal couldn't argue with that statement. Although, knowing that the man likely had something planned that would keep Cal from enjoying any part of his time at The Summit stopped him from smiling and making some soothing remark about how it was always an honor to serve the people of the United States.

"Cal!" a voice to his right called. He looked over to see two senators bearing down on him and Beni.

"I'll leave you to it, Calvin. As always, it's good to have you here supporting your party," Connaught said before walking away toward the open bar.

"Passive aggressive much," Beni muttered, making Cal smile.

"Connaught wants to hate me for teaming up with Anne-Marie, but our approval ratings are so high that it's in his best interest to at least appear to support me," he said, as the senators closed in on them.

"Playing the wolf in sheep's clothing, then," Beni said, plastering on a benign smile.

"Yes, but at least now we know those clothes don't fit," he said.

"You best not be telling this woman that her dress doesn't fit. I don't know who you are, but you look amazing," Senator Alex Vivent said, eyeing Beni. The young Senator from New York was as flamboyant as anyone could be and there was always speculation about his sexual orientation because of it. Alex, himself, had never weighed in on that particular conversation and Cal had never asked, preferring to focus on the man's ability to craft policy and debate Senate Republicans. Actually, watching Alex debate anyone was one of Cal's favorite pastimes —he was equal parts wise, intelligent, witty, and scathing.

"Thank you," Beni said. "Benita Ricci, an old friend of Calvin's," she said, holding her hand out.

Cal didn't miss the look Alex sent his way as he took Beni's hand. "Alex Vivent," he said. "And this is my colleague Marilyn Klein. So, Calvin is always *so* good about not prying into our lives, but I'm not going to return the favor and I want to know *everything*. You can tell me on the way to the bar." As he spoke, he hooked an arm through Beni's and pulled her away.

And so it went for the next ninety minutes. Donors, politicians, and guests all clamored to talk to him and Beni. For the most part, many of them were wanting to bend his ear to one topic or another, but more than a few were interested in Beni and just who she was to him.

Beni was back on his arm and, having just escaped a pointless conversation on the merits of having celebrities speak in support of politicians, they were headed out to the garden when Isiah approached them. The grim look on his face told him that Cal's presence may have provided the distraction the team had hoped, but not all was going according to plan.

"What's wrong, Isiah?" Beni asked, directing them all into an alcove.

"Vera's not feeling well. She thinks it might be a touch of food poisoning and Jasper snuck out an hour ago to go see some local musician he's been wanting to hear. Vera knew he'd gone, but figured she could come home with us," Isiah said.

Beni frowned. "Is it serious?"

Isiah started to shake his head then stopped. "I don't think she needs to go to the hospital, but I do think she needs to leave. Alexis has texted her dad and wants to check them both into a hotel for the night. With how upset Vera's stomach is, we don't think it's a good idea for her to stay on the boat."

"Then you need to go do that," Beni said.

Isiah gave them a ghost of a smile, then held a small clutch out to Beni. Cal's heart sank. He had a rough idea of what the team had planned to do with Connaught's computer, and though he'd been concerned about Alexis partaking in the task, that concern was nothing compared to the adrenaline now flooding his system. Because if Alexis couldn't do it, then that left it to Beni.

"Tell her not to worry," Beni said. "Take care of Vera and we'll see you both back on the boat in a few hours."

"Do you want us to come back?" Isiah asked.

Both Cal and Beni shook their heads. Cal didn't plan to stay much longer and was glad Beni seemed to concur. "We'll head back within the hour. I'll text when we leave," she said.

"You sure?" Isiah asked, holding Beni's gaze. Cal appreciated the man's concern, but that concern didn't make him feel any better about the situation. If Isiah didn't think something could or would go wrong, he wouldn't look so worried.

"I am," Beni said. "Go, it will be fine. I studied the schematics of the house with her this afternoon. I may not have been planning to run the op, but I am prepared to do it."

"You'll call if there's a problem?" Isiah asked.

"There won't be any problems," Beni replied. "Now go take care of Vera and we'll see you in a little over an hour."

Isiah lingered for a moment. His gaze flickered to Cal's and Cal caught hint of an apology in his eyes, but then the former SEAL nodded and walked away. Leaving him with Beni and the knowledge that not only was she going to snoop around Anthony Connaught's house, but that with Alexis gone, she was going to do it without backup.

"Fuck," he said.

Beni turned toward him and without thought, his hands landed on her waist. "It will be fine," she said. "I have it under control."

He looked down into her steady gaze. "I don't doubt it for a second, but *I* may need a little time coming to grips with it."

"Unfortunately, you don't have a lot of time, but maybe I can help with a distraction." And with that, she slid a hand around the nape of his neck and pulled him down into a kiss. A real kiss, not the soft brushing of their lips together, but a soul-searing, tongue-tangling kiss that made him want to back her against a wall and feel every inch of her.

When they finally pulled apart, he couldn't help but smile because it wasn't Beni who had her back to the wall, but him.

He didn't mind at all, though, since she was pressed into his front.

They stared at each other for one breath and then another. Then Beni's kiss-softened lips smiled. "If I'm not back in fifteen minutes, come find me."

Before he could utter one word, she pulled her phone from his pocket, where he'd been carrying it for her, slipped from his embrace, then darted back into the house.

———

Beni was grateful for the shoe advice Alexis had given her that afternoon when they'd shopped for the right pair to go with her outrageous dress. Actually, Beni kind of liked the dress that hung from her shoulders by thin, barely there, straps, then draped down her back and over her body before landing at mid-thigh. It was lovely in its simplicity but, if Cal's gaze on her was anything to go by, it was sexy as well.

Her shoes were something special, though. And for that she would buy Alexis a case of her favorite beer when they got back to Tildas. The brushed gold sandals matched the gold threading in her dress and circled her ankles before tying on the sides. What made them really special, however, was the low heel and soft sole. The combination made it so that her feet didn't protest too much about being stuffed into something other than boots or flip flops, but it also let her move quietly along the travertine floor of Anthony Connaught's home as she made her way up a flight of stairs and toward one of the residential wings of the house.

Thankfully, Connaught was vain enough to want people to wander around his house and gawk, and about twenty people lingered on the third-floor landing where a bar had been set up to take advantage of the spectacular view of the moon rising over the ocean. Beni considered rushing past, but then changed her tactic and decided to casually stroll through the area, stop for a drink, then make her way to the north wing.

She smiled at the bar tender and asked for a glass of white wine. When she had it in hand, she wandered toward the floor to ceiling windows and began to make her way toward her destination, smiling and nodding at a few people she'd met earlier.

Then feigning a phone call, she reached into Alexis' clutch and pulled her phone out. Setting her drink down, she wandered down the hall, phone to her ear, as if she were looking for a quiet place to talk.

As soon as she turned the first corner, she slipped into the second door on her left, Connaught's office. The room was unlit, but the moonlight shining through the window was enough for her to be able to make out the details of the room.

Bookshelves lined the wall to her right and to her left was a heavy mahogany desk with a second set of shelves behind it. Making her way to the desk, and presumably Connaught's computer, she drew up short when she saw his desktop was empty.

She paused to listen for signs that anyone was coming and when she heard none, she proceeded to open each of the six drawers of the desk in search of either a laptop or any sign of a computer. To her chagrin, she found neither.

Taking another slow look around the room, Beni's frustration ratcheted up. Unless there was a hiding spot—which was possible—it didn't look like Connaught kept his computer in his office. Which meant that he either *had* a hiding spot, or it was kept somewhere else—neither situation boded well for her plan to be in and out of the private space quickly enough to not have her absence noted.

Moving to the middle of the room, she forced herself to slow her racing mind and think. If the laptop was intentionally hidden, it wasn't likely she was going to find it or, if she did, that she'd find it in time to also be able to have the device Lucy and Brian had sent do its thing. Her other option was the possibility that Connaught kept his computer somewhere else, or maybe just moved it for the night.

The jarring sound of a glass shattering on the tile floor filtered down the hallway, startling her. When her brain recognized that it wasn't coming from close by, she took a deep breath and considered her options. She didn't have a lot of time left to search. Realistically, assuming Connaught had just moved the computer, rather than hidden it, she had one shot to find it.

But where would he move it? Within the space of a heartbeat, Beni realized she had no idea where a man like Connaught would keep his computer, other than on his desk or in a safe. But if it were *her* computer, where else might she keep it? Answering *that* question was a little easier and, well, there was only one logical option.

A second later, she was standing with her ear to the door, listening for any sounds in the hallway. Taking heart from the quiet, she cracked it open and stepped out. After shutting the door behind her, Beni left her hand on the knob as she gave herself another fifteen seconds to listen.

When no one seemed to be coming her way, she proceeded to the last door at the end of the hallway...Connaught's bedroom. Because if it were her, that would be the only other place where someone would find her laptop.

Glancing back and seeing no one, she placed her ear to the door again, this time listening to see if someone might be inside. She heard a muffled laugh and the rumble of a man's voice and disappointment lanced through her. There was no way she could just walk into Connaught's room if someone was in there.

Or were they?

Beni leaned closer to the door, just as a bump sounded from behind her. Keeping her reactions in check, she turned slowly.

Just as another bump and muffled groan echoed into the hallway. A groan?

Beni paused, feeling the seconds—and her opportunity—ticking by. Then when she heard the sounds again, she nearly laughed out loud. She didn't know who was occupying the room beside Connaught's, but the couple were obviously having a good time. With a grin and one last glance down the hallway, Beni silently entered Connaught's domain.

The room was pristine with no signs of any habitation. Except for the laptop sitting on the bedside table.

Not giving herself anytime to feel triumphant, she glanced at the clock on her phone as she crossed the room. Five minutes, she'd give herself five minutes. She'd be cutting it close with Cal, and Lucy had said it shouldn't take more than three minutes to get the copy, but she wanted to be sure.

Clicking the small device on and leaving it in Alexis' purse, Beni set the clutch down on top of the laptop. She had no idea how it intended to capture and copy the data from a computer that appeared to be turned off, but Lucy had assured her that the device wouldn't have a problem. Well, to be precise, Lucy had said that *if* the device did have a problem—being a prototype—it wouldn't be caused by the laptop not being powered on.

Keeping the phone in her hand to keep track of time, Beni left the device to do its thing—assuming it was doing its thing—and stepped over to the windows that made up a good portion of both the north and the east facing walls. With the moon reflecting on the ocean and the waves glowing in the light, Beni acknowledged that it wouldn't be a bad place to fall asleep at night. Then again, with the sun rising over the eastern horizon, she'd definitely need light blocking shutters on those windows.

She was just pondering whether or not Connaught had a way to open the windows and listen to the waves when she heard a familiar laugh.

Cal.

She glanced at her phone and, according to the time, she still had six minutes before he was supposed to come looking for her. Which could only mean one thing, something was just about to go wrong.

"Maybe she slipped into a room," Cal's voice was clear and concise but not so loud as to obviously be issuing a warning. She still had a minute left for the device to finish its job.

Someone was obviously with Cal and she heard a man's voice. She assumed Connaught's, though she couldn't make it out.

Forty-five seconds.

"Fuck," she muttered to herself, running through a quick sitrep. Unfortunately, only one option came to mind.

CHAPTER EIGHTEEN

WITH HIS HEART attempting to climb up and out his throat, Cal swung the door to Connaught's room open and maintained a jovial smile. His blood pressure had spiked when they hadn't discovered Beni in Connaught's office—he was glad they hadn't caught her, but not knowing where she was, was wreaking havoc on his nervous system.

"I don't know why she'd be here, but it can't hurt—"

And there she stood, in her sexy as hell dress, looking cool as a cucumber with the phone pressed to her ear. She smiled at both of them and held up a finger to ask for a minute. Beside him, Connaught's body had gone rigid. Then just as quickly, he appeared to catch himself and he visibly forced himself to relax.

"Love you, too, and have a glass of champagne on me," Beni said.

Cal frowned. Who the hell was she talking to?

"Sounds good, I'll give you a call when I'm back on Tildas and yes," she said, her dancing eyes catching Cal's, "I'll let him know you said hi."

She ended the call then looked at both him and Connaught. "Everything okay?" she asked.

Cal was honestly unable to respond to that. He was a politician; he was good at half-truths and dissembling. But this game was new to him.

"Might I ask what you're doing in my room?" Connaught asked, keeping his voice level.

Beni frowned and made a show of glancing around the space. "Oh, I'm sorry. It didn't look occupied and I wanted to make a call. It's my mother's birthday today and I wanted to catch her before she and her husband headed to dinner. By the way, she said to say hello to you, Cal."

Cal blinked at that and filed through the facts stored in his mind only to realize it was, indeed, Beni's mom's birthday. Though, he'd wager the next election Beni hadn't been talking to her.

"Truly, I'm sorry," Beni said, walking toward them and swiping up the clutch that sat on top of the laptop as she passed. "I didn't know it was anyone's room, though I can see why it would be, the view is spectacular."

She came to a stop beside Cal and he reached for her hand.

"You weren't carrying a purse before," Connaught said.

And, his heart rate kicked right back up again.

Beni frowned at Connaught's comment. "No, I wasn't. This is Alexis Wright's."

"Was she up here, too?" Connaught asked.

Beni's head cocked to the side. "No," she drawled. "She went home about fifteen minutes or so ago. Her mother wasn't feeling well. I understand this is your private space, Mr. Connaught, and I know I'm not at this event as an agent, but I have to ask, is everything okay?"

Cal's hand tightened on Beni's. Reminding Connaught she was an FBI agent didn't seem like such a great idea, but then again, when Connaught took an audible breath and his shoulders released a fraction, Cal acknowledged that maybe it was the right tactic.

But Connaught's eyes wouldn't leave the clutch Beni held in her hand. For several beats, the three of them stood there, Cal watching Beni, Beni watching Connaught, and Connaught watching the clutch.

Finally, Beni raised the small purse and opened it for Connaught to see. "I didn't have a purse of my own to match this dress, so she carried my tampons for me," Beni said. Connaught drew back so fast, Cal almost laughed. "Like I said, Mr. Connaught, I understand this room is your private space and I'd be a little disconcerted to find someone in my room uninvited as well, but your concern seems a little, well, as an agent, I just have to say it's making all sorts of warning bells go off."

Connaught's gaze snapped up to meet Beni's. She studied him, unabashedly. Cal didn't know what game she was playing, but he had no intention of stepping into it. After another beat, she leaned closer to the chairman and spoke quietly.

"If there is something going on that has you worried or concerned, Mr. Connaught, please know you can come to me anytime. I won't press you now, because you're in the middle of hosting a party, but I'll be here on Nassau tonight and tomorrow. Even after that, you can always find me on Tildas. If you need help with *anything*, I hope you'll keep me in mind."

Connaught blinked and in the space of a second, relaxed completely. Beni had played him perfectly. She'd cast him as a man important enough that others might want to target him for disreputable reasons, while also shifting his view of her from that of someone to suspect to someone he needn't be concerned with.

"Thank you, Ms. Ricci. I apologize for being so inhospitable, it just caught me by surprise to find someone in my room. As you said, it's a private space."

"Of course, Mr. Connaught. And again, I apologize, I really had no idea it was occupied. My mother used to clean houses for a living and even *her* room wasn't as tidy as this. Now, I left a glass of white wine out on the landing when I started speaking to my mom, any chance it's still there?"

Anthony ushered them out of his room, closing the door behind them. "I should certainly hope not, but I can assure you that we have plenty to go around and a bartender who'd be happy to pour you another."

"That sounds like an excellent plan. Would you mind pointing me to the bathroom, though, before we head back?" Beni asked. "I wouldn't want to walk into the wrong room again," she added with a smile, making Anthony laugh.

"This one, my dear," he said, gesturing to a door not far from the landing. "Why don't Cal and I order you a drink while we wait. White wine, you said?"

Beni nodded then slipped into the bathroom, leaving Cal and Connaught in the hallway. The bathroom wasn't that close to the landing, but they'd be able to keep an eye on the door from the bar.

With a nod in the direction of the bar, Cal spoke, "Shall we?"

"She's quite a woman you have there, Calvin," Anthony said as they walked.

"That she is," he concurred.

"Are you sure that dating an FBI agent is what you want to be doing?" To his credit, Connaught sounded more curious than critical.

Cal glanced over his shoulder in the direction of the bathroom. He wondered how Beni had even found the computer in the first place since it hadn't been in the office as they'd all supposed. He also wondered if she'd managed to get the device to work and then considered how quickly she'd adapted when her original plan had gone to shit.

Then with a flash of heat, he remembered the feel of her pressed against him, the taste of her on his lips.

He smiled at Anthony. "There's no doubt in my mind that dating Benita Ricci is exactly what I want to be doing."

"You hanging in there?" Beni asked thirty minutes later. They'd finally rid themselves of Connaught and were back outside in the gardens. She couldn't help it, but her mind flashed back to the kiss they'd shared less than an hour ago. She knew Cal had wanted to leave as soon as they'd descended from the third floor to the ground level. She hadn't wanted to take any chance of appearing that they were fleeing the scene, though, so she'd made him stay.

"Do we have to be here much longer?" he asked. Well, whined, to be more precise. His tone made her laugh, and he cast a baleful eye on her. "Seriously, wouldn't you *much* rather be back on the boat, in our room, you know, making up for lost time?"

"I would," she said, ignoring the hunger she saw flashing across Cal's features at her admission. "But we're not going to make up for sixteen years in one night, so another thirty minutes won't hurt."

He mumbled something that sounded suspiciously like "that's what you think," but she ignored the comment.

"Cal!" a voice called. Turning, Beni saw a man heading toward them, towing a woman behind him. With the light at his back, she couldn't get a good look at his features, but she felt Cal's body go rigid beside her.

"It's show time, again, Nita," he said just loud enough for her. "Hey Duncan, how are you?" Cal said as the man approached.

Now, standing two feet away, Beni came face to face with a man she knew more about than she should, given that they'd never met. Duncan Calloway looked exactly like his pictures, except his face was maybe a bit shinier which she could chalk up to the tropical heat. She'd never met anyone before who looked exactly like their pictures and she had to admit, it threw her off for a moment. A moment when she considered if maybe he'd had some work done. Why that thought flitted through her mind as Duncan and Cal shook hands, she didn't know, and in an attempt to shake it off, she switched her attention to the woman Calloway had dragged along with him.

Whoever she was, she was petite in the fine boned and short kind of way—coming in at no more than five-foot-four, in her heels. Her nearly black hair was cut into a stylish, chunky bob that ended at her chin and her grey eyes bounced from Cal to Duncan with more than the usual interest of someone who was about to meet the Vice President of the United States.

Hmm, that was interesting.

As if sensing Beni's scrutiny, the woman shifted her gaze and met Beni's eyes. Beni didn't know who she was, but there was no way she could miss the very subtle twitch of the woman's eyebrow, and the hint of a grin and eyeroll, as she inclined her head a fraction of an inch toward Calloway.

"Duncan, this is Benita Ricci," Cal said, bringing her attention back to the men.

"We don't usually see Cal bring anyone to these events," Duncan said, shaking her hand.

"Guess he was just waiting for the right guest," Beni said. Again, Beni didn't miss the little twitch of the woman's nose, as if she was trying not to laugh.

"Uh, I guess," Duncan said, slightly surprised by her answer.

"Benita Ricci," Beni said, taking charge and holding her hand out to the woman since Calloway looked to have almost forgotten her.

"Cynthia Forge," she said, her voice carrying the mark of the British upper class. "It's lovely to meet you."

Beni murmured something similar in return though her mind was working through just who she might be. If her little signs were anything to go by, she knew more about the situation than...

"I think I'll go grab one more drink while you two catch up," Beni said. She cast a quick look at Cynthia then looked to Cal. She could see the question in his eyes, and thankfully, his quick intelligence took over before his innate chivalry did. Rather than offer to get it for her, which would be his normal response, he nodded.

"I'll join you," Cynthia said. "You two need anything?"

By the glazed look in Calloway's eyes, Beni guessed he'd had enough already but he asked for another beer. Cal raised his still half-full gin and tonic and shook his head.

They were out of earshot before Cynthia leaned in and said, "Franklin Cavendish and Sunita Shah go way back," she said, confirming what Beni had sorted out. Cynthia Forge was the additional resource Shah had called in to stick close to Calloway.

"And Franklin is?"

"British Intelligence. My boss. And my uncle," she added, making a face.

"There are so many questions I have for you and we both know this isn't the time or the place, but please tell me that you don't actually have to sleep with him while doing this?" Why that seemed like such an important thing to ask right now, Beni didn't know, but she supposed she wanted to make sure that the agent wasn't being forced by her employer to use her body—especially not on an op run by the task force.

Cynthia shook her head as they approached the bar. After ordering a beer and two glasses of white wine, she answered the question. "I'm very inventive about ways to avoid it, though it is getting to the point where I might need to do something a little more drastic. We'll see."

The bartender returned with their drinks, tossed them a

wink that had both women laughing, then left to help an older couple at the end of the bar.

Grabbing her wine, Beni then reached for Calloway's beer, but Cynthia waved off her offer of help and picked up both drinks. "What's your plan for the night?" Beni asked as they wove through the guests on their way back to the garden.

Cynthia lifted a shoulder. "Not sure. I have a room in town, but I'm more of a fly-by-the-seat-of-your-pants-kind-of woman than one who plans things. I know as former Army that probably goes against your grain, but it's worked for me so far. Actually, I'm not sure I could even plan something if I wanted to," she added, sounding a little perplexed by her own observation.

"Plan what?" Duncan asked, obviously having overheard that part of the conversation as they'd approached.

"Anything much more than a day or two ahead of time," Cynthia said with a shrug and a grin as she handed Calloway his beer. "Life's more fun when it's unplanned," she added.

Duncan half snorted. "Cynthia is what one would call an heiress. Doesn't have the same kind of responsibilities that we do," Duncan said to Cal. Cynthia may or may not be an heiress, but Calloway casting himself in with Cal as a man of responsibility was laughable.

"How'd you two meet?" Cal asked, holding out his hand for her. Beni gladly took it as she stepped to his side.

"At Heathrow," Calloway said. "I was on my way home and we happened to be sitting in the same bar and catching the same flight. We got to talking and one thing led to another."

"Now, here you are," Cal said, his voice carefully neutral.

"Now, here we are," Cynthia repeated, raising her glass in a toast. "Duncan said he was coming to this event and I have a friend who has a place on St. Barts, so I thought I'd come with him and maybe head down there after. Or who knows, maybe I'll head back to DC. We'll see." She shrugged as if she hadn't a care in the world then took another sip of her wine.

"Are you staying in Nassau long?" Beni asked.

Duncan shook his head. "My half-sister comes into Miami tomorrow. I had already planned to meet her when I got the invite to attend this. Since I was going to be in the area, I decided to come to the party, but I'll fly out to Miami tomorrow. What about you?"

Cal looked to her to answer and she leaned into him ever so slightly as she did, wanting to convey that their travel plans were purely personal. "Cal and I both have to get back to work tomorrow, but we're staying with friends tonight on their yacht. Do you know the Wrights?"

Duncan blinked, then smiled. "Vera and Jasper Wright? Jasper is *such* an amazing musician. I've met him once before, at another political event. Are they here?"

Beni shook her head. "They were here earlier, but Vera wasn't feeling well. I'm here with her daughter, my friend Alexis. We're staying with Alexis and her partner tonight on the boat."

Duncan grinned and swayed a little. "I've heard rumors about that boat. Is it true it has a dance floor?"

"That and a whole host of other luxuries," Cal said.

"You should come back with us," Beni said, spur of the moment. Cal's hand tightened around hers in surprise. "I'm sure Alexis won't mind. We could have an after-party that's a little more, well, not to put too fine a point on it, but this one's a little stuffy for my taste," she said. Then she threw a grin at Cal. "Sorry, babe." The look he gave her told her he knew she wasn't apologizing for the dig at the party, but for dropping the after-party idea on him.

"That would be amazing, wouldn't it?" Calloway said to Cynthia.

"Sure," Cynthia said, sounding remarkably American. "I met Alexis a few times growing up. Haven't seen her in probably fifteen years, would be good to catch up."

Beni blinked, that was news to her. Then again, Alexis had spent much of her childhood in Europe and if Cynthia really was an heiress, chances were the two would have run in similar circles.

"Why don't I just call Alexis and confirm?" Beni asked, stepping away and walking toward a low stone wall that separated the grassy garden area from the beach beyond.

Alexis picked up on the second ring. "Did you get it?"

Beni smiled. "There was a little surprise, but if the device was working, I got it," she answered, referring to the download of Connaught's computer. "I'll send it to Brian and Lucy tomorrow." For security purposes, the device only drew data in. It needed a special docking station—one that only Brian and Lucy had—to download the information back out, so the device had to be in their physical presence to know if it had worked. "I have another question for you, though," she said, then went on to propose her plan. Alexis wasn't thrilled with the idea of having Calloway onboard her parents' yacht, but in the end, she agreed. Mostly because, after Beni's description, she figured out that Cynthia Forge was, in fact, Cyn Steele. The two women *had* known each other growing up, though Alexis hadn't known she'd gone to work for British Intelligence.

An hour later, Alexis was ushering them onboard the yacht, hugging Cynthia as she passed. Her staff took Calloway's and Cynthia's bags, and the five of them made their way to the main lounge where Isiah was standing at the bar mixing drinks.

"Cal, Beni, just in time. I have a couple of GnTs for you," he said, holding out two glasses. Beni took a sip then thanked Isiah for his forethought—the drinks were nothing more than sparkling water though they looked like GnTs.

"Duncan, Cynthia, nice to meet you, what can I get you?"

Calloway, who'd changed into a pair of shorts and t-shirt when they'd stopped by his hotel, threw himself onto a chair and grinned at everyone. "Got any bourbon?"

Beni cast a glance at Cynthia who winked. Chances were, Calloway had been drinking beer all night, a switch to liquor might help get his tongue loosened up.

"Three kinds," Isiah said, holding the bottles up. Calloway pointed to the one on the left. As Isiah poured, he looked at Cynthia.

"I'll have a white wine if you have it?"

"You and me both," Alexis said, pulling a bottle of wine from a small wine cooler and pouring them both a glass.

Under the pretense of catching up, Alexis and Cynthia wandered outside together while Beni took a seat on a love seat with Cal beside her. Isiah stayed standing, leaning against the bar.

"Back in those days at college, you ever think we'd end up like this?" Calloway asked, throwing his arms out in a wide gesture and spilling a little bit of his drink as he did. "I mean, you were always so into debate and the politics and all, but seriously, did you ever see yourself hanging out on Jasper Wright's yacht while being the VP of the United States?"

Cal let out a chuckle that wasn't entirely forced. "I think it's safe to say that I did not picture myself in this exact scenario, no."

"I guess you should enjoy it while it lasts," Calloway said.

Other than to glance at Isiah who, out of Calloway's line of sight, arched his eyebrows at her, Beni didn't react.

"All good things do eventually come to an end," Cal said. "But hopefully not for at least another four years."

Calloway held his gaze then smirked as he raised his glass. "Here's to the election. May you get all that you deserve."

Calloway sipped his drink and Beni considered if, perhaps, Calloway wasn't as drunk as she'd thought. He was being pointedly obtuse which made her think he had some control over his faculties.

"Have another," Isiah said, walking over with the nearly full bottle of bourbon he'd poured from earlier. Giving Calloway another two fingers worth, Isiah set the bottle down on the end table and within arm's reach.

"Thanks, man," Calloway said. "So, you're dating Jasper and Vera Wright's daughter? She definitely got her mom's looks, didn't she? With just enough of her dad in her to make it interesting."

Isiah's jaw clenched, but he raised his glass and took a sip. "Yeah, Alexis and I are together."

"How'd you meet? I mean, Beni told me you own a bar on Tildas Island. I guess women probably throw themselves at you all the time. Maybe you just picked a good one?"

"We did meet at my bar, but I knew Alexis for seven months before we started dating. Nobody was throwing themselves at anyone," Isiah answered.

Calloway chuckled and poured himself another drink. Beni's earlier concerns waned. It was possible that when they'd boarded the boat Calloway had more possession of his faculties than she'd thought, but at the rate he was going, it wasn't going to be long before that changed.

"Playing the long game," Calloway said with a grin, and again raised his glass as if to toast Isiah. "It's a pain in the ass but totally worth it, don't you think?"

"So, what are you up to these days?" Cal asked before Calloway went too far over the line with Isiah. Isiah could be as cool as a cucumber, but Beni was glad Cal intervened.

"I just saw you, like, three weeks ago," Calloway said.

"I see you all the time. You always seem to be at the events I'm at, but so are a lot of other people. It's not like we ever catch up at those," Cal replied.

Calloway's eyes flickered over to her, then shifted back to Cal. "A little of this, a little of that," he said, waving his hand. At least he managed not to spill this time.

"So, nothing holding your attention?" Cal pressed.

Calloway's head fell back against the chair and he closed his eyes. "I have a lot going on, Cal. All very...interesting things. So," he said, snapping his head back up, "what's it like being back together after having been childhood sweethearts and all? I mean all those teenage hormones probably made for some unforgettable times, but then again, at our age, we actually know what we're doing. Although," he paused, then smiled to himself, "there's definitely something to be said about younger women."

"I'm going to assume that wasn't a dig about me," Cynthia said, rejoining them in the lounge with Alexis following. Alexis walked to Isiah's side while Cynthia made her way to where Calloway sat.

He grinned up at her, now clearly shitfaced. "Nope, just reminiscing. Youth is wasted on the young and all that."

Cynthia glanced around the room then let her gaze fall on Calloway. "I don't know that I totally agree with that. There are some things that are much better with age. Or at least experience. Why don't we make our way to our cabin and call it an early night, luv?"

Calloway stared at Cynthia then knocked back what little was left in his glass and rose. Once standing, he swayed, but Cynthia slipped under his arm like she wanted to be there rather than as if she were holding him up.

"Keith," Alexis called, and instantly a man appeared in the hallway leading from the lounge to the private quarters. "Would you mind showing Ms. Forge and Mr. Calloway to their room?"

"Of course. Please, follow me," the man said.

Cynthia guided Calloway from the lounge and when they were well out of earshot, Beni cast a horrified look at her colleague. "She is *not* going to sleep with him, is she?"

Alexis shook her head. "No, she has a little something she'll give him that will help him sleep. She'll just make it look like they had sex, or at least slept together. I have another room made up for her."

"Uh, what's going on?" Cal asked.

Beni looked at him and realized he had no idea who Cynthia was. Taking a minute, she updated him on Cyn's role, with Alexis adding a little more detail as they talked. They were just finishing up their drinks when the woman in question reappeared in the hallway.

"He's out. Ready ladies?" she asked.

"Ladies?" Isiah asked, directing his question to Alexis.

"What are you doing?" Cal asked Beni.

Alexis leaned up and kissed Isiah on the cheek as Beni answered Cal with a grin. "We're going to search his belongings."

CHAPTER NINETEEN

CAL AND ISIAH both looked toward the hallway when they heard Alexis' voice. They couldn't see the three women yet, but they could hear them talking as they made their way back to the lounge.

"There's an empty room just next door to where I put you two. I had it made up for you if you want, but I'll leave it to you where you want to sleep," Alexis was saying.

Cal and Isiah had been sipping on single glasses of whiskey for the last hour while the women searched Duncan Calloway's belongings. Cal had tried to subtly pull information about Beni from Isiah as they'd passed the time, but the former SEAL was on to him and hadn't given up much. He respected the man for it, but still, Cal felt starved for details about Beni's life in the past sixteen years.

"That's Alexis being polite," Beni's voice floated toward them as they came into view. All the women had changed out of their cocktail dresses and were now wearing casual shorts and t-shirts. "What she really means to say," Beni continued, "is that that man is a piece of work and no one in their right mind would want to curl up next to him and his wee flaccid—"

Cal cleared his throat. "I lived with Duncan in the fraternity house for a year. I know *exactly* how that sentence is going to end. I'm just curious how you know?"

Beni laughed as she made her way to his side then perched on the arm of the chair he sat in. He should have grabbed a seat on the couch so she could have sat beside him. Then again...he hooked an arm around her and pulled her onto his lap.

Alexis gave them a gentle smile as she joined Isiah and Cyn took one of the bar stools.

"I undressed him," Cyn said. "When he wakes in the morning, I want him to believe we had sex. I can hardly be blamed if he doesn't remember it," she added with a shrug.

"Honestly," Beni said, "if you had sex with that, you probably wouldn't even notice."

The women snorted with laughter and Cal cast Isiah a look. He just shook his head and took a sip of his drink.

"Did you find anything?" Isiah asked, wrapping an arm around Alexis and pulling her up against his side.

"No smoking guns, but a few things that might be interesting," Alexis answered. "We'll look into them when we get back to the office tomorrow."

At the reminder that they'd part ways tomorrow, that Beni would go back to Tildas and that he'd go back to Washington, Cal's hand twitched against her hip. It couldn't be any other way, but they did have tonight and everything she'd all but promised him. It was only ten o'clock. He had twelve hours before he had to be on a flight back north.

Startling Benita with his sudden move, he rose from his seat, catching her arm as he did to steady her.

"As much as I'm enjoying the relaxing night and the company, I think it's time for bed," he announced.

"Subtle, Cal," Alexis said with a grin.

"Not trying to be," he said, taking Beni's hand and tugging her toward the hallway that would lead to their room.

"Seriously, Cal, a little decorum would be nice," Beni said, but with a laugh.

In response, he set his glass down on the bar as he passed, giving Cyn a wink. Then bending down, he picked Beni up and slung her over his shoulder, eliciting an honest-to-god shriek. It was a short one, but a shriek, nonetheless.

Entering their room, Cal tossed her on the bed then followed her down until he lay with his body covering hers. After all these years, he could hardly believe he—they—were here again. Her body pressed against his, the pressure increasing and decreasing with each breath she took. He held her gaze as he slowly dipped his lips to hers. His fingers twitched against her waist as she responded, but he didn't take the kiss much further than a gentle press of his lips to hers.

When he pulled back, he expected to see his usual confident, almost-cocky, Nita staring back at him. But that wasn't what he saw.

"Have you changed your mind?" he forced himself to ask. There was no disguising the hesitation he saw on her face.

A beat passed, and then she slowly shook her head.

"This will change things," he acknowledged. "For both of us. As much as I hate to say it, we both know you'll bear the brunt of the upheaval. I'll understand if that's not something you want to take on." It just about killed him to say those words, but he needed to let her know—he needed her to believe—that whatever might happen between them was her choice and that he'd respect that. Because Jess was right, Beni had a lot more to lose than he did.

Also, a selfish part of him wanted the decision to be hers. How he felt about her had never been in question, not when they'd been kids, not during the years they hadn't seen each other, and definitely not since he'd first touched her again that night at The Shack. She'd fought him at first, then seemed to arrive at some sort of resigned acceptance that what lay between them had never gone away. He didn't want resignation from her, though. He wanted her to make the choice. He wanted her to *decide* to be with him. If she did—and only if she did—would they have the foundation, the understanding between them, to weather the storm their relationship would create.

She reached up and trailed a finger down his cheek and over his bottom lip. "I made that decision—and accepted the consequences—when I agreed to come tonight, Cal."

He closed his eyes and dropped his forehead to hers, savoring the moment and the feel of them together.

She ran a hand through his hair and tipped her head to brush her lips against his. "It's just that I never expected this," she said. "I walked away all those years ago because we both had things we needed to do. I'd made my peace with losing you, though it was one of the hardest things I've lived through. And that's saying a lot considering what I've been doing the past sixteen years," she added with a wry smile.

Cal pulled back to look at her as she continued.

"In a million years, I never thought we'd be here again. I comforted myself by following your career and seeing all the good you've done. Every victory you had, every healthcare bill you got passed, every regulation to protect the environment, every budget allocation for education, was a validation of the choice I made. And I was okay with that."

She hesitated, then brought her fingertips back to his cheek. "I *made* myself be okay, because you were off doing what you were supposed to be doing. Something you probably couldn't, or wouldn't have done, if I hadn't left. I missed what we had, though. I missed you.

"But now we're here. Again. Just you and me. You've done—are doing—what I've always known you were born for and I'm in a place in my own life where I can make a different decision. I *know* this isn't going to be easy. I know the media is going to have a field day, I know the public is going to judge us for any myriad of things—for the fact that I'm part Hispanic, for the fact that I barely finished my bachelor's degree, for the fact that I'm a strong woman, for the fact that I was in the military and now in the FBI. But we're stronger now. I know it's only been a few weeks since we've been in each other's lives again, but not only are we stronger individuals, we're stronger together. We can weather the storm now in a way we never would have been able to back then.

"So, yes, I'm choosing you. I'm choosing us. I just never thought I'd ever have that opportunity again, and sometimes, like right here and right now, when it's just the two of us, it feels a little surreal. Like I'm not sure how we got here. And sometimes, I'm just a little afraid it *isn't* real."

He stared down at Nita as her hazel eyes studied him. *They* were real, what was between them was real. He knew Beni knew that or she wouldn't be here with him right now, but that didn't mean he didn't understand what she'd meant.

"I think it's good to be a little afraid," he said. "Believe me, I'm just a little terrified that you'll wake up tomorrow, or sometime next year, and decide you're better off without me; that I'm just a complication for you. Or worse, you'll decide that I'm better off without you. Which, let's be clear, will never be the case."

A ghost of a smile teased her lips at his stern pronouncement.

"But if we want this—and I know we both do, because you wouldn't have said everything you just said if you didn't feel the same way I do—then I think a little fear is a good thing. We know what we have to lose, and we know what we have to gain. We also know that what we have is worth fighting for. There's no way we would be here right now if it weren't, Nita."

Again, she studied him. He didn't press her any further, he wasn't trying to convince her of anything. He didn't need to. What he did need to do was give her this moment, give her the time and space to let the fact that this was real—*they* were real—settle into her soul.

Slowly, a soft smile spread across her face. "This is really happening, isn't it?"

He couldn't help his own smile at her comment. "It is," he said, lowering his lips to capture hers. This time the kiss deepened, and his hand slipped under her shirt to feel the bare skin at her waist just as her hands began unbuttoning his.

When her palm flattened on his bare chest, he pulled back. Her eyes were hungry, her lips kiss-swollen, and he wanted nothing more than to bury himself in her over and over again.

"What are you thinking up there?" she asked with a knowing smile.

He grinned down at her. "That this is really happening. Like right now," he added with a laugh as he pulled her shirt over her head.

"Well thank god for that," she said, as he kissed his way down her belly and began unbuttoning her shorts.

He paused and looked up at her. She was smiling at him, her fingers toying with his hair. She still wore her bra, a navy lace confection, and she looked ready to be loved. By him.

His lips quirked into a grin. "Yes," he said, divesting her of her shorts to find a pair of bikini underwear that matched her bra. "Thank fucking god for that."

And then he proceeded to spend the next several hours showing her just how thankful he was.

CHAPTER TWENTY

SEVERAL DAYS LATER, Beni and her teammates sat in the largest conference room in their office staring at the data on the screen. Rather than continuing to work from their home in Boston, Brian and Lucy had decided to fly down to Tildas the same day Beni, Alexis, and Isiah had returned from Nassau. Now, the pair stood at the front of the room, holding everyone's attention. Their arrival had been a serendipitous godsend since there was no way the team could have focused on the data the little device had collected from Connaught the way the couple had. Not while simultaneously fulfilling all their obligations to The Summit.

"So that's that," Lucy said, glancing at Brian who nodded. Her straight, black hair was up in a ponytail and it swung as she moved. For a moment, Beni pondered what it would be like to have hair that didn't look like she'd stuck her finger in an electric socket every time she set foot outside in the tropical humidity. It was an inane thought, but easier to contemplate than what Lucy and Brian had just walked them through.

"So, let me summarize," Jake said. "We have two factions, one led by the chair of Cal's party and the other by the chair of the president's party. They are working together, but they have different ways of supporting their activities. The Democratic faction works through Wainwright Holdings and they own the island in the BVI where Dominic and Damian were almost blown up as well as the warehouse where the hitman who killed those men from The Bank of DC was staying. Then there's Imperium Holdings, which is the entity the Republican faction works through. They own the island where the drug bust happened as well as the hotel Oscar Olde, my beloved godfather, pointed us to," he summarized, referring to one of the most powerful men in the world of organized crime who was most definitely not beloved, even if he was Jake's real godfather.

Picking up the thread Jake had started, Alexis jumped in. "They used donations they received as part of their regular fundraising efforts to fund the properties they acquired. Then, once the properties started making money, they returned the initial investment so that it didn't appear that anything was missing from the party coffers. All the additional funds that have come from those initial investments have been used to fund the activities of people like Duncan Calloway and Patrick Dearil."

Brian and Lucy both nodded. "There were some initial personal contributions by both Connaught and Egerton, but that about sums it up," Brian said.

"Is there any indication that the donors knew where their money was going or what it was funding?" Shah asked.

Lucy's gaze drifted to the data and chart on the screen behind her, then she shook her head. "For the run of the mill donor, like Alexis' parents, no. For those who are on the boards of Wainwright and Imperium Holdings," she paused, her head tilted as she studied the data, "well, it's not quite as clear. We have evidence that about half know what's going on."

"As for the other half," Brian stepped in, "we either haven't found the evidence or they don't know."

"If they don't know, I'd ask if that's because they intentionally don't want to know or if they truly don't know," Beni said. Both Brian and Lucy nodded in agreement.

The room fell silent then Beni spoke again. "I think we can all agree we need to keep following the leads Brian and Lucy are uncovering, but unless we find enough evidence to go after both committee chairs before The Summit starts, we need a plan to protect Cal from whatever it is those men are planning. The conference starts in less than two weeks, we need a back-up plan."

"I agree," Shah said. "We'd need airtight evidence to stop them and, unless there's a smoking gun somewhere, that takes time. I think we all know we don't have much of that. Anika, Dominic, you were looking into the trafficking angle with Serena, have you been able to find anything to indicate that might be how they intend to go after the vice president?"

Dominic glanced at Anika, who pulled out a piece of paper from a file. "Based on the information Alexis and Beni discovered in Calloway's belongings while he was on the boat, we have confirmed that he's been in contact with both Andrew Smythe and Fredrick Towers. If you recall, they were both on the list of names connected to the trafficking ring that Abdul Aziz controls."

"Just this morning," Dominic said, picking up the report, "we received notice from the food service department at Hemmeleigh that there's been a request to bring on a new employee."

"What reason did they give?" Damian asked. "They know there's been a lock down on hiring employees for the last two weeks." As part of the security precautions, the resort had agreed that in the month prior to The Summit they wouldn't hire any new employees.

"One of their people quit unexpectedly and one had a heart attack two days ago. They wanted to bring on two people so that they weren't short staffed, but knew that would be pushing their luck, so they only asked for one," Anika answered.

Shah looked at Jake, and he nodded. "I'll look into the two who left." Judging by the looks on her colleagues' faces, there was very little doubt that both the abrupt departure and the heart attack likely had some help in coming about.

"Who is the employee they want to bring on?" Shah asked.

"Smythe's girlfriend's youngest brother," Dominic answered.

Beni couldn't help but snort. "So, they are going to try the whole sneak-a-young-girl-into-the-room-under-the-food-trolley cliché?"

Both Anika and Dominic smiled before Dom answered. "We've made it a condition that there not be anything obstructing the view of the entire food trolleys, but there is a shelf and yes, if they ignored the rule we've set down, they *could* sneak someone into the room."

"Seems haphazard, at best, to me," Alexis said.

"Isn't that in line with nearly every other crime we've seen this group commit?" Dominic countered.

"He's right," Jake said. "Remember, it's irrelevant whether the crime actually takes place."

"It just needs to look like it could have," Beni finished. "So, maybe we should let that happen and set a trap?"

"You sound like Fred from Scooby-Doo," Jake said. Beni flipped him off, eliciting a low laugh from everyone in the room despite the serious topic being discussed.

"I do think we need to set a trap, but I don't want to do that at the resort," Damian said. "If something *were* to happen during the operation, can you imagine how that would look when it came to light that the FBI intentionally allowed a breach of security?"

Beni understood Damian's point, and he was right. It might make things more complicated if they couldn't set a trap at the resort, but there was no way they could intentionally let a security breach happen.

"What if it happened beforehand?" Alexis asked.

"He's not scheduled to be down here until the day The Summit opens," Beni said. It was a little bit of a bone of contention between her and Cal—he wanted to come down a few days early to see her, but she didn't see the point because she was going to be so busy with both the investigation and The Summit that she wouldn't be able spend time with him.

"Right now, he is," Alexis agreed. "But we're all going to be based at Hemmeleigh beginning three days before The Summit, which leaves my house completely open. Why doesn't Cal use it to host an early kick-off dinner the night before and he can invite a few, select guests."

"Guests we choose," Jake said, picking up on Alexis' train of thought.

"Exactly," Alexis said. Beni knew exactly where her friends were going with the suggestion, too, and though she saw the benefits, she wasn't quite ready to jump on board.

"It would set a trap without compromising the security of The Summit," Damian mused.

"We all know how secure Alexis' place is," Dominic added.

"We could set up in the gatehouse with Alexis' security to keep an eye on things," Jake chimed in.

"What about the guy who's supposed to be starting work? Smythe's girlfriend's brother? If we deny him employment and then suddenly Cal is hosting an offsite dinner, don't you think they might get suspicious?" Beni asked.

"If we don't deny his employment, it will be even more suspect," Shah said. "The hiring freeze has been our policy from the very beginning. If we don't enforce it, people might start to ask why."

"I'm sure your security is top notch, Alexis, but we'd be

happy to spend the next few days working with your team to bolster it, if needed," Lucy offered.

"I know it's uncomfortable, Beni," Anika said softly from beside her. "But if we deny employment to the person they think is going to be their man on the inside, they'll be desperate for a backup plan. Having Cal host this party at Alexis', which is a controlled environment, is our best option."

"If he goes for it," Jake said.

Beni looked around the table. There was no question in her heart or her mind that other than a few buddies from the Army there was no one she trusted more than the people sitting in the room with her. But the set-up didn't feel good and, even if it was a controlled environment, she didn't like putting Cal in the line of fire. He had so much to lose if they lost even a little bit of that control.

But they were right.

She sighed. "He'll do it. I know he will," she said. "I'll go call him while you all sort out who he needs to invite and a good justification for why he's inviting them. It can't look too contrived." Jake made a face at her and she raised a hand to stop his objection. "I know I'm not telling you anything you don't already know, but this *matters* to me. Please, humor me."

Jake pursed his lips and nodded.

"We're assuming the goal is to insinuate that the vice president has a thing for young women—possibly even girls," Anika said. "And that he has connections to the trafficking circle to provide him access to those young women. What we need to find out, once the dinner is put in play, is who they are planning to use and how they plan to get her into the house."

"I think we need to keep close tabs—and by that, I mean monitor every piece of the invitee's electronic traffic—once Cal issues those invitations," Brian said. "As you pointed out, Anika, they'll be desperate for a Plan B, and I bet we'll learn a thing or two that will help us intercept the woman."

"And maybe replace her with one of our own. Well, one of *your* own," Lucy said, adding that last bit with a wry smile.

"So, we have a plan?" Shah asked, though everyone knew she wasn't really asking.

"I'll go deny the request for the new hire," Dominic said. "Then I can help the others sort through who Cal should invite to the dinner." He rose and left the room, Anika and Jake trailing after him.

"I'll need to alert Yael and Eric," Alexis said, referring to her head of security and in-house chef. "Brian and Lucy, if you'll come with me, I'd like to introduce you to Yael and then maybe you can head to the house to do a walk through?"

Both the consultants nodded and followed Alexis out of the room.

"We'll reconvene tonight to go over the progress," Shah said before leaving herself. Everyone but Damian had gone and, rather than rushing out to his tasks, he was studying her, his expression one of concern.

"You doing okay?" he asked.

She sifted through her emotions as best she could on the spot. It was a good plan, it was the *right* plan, but she wasn't loving it. Then again, just over a year ago, Damian had walked into an abandoned boathouse, with Charlotte by his side, knowing full well it was a trap, but also that it was the only way to put an end to the situation they'd found themselves in and truly keep Charlotte safe. The team had had his back then, just as they'd have hers now.

"I wish I could wave a magic wand and make it all go away, but since I left my fucking faery dust in Boston, I guess this will have to do," she said, making him smile.

"You have something better than faery dust or magic wands, anyway," Damian said, rising from his seat.

"Oh yeah? 'Cause I gotta say, either would be very welcome at this point," she replied, rising as well.

"You do," he said, throwing an arm around her shoulder. "You have us. We put that fucking faery dust to shame."

"I'm in, but you knew I would be," Cal said to Beni. She was standing with her phone to her ear, watching life on the streets of Havensted from the window of the FBI offices five floors up. "You don't like it, though, do you?" he asked.

She sighed. She and Cal had talked every day, sometimes more than once, since they'd parted in Nassau. They might have a few years to catch each other up on, but it was almost eerie how well they knew each other already—sliding right back into being a couple wasn't nearly as jarring as she'd thought it would be.

"It's the best plan. I don't love it, but I agree with my teammates that it's the plan most likely to succeed."

Cal laughed. "You make it sound like one of those high school yearbook things. Do you have 'best looking plan' or 'the plan with the best body?' Can you believe we actually voted on that shit in high school?"

Beni laughed, as Cal had intended.

"That's a sound I like," he said. "So now what?"

"Now, I have Brian and Lucy scrub your security team to see who should be brought into this. I'm sure they are all clean, but we want to keep the number of people who know about the plan small and we want to be beyond certain that those people are trustworthy."

"I'll send you a list of names once we're off the call," he said.

"Jake, Anika, and Dominic are looking at folks we think are involved in order to come up with the best guestlist. We should have something for you in a few hours. Once we have the security team in place and up to speed, then you can start issuing invitations, probably tomorrow morning."

"Sounds good. The dinner is a week away though, eight days, actually. I want to see you before that," Cal said.

His tone bordered on being whiny and it made Beni laugh. "We've had this conversation before, Cal. You can't be flying down here all the time. Even though the cat is out of the bag about us, I don't have a lot of free time on my hands and you don't need to look like you're spending taxpayer money to visit your girlfriend."

"I like the sound of that."

"Spending taxpayer money?" Beni asked, knowing that couldn't be what he meant.

"Ha, no. You being my girlfriend. Kind of a weird word given we're in our late thirties—well, just forty for me—but whatever."

Beni smiled to herself. The world now knew Vice President Calvin Matthews was seeing someone. There hadn't been any media at Connaught's party in Nassau, but there were a lot of people who liked nothing more than to gossip. The fallout—or media swell—hadn't been too bad yet, but Beni suspected there were two factors behind that. First, she and Cal hadn't been spotted together since Nassau. And second, Jess had helped by putting Beni in touch with one of her colleagues who covers the personal side of politics. By speaking to a (relatively) trusted journalist, Beni and Cal had ensured that their story would be reported in the least salacious way possible. At least at this point in time.

And to Jess's credit, the reporter had come through. A picture of the two of them from the party—Cal with his arm loosely draped around her waist, leaning down and saying something to her as she smiled—accompanied an article that gave the bare bones of their story. Who she was, their history, and how they'd reconnected. It highlighted the fact that Beni was still working and would be for the foreseeable future. What she hadn't printed, which Beni was grateful for, was anything about her special assignment on Shah's task force or her role in the security of The Summit. It wouldn't be hard to find out if someone dug for it, but that information didn't need to come from—or appear to come from—her or Cal.

"We both know that I don't spend taxpayer money without good reason," he said, bringing her back to the issue they'd covered more than once in the past few days.

"I know the first time you visited it was a legit expense tied to an FBI request. That's hardly the case now, is it? I don't think the taxpayers want to pay for you to spend the night with your girlfriend."

"They won't. Brian's cousin is a pilot. I've already talked to him about the cost of chartering a flight. Alexis has offered one of her planes, too. Her parents keep one in New York and it can pop down and pick me up."

That startled Beni. "When did you talk to Alexis?"

"You're getting off topic, Ricci. I want to see you."

Hearing the genuine longing in his voice, she paused then let out a long breath. "I know. I want to see you, too, but I think we both know that can't happen. You probably have access to dozens of ways to get down here, but unless it's an official trip, your security isn't likely to let that happen. The Summit will be over in just over two weeks. We'll have some debrief activities after that, but maybe you can plan an actual vacation and we can go somewhere together?"

After a beat, Cal sighed. "I know I should be more patient, but it's hard. We missed so many years that I don't like the idea of missing any more than we have to. But I guess that's your point. Right now, we're at a time where we 'have to' be apart. I'm sure there will be other times in our relationship where we won't be able to be together and we'll figure it out. I just hate that this is happening right as we've found our way back to each other."

"Two weeks, Cal. I wish it were different, but all we need to do is put our heads down and make it through and then we can decide what our future looks like," she said.

"Something else I like the sound of."

She heard the smile in his voice as he said this, and she agreed. She didn't know what their future would look like, or, more specifically, what her professional future might look like, but she liked the idea that they were both in a place in their lives where they could plan one together.

"Send me that list of your security detail," she said. "I'm sure Brian and Lucy can get their hands on it, but they're off reviewing the security at Alexis' house, so getting it from you might save some time."

"You'll have it in ten minutes."

"Once Lucy and Brian cull through it, we'll set up a call with you and the selected members of the team and by then, we'll have a list of the invitees."

"I'd say that sounds good, but it's all kinds of fucked up, so I'll just say thank you to you and everyone working on this. I know this is your job, but I have a hard time believing that when you agreed to be on the task force that you foresaw this happening."

Beni chuckled. "I think that's a pretty safe assumption. But being the control freak that I am, I'm glad it was me and this team that uncovered this mess. There's no one I would trust more with your safety than me and my teammates."

"You and me both, Nita."

Silence hung between them for a beat. It was always this way when they neared the end of their calls—neither one really wanting to say goodbye.

Finally, Cal cleared his throat. "I'll get that list to you and we'll talk later."

"Sounds good. And Cal?"

"Yeah?"

"Love you."

"Love you, too," he replied on a heartfelt sigh.

After ending the call, she remained at the window for a few minutes, watching the traffic and people below. The offices were on the north side of town, away from the beach, so most of the foot traffic was locals or businesspeople. Still, every now and then, the odd tourist ventured their way, like the two women she now watched.

They were pointing to something up the hill, gesturing. One held a piece of paper and by the way the two studied the paper then looked up the hill, Beni suspected they were either historians or archeologists. There were lots of ruins up in the hills of Tildas Island. Remnants of the island's colonial history.

As she watched the women, her mind drifted to what Cal had said. He was right. When she'd agreed to take the job with the task force, it hadn't been about the security work for The Summit. She'd done so only for the opportunity to work with Sunita Shah.

So much had changed since then.

She'd certainly learned from Shah, but more importantly, she'd gained friends and trusted colleagues. She'd helped investigate several major crimes from start to finish, and she'd helped uncover a conspiracy. And most unexpected of all was that she'd reconnected with Cal. No, it was safe to say that when she signed up for the task force eighteen months ago, she hadn't expected any of this—except the Shah part.

And there was no way she'd have it any other way.

CHAPTER TWENTY-ONE

"So, we have Calloway, Andrew Smythe, Victor Hernandez, and Peter Loughlin on our list," Beni said. Cal and the four members of his security team selected by Lucy and Brian were on speaker phone.

"Sir—" one of them said.

"I'm doing this, Craig, so you just need to get over it," Cal cut the man off. Beni felt a little sorry for him. If she were part of Cal's security detail, she'd be throwing up every objection she could, too. "Why those four?" Cal asked. "I get Calloway, but what about the others?"

"We wanted you to be able to frame the event as a potential way to garner support from younger members of the party. Because of that, we chose to keep the invitees to a small group of men approximately the same age as you. As to the specific men, as you noted, Calloway was a given. We chose Smythe because he's linked to the trafficking ring, and it was his girlfriend's brother who they attempted to insert into the Hemmeleigh staff," Beni answered.

"Fair enough," Cal replied. "What about the others?"

"Hernandez runs the second largest infotainment media

outlet in the US. If Connaught and his counterpart, Egerton, are looking for media to blast the story they're concocting, he's a likely candidate. He also spends a lot of time with Calloway and there are indications that he's aware of—though may not be directly participating in—the conspiracy," Damian answered.

"Last but not least is Peter Loughlin," Alexis said. "He runs a hedge fund, several actually, and invests heavily in the defense industry. He's a man who reaps massive benefits when the country is in conflict. He's also on the board of several institutions, including The Bank of DC."

"So, with his connections to The Bank of DC, are you saying that he's more likely to be directly involved than Hernandez is, though not as much as Calloway?" Cal asked.

Beni almost laughed. "Other than Connaught and Egerton, *no one* is more involved than Calloway. To answer your question, though, we're not sure. Loughlin is certainly positioned better than Hernandez to be directly involved, but he's also the kind of guy who probably prefers to just let other people do his dirty work."

"Sounds like my kind of guy," Cal muttered, sarcasm thick in his tone.

"Despite your differences, it should be easy to sell the invitation as a pre-conference dinner with like-minded young blood of the party," Shah said, joining in. "You're the youngest of the group, Mr. Vice President, but none of the men are older than forty-five."

"Will inviting them down make them suspicious if they aren't already attending the event?" Cal asked.

"That's the beauty of it," Jake responded. "Loughlin was already planning to attend as part of the US delegation."

"Charlotte turned us onto him," Damian said. "She tried to have him blocked because she has some experience with his lack of ethics, but she was overruled."

"Bad for the conference, but good for us," Jake said. "As for

Hernandez, his media outlet was also already planning to attend the event. Not the hard news part of it, but you know, the glitz and glamour of it. His team will be at both the opening and closing receptions. He normally wouldn't come down, but inviting him won't seem unusual."

"And Calloway will go wherever we lead him," Alexis said. "Given that you just saw him, it won't seem weird for him to be invited for another catch-up. Also, conspiracy aside, there's no way he'd miss the opportunity to say he's having a private dinner with the vice president at the home of Jasper and Vera Wright."

Judging by the way Calloway had all but salivated at the idea of staying on the Wright's yacht, Alexis was spot on with that assessment.

"What about Smythe? I just met him in Nassau, as well, so maybe it's just extending the hand of friendship to someone relatively new to the party?" Cal suggested.

"Exactly," Dominic said, jumping in. "Of all the invitees, he's the one you'll need to spin the most. The others have their own agendas, but Smythe doesn't so you'll need to make him feel like he's special."

"Oh, he's special," Cal muttered. "Special like a tire-filled-dumpster on fire."

"Lucy and Brian will reach out to your security team after this call to go over everything," Beni said, cutting off any more of Cal's commentary. Everyone in the room agreed with his assessment, but he didn't need to be saying it to so many people.

"That's all there is to report at this time, Mr. Vice President," Shah said. Before going into the details of the dinner, they'd spent time bringing Cal's security team up to speed on the investigation. Then, once the four men had processed the breadth and depth of the conspiracy that had, more or less, been unfolding under their noses, Shah had updated everyone, Cal included, on the current activities and findings. Now, thankfully, it appeared that everyone was on the same page. Even if, in the case of some of Cal's security, it was begrudgingly so.

"Is Serena involved?" Cal asked.

Beni glanced to Anika. As strange as it was, Anika and Serena had hit it off in the past few weeks. They hadn't known each other long, but, along with Dominic, they were lock-step on tracking the movements of the trafficking ring.

"She is," Anika answered. "We're setting her up as one of the servers at your dinner. Eric, Alexis' chef will cook, but we'll have Serena and a colleague of Cyn Steele's step in as the servers."

"Cyn won't be involved, I assume?" he asked.

"Correct," Shah answered. "Though, she will be nearby should we need her. Also, with the connection to Georgina Grace, Calloway's half-sister, who is also British, Cyn and her handler want to stay close."

"Makes sense," Cal said. "I don't have any more questions, but I have some calls to make now, so if we're done…?"

"For your part, yes, we're done," Shah confirmed. "If Craig and the rest of the team could make themselves available in about fifteen minutes, we'd appreciate it."

"Of course. Go ahead and call back on this line. Beni?" He waited for her to respond before he added, "I'll call you tonight."

She ignored the smiles and raised eyebrows of her teammates, and simply said goodbye. When the line was quiet, everyone looked to Shah.

"Damian and Alexis, work with Lucy and Brian to go over the security details with Matthews' team. Conference Yael in as well, please," she said. "Anika and Dominic, I know you're monitoring the chatter, but I expect it will pick up once we've dropped this golden opportunity in Connaught and Egerton's laps. If Calloway is going to use this opportunity to try and catch the vice president in the act, they are going to need a girl or a young woman. We need to know who she is and how they plan to get her in. Then we need a plan to intercept and replace her with one of ours...who that ends up being will depend on what the intended young woman looks like."

"I know I'm preaching to the choir here," Beni said, looking to Anika and Dominic. "But finding the young woman they intend to use for the entrapment is probably the most important part. If we mess that up, we can still control what happens in the house, but it will look a lot less convincing if it's truly a young woman that's been trafficked in rather than an undercover agent."

"You know we have your back on this, Beni. Yours and Cal's," Anika said. "I'll also point out that Serena borders on being scary as shit and she has a history with these traffickers. This is more than just a job for her. I don't think I've ever said this so quickly about anyone in my life, but I trust her. If anyone can locate the young woman being used, it will be Serena."

Beni regarded her friend. Anika's childhood had included a mother who'd abandoned her at a mall then to a series of foster homes. To say she didn't trust easily was an understatement and Beni accorded her words the respect they were due.

"Thank you," she said.

There was a knock at the door, and everyone looked up to see their receptionist, Steven, who was also a retired MI-6 agent, standing in the entry. Shah waved him in.

"Here's the information you requested, Director Shah," he said handing over a file.

"Any problems?" she asked.

Steven shook his head. "He's as solid as they come and was entirely on board."

Shah opened the file and quickly glanced over it before raising her attention back to Steven. "Thank you, I'll be sure to follow up on this."

Then, with a nod, Steven turned and left.

"What's that?" Jake asked, eliciting chuckles from everyone

in the room. Eighteen months ago, everyone practically asked Shah for permission to sneeze, and now Jake was demanding to know the contents of some secret folder. It wasn't that they'd thought Shah was scary, but she was a very powerful person in the Bureau. She *still* was, but their relationships had shifted during their time together and now there was a level of trust—and familiarity—that hadn't been there before.

"Thanks to Jessica Kilkenny, this," Shah said, holding up the closed file, "is a press contact who's going to help us convince Connaught and Egerton they've succeeded in their plan so that we can get them to reveal how much they know. Before you ask any more questions, no, I'm not going to elaborate. Not right now, anyway."

Jake frowned and let out a dramatic sigh.

Shah's lips twitched. "Jake, you and Beni check in on everyone's whereabouts. I don't want to lose sight of any of our key players. While you're at it, see if you can make any headway on determining who is knowingly contributing funds to this operation versus those who believe they are still just contributing to the party."

"Aye aye, Captain," Jake said. Shah shot him a repressive look before rising.

"I'll be in my office if anyone needs me," she said as she exited the room.

Once she was gone, the remaining eight people in the room —the five members of the task force, Anika, Lucy, and Brian— all looked at each other. It was a single brief moment when everything that was at stake settled over them. But it wasn't a sense of being overwhelmed that filled the room.

In her years in the Army, Beni had seen enough grit and resolve to recognize it. And looking around the room, she knew there were no better people she'd want at her back than those who surrounded her now.

The next day was a long one. The team divided tasks, alternating between their responsibilities at Hemmeleigh and preparing for Cal's special dinner in a week's time. Beni had started at five in the morning, and it was just after eleven o'clock at night when she finally walked into her apartment.

She toed off her boots, leaving them beside the door, and dropped her keys on the hall table. It wasn't until she reached up to loosen her holster that she sensed she wasn't alone.

As quietly as possible, she unsnapped her holster and withdrew her weapon. Once her fingers closed around the familiar, cool metal, she stilled and listened for anything out of the ordinary. In the eighteen months she'd been on the island, not once had her apartment been broken into. It did not escape her attention that within a few days of going public with the news that she and Cal were seeing each other, an intruder decided to pop by for a visit.

Thanks to her years of training and experience, she controlled her fear and kept her breathing both steady and quiet. There were two doors in the short hallway, one to her bedroom and the other to the guest bathroom/laundry room combo. Both doors were closed, just as she'd left them that morning.

Assuming there was only one other person in the apartment with her, she could move past the doors and clear the living room and kitchen before going back to check the bathroom and bedroom.

And didn't the thought of some stranger in her bedroom make her feel all warm and fuzzy.

Inching forward on her stockinged feet, she stepped past the bedroom door and paused at the end of the hall just before it opened up to the living areas. From where she stood, she could see into the kitchen and the small dining area.

Both were empty.

Taking a slow, deep breath, she spun and placed her back against the opposite wall, giving herself a view of the living room. Her eyes quickly scanned the room before catching on an odd shape propped up on the arm of her sofa.

She paused and took another deep breath. It was then she recognized something she hadn't before. The vague hint of something both fresh and musky—masculine.

A scent she knew well.

"Cal," she said, dropping her gun to her side.

His head popped up from where he'd been lying on her sofa, his feet propped on the edge.

She flipped on the light and his eyes skated over her, a smile dancing on his lips. He wore dress pants and a button-down shirt. His tie was askew.

He grinned. "Is it wrong of me to be having some pretty explicit fantasies about you right now?"

CHAPTER TWENTY-TWO

"Hard to believe we're finally here, isn't it?" Alexis asked Beni as they both stood in front of a bank of monitors located inside the gatehouse to her property. On one screen, they could see Cal, Andrew Smythe, Victor Hernandez, Peter Loughlin, and Calloway all sitting on the patio enjoying a cocktail. The sun had just set, and they had another hour before dinner would be served. On another monitor, they could see Eric working in the kitchen while Nora, a gorgeous woman on loan to them from some intelligence agency neither Shah nor Nora identified, checked the table settings. On a third monitor, Serena could be seen upstairs, quietly making a sweep of each of the visitors' rooms—and belongings.

"I'll be happier when it's tomorrow," Beni muttered. By tomorrow, if everything went according to plan, the conspiracy to bring down the Cunningham-Matthews administration would be over. Not only would it be over, but those primarily responsible for pulling everything together that had brought them to this point—including the murders of innocent people— would be facing justice. Beni just hoped the hands of justice would be cold and unforgiving.

"We'll get there," Alexis assured her.

Beni knew that to be true, but she couldn't help but consider what might go wrong between now and then. Because something always went wrong. Maybe just a little thing, something that would have no consequence. But sometimes it was something big.

Everyone was prepared for something unexpected, if not the actual form the unexpected would take. Not knowing if it would be a big thing or a little thing, was definitely edging her anxiety up, though.

The sound of a door closing upstairs drew Beni's gaze upward. While the monitors she and Alexis watched had no audio, Damian and Cyn, who'd joined them in this final leg of their operation, were set up in a room on the second floor listening to the conversation on the porch. The set-up felt a little disjointed, but while Shah had wanted Alexis' usual security to remain on site as additional pairs of eyes, she hadn't wanted them hearing anything. Hence the separation. Beni and Alexis were on the ground floor with the two men who normally operated as Alexis' gate and grounds security, while Damian and Cyn were tucked in upstairs, listening and recording.

She and Alexis watched for several more minutes then finally, Serena came out of the last bedroom, which happened to be Hernandez'. She pulled out her phone even as she glanced at the camera and gave them a sign, letting them know she was done with her search and nothing dangerous—in the traditional sense, like a gun or knife—had been found.

A few seconds later, Beni's phone vibrated. Pulling the device from her pocket, she unlocked it and tilted the screen so Alexis could read, as well.

"Camera with WiFi in room four, all sort of sexual accoutrements in rooms one and two. Looks like they are planning to stage something."

There was no need to reply, so as soon as they read the message, Beni hit a button and it disappeared. Room one was Calloway's and room two was Smythe's. Room four was Hernandez', so it was hardly surprising that Serena had found a camera there. They'd even prepared for him to bring a WiFi enabled one and had scramblers set up around the house so that, when the time came, they could interfere, and prevent any wireless communications. In other words, if Hernandez tried to send any pictures, he wouldn't be able to.

The lack of anything in Loughlin's room, room three, made Beni question if he had any idea what was being planned for the evening. They'd uncovered evidence during the past week pointing to Loughlin as the creator of the fictitious Bank of DC scandal, although they hadn't yet confirmed if he knew about the overall conspiracy plan, or if he was only aware of the part he had played in it. As for the night's activities—did he know what Calloway and Smythe intended to do? Or was he only along for the ride?

Beni made a mental note to keep her eye on Loughlin then sent a message to Damian and Cyn updating them on Serena's findings. After Damian acknowledged the text, she locked her phone and slid it into her pocket. And waited.

She hated this part of any op—the waiting. She wasn't like Damian or Jake, who could still their body and mind, and go into an almost trance-like state as they waited to spring into action. She'd be fine, she could do it, she'd done it enough in her career. But that didn't mean she didn't hate it.

To pass the time as Eric finished the dinner preparations and Nora and Serena prepped the copious amount of alcohol being provided that evening, Beni pulled out a file and started to review the information it contained. None of it was new, but even so, the contents got her blood flowing just a little faster. In the week since they'd put this plan into action, the team, aided by Serena, Cyn, Brian, and Lucy, had gathered enough evidence that the Department of Justice would barely need to conduct their own investigation.

When it became clear that they had all the evidence needed to put a stop to the conspiracy, Beni had tried to call off the dinner. But neither Shah nor Cal had agreed. Shah had informed her that if they called it off so close to the event, it would unnecessarily raise red flags. Cal's reasoning wasn't quite as logical. He might have been content to let the task force run the investigation, but that didn't mean he wasn't good and pissed off about Connaught and Egerton's activities. To him, the dinner was his way of saying FU to all of them. She hadn't been happy with his position, although in some ways—many ways—she could understand it. If someone had been trying to frame her, she'd want the opportunity to bring them down a peg or two—or twelve—and make sure they knew it was her who had done it.

"They're moving inside now," Alexis said. Beni closed the file and focused on watching the dynamics of the group. Hernandez wore a hint of a smirk and his eyes kept darting to Calloway. Smythe's smile was wide, and his slightly off-balance journey from the patio to the table told Beni he'd probably already had too much to drink. So did the way his eyes blatantly tracked Serena and Nora.

Her gaze shifted to the two women. Serena could take care of herself, but Beni knew nothing of Nora other than she was a foreign intelligence agent and that her looks could very well inspire a man—particularly a drunk hetero man—to misbehave. Beni hoped Smythe wouldn't be a problem, but with his predilections, she wasn't going to count on it.

Beni pulled out her phone to send a quick message to Serena and give her a heads up about Smythe, then paused as Nora smiled at something Serena said. Nora's expression didn't change, but there was a dark edge in her eyes. Whatever the women were discussing, Beni suddenly had absolute faith that Nora could take care of herself.

She slid her phone back into her pocket and switched her gaze to a different monitor just in time to see Loughlin amble into the house. His hands were tucked into his khaki shorts and his six-hundred-dollar t-shirt—a little fact Beni only knew because Alexis had informed her of such—untucked. With his sun-streaked hair, lean build, and confident walk, he was the kind of guy who caught a woman's attention. From behind. From the front, Peter Loughlin had pinched eyes, a nose that spread over a third of his face, and nearly non-existent lips. Looks weren't everything, but given what Beni knew of him from their files, his personality wouldn't win him any points, either. Known to be petty, demanding, and even vindictive, he had no wit, no charm, and even less humility. She grinned when she saw Cal move subtly away from the man, clearly not wanting to be seated beside him at the large round table where they were gathering.

Last but not least, Calloway brought up the rear of the group. His gaze swept over the room and a ghost of a smile touched his lips. Judging by the way he inched closer to Cal, he was playing up the "we've known each other for years" card and making them seem closer friends than they actually were. There were a number of possible motives for Calloway's behavior, including showing the rest of the group how close to power he sat, or perhaps he was trying to ingratiate himself to Cal in order to more easily carry out his plan. Her personal favorite option, though, was that he was being overly friendly just so the knife would hurt even more when he stuck it in Cal's back later that night.

Because yes, betraying Cal was the plan. They'd all known that, of course, and over the last few days, they'd uncovered exactly how Calloway and his puppet masters planned to do it.

At half past ten, Calloway was going to suddenly realize that there was a rum he loved that they all *had* to try. Miraculously, he'd discover a liquor store three miles up the road that carried it. Then he'd leave under the auspices of picking up a bottle, but in reality, he would meet with his contact and collect the girl they planned to use to set Cal up. When he returned to the house, he'd encourage everyone to drink more than they should, then, once Cal was fast asleep, they'd bring the girl in for a round of bedroom photos with the vice president. Photos that would end up on all the major news outlets by morning.

Only it wasn't going to go down quite the way Calloway planned. He wouldn't be meeting the contact that Smythe had arranged, nor would he be picking up the young woman the trafficker had selected. No, those two had been identified two days ago and picked up earlier in the afternoon by Anika and Dominic. They were now sitting in a safe house on Tortola with a couple more of Shah's friends from British Intelligence.

Their replacements had been selected for their similar looks to those Smythe had hired—or forced—and they'd both been quickly read in on the operation when they'd arrived on Tildas that morning.

Beni glanced at the clock on the monitor then let out a deep breath and finally took a seat. It was just after seven-thirty, they had a long night ahead of them before Cal was firmly out of harm's way.

Alexis sank into the seat beside her. Serena and Nora brought out a round of drinks followed by the first tastings course, a mixed plate of traditional Caribbean cuisine, but all done in miniature—a roti, a pate, a dollop of mofongo, and a ramekin filled with a saltfish and dumpling stew.

"Holy god that looks good," Alexis muttered. "I haven't had a coursed meal since moving here. This is making me think we've been missing out." She gestured to the monitors as she spoke.

"I have a protein bar in my bag if you want," Beni offered.

"I think a little bit of my soul just died, Ricci," Alexis responded. "Good news, though…"

Beni looked over and Alexis held out a deck of cards.

"We can finally have that poker rematch you've been promising me for four months," she said with a grin.

While Cal prided himself on being an authentic politician—something most people believed to be an oxymoron—that didn't mean he wasn't capable of acting the part when needed. And damn if it wasn't needed tonight.

Hernandez kept casting him sly, superior looks. Despite being forty-one, Smythe had decided to play the frat boy role. Calloway was acting like his best friend. And Loughlin, well, the guy was just a complete and utter wanker. Cal might have attributed the epithet "prick" to him, but the British slang version just seemed to fit better.

Serena and Nora placed the first course on the table, a plate of miniature tastings of local Caribbean cuisine. As Nora passed by Loughlin, the man's hand brushed against her hip. Cal would like to say he was surprised by the behavior, but he wasn't—it was the behavior of a wanker. He considered saying something, as he normally would have, then realized that Calloway had a plan he needed to stick to and he wouldn't—couldn't—let Loughlin throw off the balance of the evening. If Loughlin did anything inappropriate with, or to, Nora it would definitely throw off the balance because having her around would not be conducive to the planned activities.

Or would they?

Cal contemplated that line of logic as Smythe carried the conversation, talking about some boat race he'd been in. He didn't know if Loughlin was involved in the plan for the night, but Calloway and Hernandez most definitely were. Even if

Loughlin wasn't part of it, if he somehow managed to get Nora to stay, Calloway and Hernandez could use that to their advantage. After all, as far as they knew, she was an island girl, with no ties to either party or politics. It would be hard to drum up a more perfect witness to the scene Calloway planned to stage.

As if to give voice to his thoughts, Calloway suddenly asked, "Do both you ladies live here on the island?"

Serena had just finished pouring a cocktail for him and she answered first. "I do. I've been working for the Wrights for nearly a year." She was presenting as a woman tonight and both she and Nora wore slim fitted black pants and white silk tank tops. Looking at her now, with her hair (compliments of a wig) and make-up done, it was hard to believe that she was one of the most successful assets in the history of the CIA—one who was known to most as The Gentleman, since more often than not, she dressed, and presented as a man.

"And you?" Calloway asked Nora who was now standing back, waiting for Serena to pour the last drink before the two returned to the kitchen.

Nora nodded. "I came for spring break while in college and just stayed. I can't imagine living anywhere else."

Cal knew for a fact that Nora had arrived on the island just this morning, but both women were far more versed at lying and misdirection than he would ever be.

"Lucky you," Loughlin said. "You work catering all the time?"

Nora shook her head. "No, I take jobs when they come. A little of this, a little of that. I've been here long enough that I have a big circle of friends and acquaintances. If I want to work, it's not usually hard to find a gig."

Cal briefly caught Serena's eye who gave a nearly imperceptible nod. It appeared that Nora had already caught on to Loughlin and had come to the same conclusion Cal had regarding a new role for her to play. Actually, she'd probably had it figured out the minute the men had walked in the door an hour and a half ago. He'd learned long ago from Serena that while he may play six moves ahead—which was more than most politicians—she, and other assets like her, were always ahead by at least ten. At least the ones who stayed in the game.

"Sounds like a nice life," Calloway said.

Serena joined Nora at the side of the room.

"It has its ups and downs, but like I said, I can't imagine being anywhere else. We'll let you start your meal, now." And with that, both women gave the table a little nod and stepped out of the room.

Loughlin made some comment about Nora that wasn't worth responding to. In fact, it took a certain amount of restraint not to tell Loughlin to shut the fuck up. Cal didn't need to have a sister or mother to know that talking about women—or any human being—in the way Loughlin had wasn't acceptable. He kept his mouth shut, though, knowing that letting these men show their true colors wasn't just *part* of the plan, but a necessary component of it. Regardless of how sleazy it made Cal feel.

The conversation returned to the boat race, and now Smythe and Loughlin were trying to one-up each other on boating talk. Loughlin could buy Smythe out a hundred times over, but Smythe's more genial personality gave him an advantage Loughlin didn't have.

Unfortunately, the meal progressed as Cal thought it would and the next two hours sorely tried his acting abilities. A man could only take so many sly comments from Calloway, talk of how much he was worth from Loughlin, salacious stories covered by Hernandez, and party—the traditional kind, not the political kind—gossip from Smythe.

But the length of the meal—long enough to take them well into the night, but not so long as to the give the guests something to complain about—was intentionally orchestrated, and he had to play his part. Thankfully, the food was excellent, and the drinks flowed freely. Although, by design, Cal's drinks were less potent than his guests, leaving him in that unenviable position of being the sober one amongst all the drunks. Not that it would have been much better had they all been sober. Or all been drunk.

Thinking about what kind of torture it would be to be drunk with these men, Cal glanced around the table. His gaze snagged on Calloway and Cal realized he wasn't the only one sober. Calloway might be smiling and laughing and acting a bit loose, but the sharpness in his eye hadn't dulled since he'd walked into Alexis' house several hours ago. Given that he was supposed to drive to the local liquor store in less than an hour, and likely wanted to stay sober enough that security wouldn't keep him from getting into his car, it didn't surprise Cal. But how easily Calloway could have fooled him—if he hadn't been paying attention—did.

Cal made a mental note that while his fraternity brother might be all flash and no substance, it wouldn't be wise to underestimate him.

Finally, the dessert plates were cleared, and the men retired back to the porch for cigars and another after-dinner drink. They'd chosen to serve whiskey knowing that it would give Calloway the best opening to start talking about the local rums.

As the night wore on, Cal deflected a few questions about Beni, but did engage in a conversation with Loughlin about taxes and a couple of upcoming senate races. The conversation was uninspired as Loughlin's primary interest was in whatever would make him the most money, but it allowed Cal's attention to drift to more interesting things. Like planning a vacation with Beni once this was all over.

He was answering a question about some lobbyist while also still daydreaming about the vacation when Calloway popped up from his seat.

"Does Alexis have Axeline Rum?" Calloway asked.

Cal raised his hand and signaled for Nora who opened the sliding door and stuck her head out. "What can I help you with?" she asked.

Calloway repeated his question and Nora gave the illusion of contemplating it before shaking her head. "No, that's not one we have here, but it is a good one. Very unique," she added.

Calloway pulled his phone out and started typing.

"Thank you, Nora," Cal said. He didn't miss the look she cast at Loughlin, it was a brief moment where she caught and held his gaze, before dropping her own and letting a little smile touch her lips. Cal almost laughed out loud. Loughlin's ego was super-sized enough that he took her subtle flirting as both genuine and expected. To be fair, Nora was damn good at her job and played her role well, so it wasn't so much the fact that Loughlin believed her that made Cal smile, but it was more the lazy predatory gleam in his eye, like he knew she was a sure thing when the night winded down. Cal almost wished he could be a fly on the wall when Nora did whatever she planned to do to neutralize him.

"There's a shop fifteen minutes away that carries it," Calloway said.

Cal rolled his head to look at Duncan. "Carries what?" He wanted to give the impression of bordering on being tipsy.

"Axeline Rum," Calloway said. "You have to try it. As Nora said, it's unique. Only available on Tildas Island, two locations in New York, and one in London. I'll go get us a bottle."

"Should you be driving?" Cal asked for show.

Calloway lifted a shoulder. "I'm fine, haven't had that much. Especially not compared to some of the nights we've indulged," he added, alluding to their college years. Cal nearly rolled his eyes. A man in his forties comparing himself to the man-child of his college years was a little "glory-days" pathetic, not to mention that he could count on one hand the number of parties that he and Calloway had attended at the same time.

Cal raised a dismissive hand. "Fine, whatever. If security says you can go, you can go, but you have to run it by them. I think they moved your car into the garage."

Smythe, who was probably the most drunk among them, laughed. "We can't leave without security's say so?"

Calloway ignored the comment and started toward the door, saying he'd be back with the best bottle of rum. Nora was opening the door for him when Cal responded.

"You can leave, but if you want to come back, my security team needs to know," he said. "You know, being the vice president and all, they're a little high strung about my safety."

Smythe snorted and that started an inane conversation about whether it was better to be just rich or both rich and famous. From there, not surprisingly, the conversation devolved into more society gossip, who was sleeping with who, and all sorts of things Cal didn't care about.

Thirty-five minutes later, Cal saw the gates to Alexis' estate open and Calloway's car pull back in. It paused for a moment while his team did a cursory check, then it pulled forward and into the garage. Listening to the garage door closing, Cal thought about the young woman who was now stowed away in Calloway's car. If all had gone to plan—which he didn't have any reason to think otherwise—the young woman was well aware of how the rest of the night would unfold.

But if Beni and her team hadn't figured out the elaborate scheme the two political parties had concocted together, it would be a very different sort of young woman in the car. It would be a woman, or perhaps a girl, scared, likely being threatened, maybe even kidnapped. She'd be lying in the dark in the back of a car, waiting to be fetched and taken to her fate—a fate she probably would have been able to guess at. She would have been terrified, not just for what was planned for her that night, but for the days and nights that would follow.

Suddenly, the delicious meal that Cal had eaten churned in

his stomach. He set his drink down and rose from his seat, just as Calloway stepped back onto the porch.

"Going somewhere, Cal?" he asked, holding up a bottle of what Cal assumed was the rum he'd gone to pick up.

"I've got a long day coming up tomorrow. The president will be here, and she and I have briefings and meetings all day before she opens The Summit tomorrow night. I think I'll call it a night. But please feel free to remain. Eric has gone home, but both Serena and Nora are here. If you need anything, feel free to ask them, or any of the security that will remain here overnight."

Calloway's grin faltered, but then it fixed back into place so fast that Cal almost didn't see it. "Fine, but you have to have a taste before you go. After all, I did just run out especially for this." He held the bottle up again. "You wouldn't want to be inhospitable now, would you?"

The plan was for Calloway to get him drunk enough to pass out—or at least fall deeply asleep—so that he could take the incriminating photos. If Cal didn't fall in with that scheme, was there a Plan B? Beni had mentioned that she thought Calloway might try to drug him. Was that the route he was planning to take? If so, Cal needed to go along with it.

He glanced inside the house and saw Serena preparing a tray of empty tumblers. She looked up, caught his eye, and gave a tiny nod.

With a sigh, he sank back into his seat. "I suppose," he drawled, exaggerating his speech to appear more intoxicated. "One wouldn't want to be accused of being inhospitable."

Calloway's grin morphed into a shit-eating smile. "There's a good man. Now stay in your seat and I'll pour."

As he spoke, Serena entered the porch and set the tray on the table. She watched Calloway remove the seal on the bottle then held her hand out to take the torn foil. Slipping it into the pocket of the light-weight jacket she'd thrown on, she then placed the tumblers, one-by-one, on the table as Calloway began to pour.

Watching Serena and Calloway without trying to appear too interested was harder than Cal thought it should be. Then again, maybe that was because he knew this was likely the time of reckoning.

"I've got this," Calloway said, waving Serena away. "You don't have to serve."

"If you're sure, sir?" Serena asked. Despite the intense emotions swirling inside him, Cal nearly snorted at Serena's deferential tone. Never once in their relationship had she been deferential. Not even the day after he and Anne-Marie had won the election in a landslide.

Calloway waved her off then turned back to the drinks. He was facing away from Cal so other than the quick movements of Calloway's arms, he couldn't see what the man was doing.

Serena moved carefully away from the table and, taking her tray, started to circle the porch and collect the now empty whiskey tumblers. Starting on the far side of the room, she collected Hernandez' before moving onto Smythe's.

By the time she'd reach Cal, Calloway had already handed him his rum and was moving across the porch to deliver glasses to the other three men.

Cal caught Serena's eye, and she tipped her head to the side table where his empty glass now sat. He hoped he'd read her right and he set his new glass of rum beside the empty one on the table.

Just as Calloway was about to hand Hernandez his drink, a loud crash came from inside the kitchen. Everyone, including Cal, jerked in surprise and looked toward the house.

A beat passed when Cal felt a whisper of air move across his skin, but when he looked back, Serena was already moving away from him, his empty tumbler on her tray and the rum still on the table beside him.

"Please, excuse me," she said. "I'll go check on Nora." Stepping into the house, she closed the door behind her.

Once Serena was out of sight, all the men looked at each other. Then Calloway let out a laugh and finished handing out the drinks. When everyone had one, he moved to the center of their haphazard circle and raised his glass. Cal reached for his and eyed the dark caramel colored liquid swirling in the bottom.

"Here's to a night like no other," Calloway said.

Hernandez and Smythe chuckled before taking a sip. Loughlin's attention flitted toward the house where Nora could be seen on her phone as she leaned against the counter. He, too, took a sip as he studied the woman. Cal's gaze landed back on Calloway who was watching him.

Slowly, Cal raised his glass. Calloway inclined his head and both men brought their glasses to their lips.

Never taking his eyes from Calloway, Cal slowly sipped his drink.

CHAPTER TWENTY-THREE

BENI LEANED over Cal's prone body. The sheets were pulled down and he wore nothing but a pair of boxers. She brushed the hair from his forehead and his eyes fluttered. She knew what was going to happen next, but even prepared for it, the sudden movement of his hand and the grip on her wrist startled her.

His eyes flew open and they stared vacantly at her. Then he blinked once, twice. As she watched, his gaze slowly came into focus and the grip on her wrist loosened, though didn't release.

"Nita?" he croaked.

Leaning over, she reached for the glass of water she'd brought up to his room and raised it for him to see. His gaze dragged over the drink. His attention lingered, as if trying to put two and two together, then he released her wrist and sat up.

"What time is it?" he asked.

The sun hadn't yet come up and the room was dark. It was a fair question. "About five-forty-five," she answered, nodding to the clock on the bedside table. "May I?" She gestured to the lamp.

He nodded then took a sip of the water as she switched on the soft light.

She rested a palm on his thigh as he gulped down the water. She wished she'd brought a second glass. Serena had exchanged Calloway's Rohypnol-dosed rum with a concoction of her own, and while the drug she'd used was relatively benign, it did tend to make the taker very thirsty.

When he finished the water, he retained his hold on the glass, even as he raised a hand and brushed his fingers down her cheek.

"Eight minutes to sunrise," he mumbled.

She frowned at the non-sequitur. "What?"

His gaze went to the clock. "The sun rises in eight minutes. It's a special time of day because it takes about eight minutes for the sun's rays to reach us. So right now, the sun has risen, we just can't see it yet."

A soft smile touched Beni's lips. It was so like Cal to know something like that. It was also more poignant than he knew. Like with the sun and its rays, everything would soon be illuminated, but they couldn't see the light quite yet.

His eyes softened as he looked at her. "This is not a bad way to wake up. Seeing you," he said. "What happened last night?" he asked. "I don't remember much of it after drinking the rum Calloway gave me." Then before she could answer, his hand cupped her cheek as his attention went to the door. His brow dipped in confusion. "Wait, what are you doing here?" he demanded.

The realization that hours were missing from his night was starting to set in and for a man as in control as Cal, she knew the panic—panic he'd keep a tight rein on but panic nonetheless —would start to surface. Sure enough, before she even answered, his gaze was moving around the room, taking in the evidence of everything he couldn't remember. His clothes were scattered across the floor. One shoe was near the closet while the other was lying against the sliding door to the balcony. And oddly, his toothbrush was on the bedside table.

Then his gaze swept the empty expanse of the bed beside him then lingered on the pillow. The pillow with a clear indentation—indicating he hadn't been alone—and three long strands of black hair on it.

Letting his hand fall from her face, he shifted toward the empty bedside. "Nita," he said, dropping his finger to the pillow beside him without actually touching the hairs. "What the hell happened last night?"

His gaze flew back to hers and her heart broke just a little bit with the fear and panic she saw there.

Gently, she cupped his jaw with both her hands. "It's going to be fine, Cal. I promise," she said.

His eyes skated back to the pillow beside him and she could all but see him racking his brain.

"Look at me, Cal," she said, leaning forward and touching her forehead to his. After a beat, his eyes came back to hers. "Do you trust me?"

He did. She knew he did. Even so, he hesitated. Grateful that he'd given *her* enough faith in *them* to weather the minor slight, she tipped her head and brushed her lips against his.

"I'll explain everything, I promise," she said when she pulled away. "But we need to get out of here. We have a helicopter waiting for us on the east side of the island and it's taking off in thirty minutes."

Again, his eyes slid to the hairs on the pillow before coming back to hers. "You know I love you, right?" he asked.

Beni stared at the man, the sting of tears touching the corners of her eyes. It was so like him to be worried about *her*. To be worried that she might think him capable of what the evidence in the room suggested.

She blinked, willing the moisture not to fall. "I do," she said. "I love you, too. Now, trust me, you are going to want to be on that helicopter."

He studied her for a beat, as if to be sure she was speaking the truth. Then he jerked forward and kissed her, tangling his hands in her hair as he pulled her toward him. It was a kiss of desperation, of love, and of gratitude. They didn't really have time for it, but Beni gave back everything she felt coming from Cal. He needed it from her, and she needed, more than anything, to give him the only reassurance she could in this moment.

When he pulled back, his eyes searched hers. "A helicopter?" he asked.

She nodded.

"How long do we have?"

"About twenty-six minutes, now," she said with a grin.

His lips spread into a hopeful smile. "Then I guess we better get going."

Anthony Connaught poured himself a cup of coffee and sat back in his seat. The view from the lanai of his bungalow was spectacular—the blue of the Caribbean stretched out before him, palm trees swayed in the early morning breeze, and gentle waves lapped up on the white sand. His gaze might have lingered on the scene, but he wasn't really looking.

He smiled to himself as he took a sip of his drink, his other hand resting on the newspaper folded on the table. Four years ago, when it had become clear that the Cunningham-Matthews ticket was as sure a bet as anything, he'd had to stomach his dislike of Lawrence Egerton and, for the first time in his life, reach across the aisle.

What Connaught found was that Egerton wasn't much different from himself. He was a man who preferred leaving politics to others, staying nicely in the background to orchestrate platforms and campaigns, and to generally play the puppet master by controlling the purse strings.

And now, four years later, their plan had worked. Everything they'd put in place, every chance they'd taken, every alliance they'd debated, had all paid off.

His eyes drifted to the paper again and his smile grew wider. Within hours the Cunningham-Matthews ticket would be dead. Connaught didn't particularly like that they'd had to take down the politician from his own party, rather than the president. But Matthews was a jumped-up, upstart with zero respect for the current party platform and even less respect for the power Connaught wielded. As far as Connaught was concerned, if a politician from his own party had to go down, it couldn't happen to a better man.

The scandal wouldn't take down the whole party, though. He'd held back details and evidence from Egerton that would eventually cast doubt on Matthews' guilt. It wasn't enough to clear the young politician, but it was certainly enough evidence to cast Egerton's party into the shadows. To hint, but not prove, that they were behind everything. But Matthews would never fully recover, not with the evidence now printed for the world to see. The party sure as hell would, though.

His phone rang just as he set his coffee down. A call he'd anticipated.

"Did you see it?" Egerton asked, when Connaught answered.

"Yes. Exactly as we'd hoped," he answered.

"We're sticking to the plan?" Egerton asked. There were so many things Connaught didn't like about Egerton, but his need to incessantly go over every plan time and time again was far and away the most annoying. Did the man not know how weak it made him look? Weak and ineffectual.

"Yes," Connaught responded, raising his gaze as a helicopter came into view. He frowned. Arriving at the exclusive resort on the private island Imperium Holdings owned, the island where the incompetent FBI had conducted a drug bust of one of the alliance's activities, wasn't unusual, but doing so this early in the morning was.

As he watched the aircraft approach, he wondered if perhaps the broader news agencies had gotten ahold of both the story and his location and were paying him a visit. He smiled. He hadn't anticipated that, but it would definitely be a bonus.

"Are you ready?" Connaught asked as the helicopter circled around to the landing pad. They'd planned for a media firestorm, though perhaps not so quickly. Regardless, he and Egerton had a story prepared as to why they were both at the same resort when the story broke. It was a simple one, really—they'd heard rumors that Matthews was engaged in the kind of behavior that, thanks to the story, they now had proof of and were already in the process of discussing what it would mean to the parties if it were true.

"They're here already?" Egerton's bungalow was at the other end of the resort and if he were inside, he wouldn't have heard the helicopter. Although, as it descended to the landing pad located on the back side of the resort, he'd be hard pressed to miss it if he only listened.

"I believe so," Connaught said.

"I'll be there in five minutes," Egerton said before hanging up. The man, who had nervous tendencies, had likely been up long before sunrise and was dressed and ready to go.

Unlike Connaught.

He glanced down at his robe, at the way it fell, revealing the thin, wrinkled skin of his legs. With a sigh, he rose and made his way back into his bungalow. He'd been looking forward to this day for years, but even so, he wouldn't have minded a few more minutes to enjoy another cup of coffee with his triumph.

"You ready?" Beni asked Cal through the headset as the helicopter descended the last twenty feet.

He looked over at her and couldn't help but smile. There had never been a doubt in his mind about just how strong and capable Beni was—but having her strength and ability helping him, backing him up, was something that, in the past sixteen years, he hadn't allowed himself to dream of. Now that he had it, though, he wasn't ever going to let it—or her—go. No, he'd told Beni that first night that he had no intention of ever letting her go again. He'd meant it then and he knew it to the bottom of his soul now.

"As I'll ever be," he answered. Then asked, "She's here?"

Beni nodded as they touched down. Removing their headsets, they allowed two of his security detail to disembark first, then he and Beni followed, with two more security bringing up the rear.

When they were far enough away from the rotors to hear, she answered. "She arrived late last night by boat. She's waiting in her suite."

Cal nodded and followed Beni and his security as they wound their way through a series of paths toward a large bungalow. When they arrived, a man standing on the lanai nodded to them and swung the door open.

His security team peeled off, but Beni remained at his side.

"Ready?" she asked.

He glanced over, taking in the woman he never thought he'd be lucky enough to have by his side again, then nodded. "Let's do this," he said. And together they stepped into the room.

Despite having met President Cunningham once before, the awe of being in the presence of a leader who was both immensely powerful but also *good*, hadn't dimmed. Feeling a bit starstruck, Beni straightened as she and Cal came to a stop before her.

The president stood with the morning sun shining through the window behind her, making it hard to see her face. In her hand, she held a newspaper. *The* newspaper.

"It seems we have an interesting problem on our hands," she said, striding over and handing the paper to Cal. "You've seen this?"

He nodded but didn't take the paper. "Benita had it waiting for me on the helicopter."

President Cunningham withdrew the paper and looked at the cover picture. A picture of Cal, all but naked, with a young— very young—woman draped over him.

"Not a bad picture," President Cunningham said.

And it wasn't, not for their purposes.

"You ready?" President Cunningham asked.

Cal grinned. "You have no idea."

Beni fought her own smile as she moved away, not entirely sure if she'd be welcome to stay. She and the task force might have played an integral role in getting everyone to this crisis point, but that didn't necessarily mean she'd be invited into the room when it all came to a head. Everything was being recorded, though, so if she was asked to leave, she could always listen later.

"Go ahead and call them," the president said to a woman sitting at a small table with a laptop open in front of her. Beni vaguely recognized her and thought she might be the president's press secretary. The woman nodded then picked up a phone.

"Agent Ricci," President Cunningham said, halting Beni's progress toward the door. Beni turned around. "I'd like you to stay, but perhaps take a seat there?" President Cunningham gestured with her head toward an upholstered chair in the corner where she'd be visible, but not in the middle of things.

Beni nodded and started toward the chair. She made it half a stride before Cal caught hold of her arm and swung her around, pulling her flush against his body.

Her hands came up for balance and landed on his chest. His heart beat strong and steady under her palm. She looked up to find his blue eyes staring down at her.

"Thank you," he said. He wasn't just referring to the situation they were now in. No, he was thanking her for everything, for not walking away all those weeks ago, for giving him a chance, for letting him in. For loving him.

Ignoring the fact that the president was fifteen feet away and the room was filled with officials and security, Beni rose up on her toes and kissed the man she loved. The man she'd always loved. The man she *would* always love.

"Thank you," she whispered.

His eyes glistened but she didn't have a chance to appreciate the emotion in them because he dipped his head and kissed her again. Only this kiss was for more mature audiences than the one she'd laid on him.

A throat cleared behind her and she pulled back. Cal grinned down at her. Beni chanced a glance over her shoulder to find the president standing there with an arched eyebrow and her own grin. Beni looked back at Cal. "While that was nice, don't ever do that again in public."

Cal seemed to consider her comment, then brushed a quick kiss across her lips. "I'm not promising anything," he said, then let her go.

She opened her mouth to say something, but the president cut her off.

"I'm kind of with her on that one, Cal," she said. "I mean, I'm all for love and the press is going to have a fucking field day with this, but maybe keep things G-rated for the little ones."

Beni quickly slipped from Cal's embrace and made her way

to the chair the president had directed her to. After she sat, she looked up to find Cal's gaze had tracked her. He grinned again.

"Sorry, Anne-Marie, if I'm not going to make that promise to her, I'm certainly not going to make it to you. We'll just have to see how things unfold."

The president snorted and Beni was sure she heard a couple of the security folks, and the press secretary, hiding laughs behind coughs.

"Yes, let's get through this disaster of epic proportions and see how things unfold," she said. Then turning to one of her security, she asked, "How long?"

"They are both coming up the path, now, Madam President. Two minutes out," he answered.

The president looked back to Cal and gestured with her head to the spot next to her. "Why don't you come stand beside me so we can present a united front when we take these fuckers down."

In the few moments they had before the shit hit the fan, Beni laughed. Never, in her wildest thoughts had she envisioned the eloquent, poised leader of her country, swearing so freely. It made Beni like the woman even more.

CHAPTER TWENTY-FOUR

THE DOOR swung open and in walked both Anthony Connaught and Lawrence Egerton. Despite him being the chair of his own party, Cal had never had much respect for Connaught. And while Egerton certainly liked to pretend that he pulled the strings, he'd always struck Cal as more of a follower than a leader—probably why some of the more ambitious and aggressive members of the party had selected him as chair, he was easy to bully.

Connaught paused inside the door, his gaze flickering between him and Anne-Marie. Egerton came to a stop behind him. Predictably, Connaught was the first to speak.

"We have a problem," he said, striding forward and slapping the newspaper down on the table. "I assume that you heard rumors of his activities like Lawrence and I did?" He directed the question to the president.

Standing beside Cal, she smiled. "Oh yes, you could say I heard something. I assume that's why you're both here?"

Connaught nodded. "Yes, we have some fixing to do and since this implicates both parties, we thought it would be better to do it together."

"*That* just happened last night," Cal said, tipping his head toward the paper. "It wasn't what brought you down here. So, what did?"

Connaught narrowed his eyes at him. "I hardly think that matters now that *that's* hit the front page," he said, mirroring Cal's move with a nod toward the newspaper.

"Let's be honest," Anne-Marie said. "More than one politician has survived a sex scandal. The events of last night weren't what brought you down here. What rumors have you heard?" Anne-Marie asked, then continued without waiting for an answer. "We all know rumors are a dime a dozen in politics, so it had to be something more than that; something substantial enough to get the two of you down here to strategize together. And since presumably, you're here to discuss dismantling my administration, I'd like to know what you heard, from whom, and what evidence you have to back it up."

"You don't think that's evidence enough?" Again, Connaught gestured to the newspaper, this time with his bony finger.

Anne-Marie arched an eyebrow at him.

Connaught let out an aggravated sigh. "Listen, Madam President, with all due respect—"

"With all due respect, Mr. Chairman, answer my question," the president cut him off.

A tense silence fell over the room and Cal wondered how long it would take Egerton and Connaught to start to question why the president was pushing back. Because surely, if their plans had truly succeeded, she'd be the first one to want to throw him to the wolves.

Finally, Connaught answered. "A month ago, I received a tip that a man by the name of Duncan Calloway had engaged in several illegal activities. Evidence was provided that led me and Lawrence to agree that Calloway's activities were intended to enrich and protect the vice president and had been undertaken at his express direction."

Ah, so that was the tactic they were going to take. Beni had pointed out a few weeks ago that Calloway wasn't ever meant to survive this scheme intact. Even so, Cal was surprised at how quickly Connaught had brought his name up. Even if just to throw him under the bus.

"How well do you know Calloway?" the president asked.

Connaught frowned. "Not at all. He comes to political events on occasion. He was even at my home in Nassau less than two weeks ago. Other than the fact that he likes to drink, the only thing I really know about the man is what our investigation uncovered."

"Your investigation?" Anne-Marie prompted.

Connaught nodded. "We weren't about to take anyone's word without doing our own due diligence. We investigated further and came to the same conclusion that had originally been presented to us. We chose to meet at this resort to discuss our options because the Virgin Islands is neutral territory, so to speak—they have no representation in congress and can't vote for president, so don't have the same dog in the fight as one of the states. We thought our presence here would go unnoticed, but clearly, that's not the case."

"You'll hand over everything you found in your investigation?" Anne-Marie asked.

Connaught glanced at Egerton who nodded. "Of course."

"We'd appreciate that," she said, then winked at Cal out of sight of the two chairs.

"I think there's no question that you'll resign," Connaught said, directing the comment to Cal.

For the first time since Beni had woken him early that morning, Cal was actually looking forward to what would come next.

"Why would he do that?" Anne-Marie asked.

Connaught blinked. "You want to keep a man who hires trafficked women—girls—to have sex with as your vice president? As much as it pains me to say it, you would have been better off with one of your own party, Madam President."

"Point of fact, Mr. Connaught," Anne-Marie said, "if she was a girl, or trafficked, or unwilling in any way, it wasn't sex, it was rape."

Connaught drew back at that. His eyes went between the two of them, then drifted over to Beni, who sat quietly in the corner, before shifting his attention to the press secretary. The smarter of the two men, Cal could see the questions finally coming into Connaught's eyes. There was too much at risk, though, for him to start doubting, so, infusing his voice with as much disdain as possible, he responded.

"Call it what you will, and that actually makes it even worse. If you want to keep him, go for it. The party, however, will decry him and call for his resignation."

"It's not just the woman—girl," Egerton said, finally stepping into the conversation. "Our investigation uncovered so much more—nepotism, the selling out of our intelligence assets, drugs, and even murder. At the very least, there will be a criminal investigation, if not a full trial. But for now, this," he said, pointing to the picture on the front page, "is enough for both parties to demand that you call for his resignation."

"They can try," Anne-Marie said, holding a hand out toward her press secretary. Veronica Mendoza had always been one of Cal's favorite members of the president's staff. Unflappable to the core, she possessed a wicked sense of humor and her intelligence was sharp enough to cut glass.

Veronica placed a file in the president's hand, and she opened it. Perusing the contents, contents Cal knew Anne-Marie had probably already memorized, she remained silent.

"Would you like to know what I have here?" she finally asked, holding up the file.

"If it's your press statement calling for his resignation and an investigation into his activities, then yes, I think I should see it," Egerton said, stepping forward with his hand stretched out.

Anne-Marie raised the file out of his reach and one of her security detail stepped forward. Egerton paused, then stepped back.

"I was thinking of dragging this out a little bit, Mr. Vice President," the president said. "Only now I find it's not all that interesting and this meeting is making me lose my appetite. Would you care to do the honors?"

Anne-Marie handed him the file and he opened it, much as she had. Like her, he also already knew the contents. He wanted a second to decide where to start, though.

After a beat, he pulled two pieces of paper from the file then closed it. Deciding that, like his colleague, he had no stomach for drawing this out, he launched his first attack.

"As we speak, there are arrest warrants being served for these members of each of your parties." As he spoke, he handed each man one of papers he'd removed from the file.

The chairmen looked down and their gazes darted across the lists. Cal watched both men closely, but in particular, Anthony Connaught. He was gratified when the older man's pulse started picking up speed, something easily visible under the thin skin of his neck.

"On what grounds?" Connaught asked.

"Several, actually," Cal answered. "Everything from fraud, racketeering, drug trafficking, treason, sedition, murder, and yes, conspiracy to commit illegal acts. It seems someone was engaged in illegal activity and it sure as hell wasn't me."

Egerton choked and loosened his tie. Connaught eyed Cal. "What does this," he said, holding up the paper, "have to do with the story covered this morning?"

"Oh, that story?" Cal asked, his gaze lazily drifting to the newssheet. Beside him Anne-Marie shifted and looked away, no doubt to hide a grin. "We thought it would be a good conversation starter. You know, lull you and Egerton into thinking you'd won. The thing is, though, that young woman—and she is a woman, though barely—is a member of an intelligence agency that was happy to lend her services to help bring down a conspiracy targeting American Democracy. The conspiracy led by the two of you."

Egerton went pale and took two steps back. One of the security detail stepped in front of the door. Cal didn't think the man would do a runner, but it couldn't hurt to be sure.

Arrogant to the last—and Cal hadn't expected any different —Connaught laughed. "I'm not sure what you're talking about, son. There's no conspiracy and there's no way the American people are going to believe that picture is a set up. Some may eventually believe something, but you know how it works, once it's printed, it's the gospel. You'll never recover."

Cal smiled. "I don't need to recover. The only people who have seen this version of today's local paper are either in this room or part of a select group of FBI agents," he responded.

"You may have been able to recall a newspaper, but you know as well as I do, that that article went live on the internet the moment it was printed. There's no way you can recall that," Connaught shot back. Cal had to admit to being just a little impressed with the man's persistence. And his knowledge of the internet.

"No, you misunderstood me," Cal said. When he was sure he had Connaught's attention, he continued. "That paper is a ruse. The man who owns the local media is a friend of a friend. He printed exactly four copies of that paper. If you're interested, I'm sure Ms. Mendoza has today's real paper."

Veronica slid from her seat and stood, holding the true version of the day's paper. She didn't bother to hand it over to

Connaught. Instead, she held it up for them to see the headline, then turned it around and perused the front page. A front page that did not include a picture of him in bed with a young woman.

"It seems the Virgin Islands are very excited about your visit, Madam President," Veronica said. "It's all they can talk about. They seem to be hoping it will be good for tourism."

She flipped the paper back around for both Connaught and Egerton to re-read the headline which was, indeed, about the president's pending arrival on Tildas.

Connaught's eyes widened so big, they bugged out. Cal had thought that phrase was nothing more than literary hyperbole, but Connaught had just proved him wrong. *Hmm, learn something new every day.*

He chanced a glance at Beni who was leaning back in the chair, her legs crossed, her chin resting on her hand. She winked at him.

Turning back to the two men who, in their greed for both money and power, had wrought so much destruction, Cal let his disgust show.

"We have evidence, more than you could possibly know," Cal started, wanting to bring these two men to their knees. He'd never considered himself a vengeful man, but what these two had done in the name of politics and power was unforgivable. People had died because of them, the integrity of the CIA and FBI was now in question, and thousands of donors had been defrauded—donors who'd thought they were giving to the party for legitimate reasons only to have their funds used to perpetrate the crimes committed by these two men. And if that wasn't enough, the fact that it had all been done in order to undermine duly elected leaders—leaders chosen by the people the parties were supposed to speak for—was the final straw.

"We know your connection to Calloway goes much farther back than just a month, but thanks for confirming you know him—it will be interesting to see what the DOJ thinks when they compare the evidence we have proving your long standing association with the man to the statement you made that you barely know him." Cal paused and glanced down at the file in his hand before once again facing Connaught and Egerton. "We also know about his lackey, Westoff. We know about Gregor Lev and the drugs that you paid him to develop, and we know that you were involved in selling the identity of one of our CIA intelligence officers. We know that the investigation into The Bank of DC was fraudulent and we know you hired a hitman to kill three men in order to make it look like I was cleaning up loose ends. We know it all, Anthony and Lawrence."

While his words were mostly true, he considered whether Calloway would turn on the two men who had paid him millions over the last four years. It wouldn't matter if he didn't —they had enough evidence for the DOJ to prosecute—but it would help if Calloway decided to save what little bit of his own skin he could by turning on Egerton and Connaught and filling in what few gaps were left in the investigation.

"You can't," Egerton said.

"Shut up, Lawrence," Connaught cut him off. Being the smarter of the two, Connaught might recognize he'd lost, but he had no plans to go down without a fight. Too bad for him, he'd teamed up with a man whose spine was about as firm as jelly. Connaught might not break, but Egerton sure as shit would.

"This isn't the end," Connaught said, as several FBI agents who'd been flown in from the Miami office to lend assistance, entered the room. Beni's own team still had the security of The Summit to attend to and none of them were hung up about being the ones to actually arrest the men they'd been hunting for over a year. What would be important to them was simply that they *were* arrested and the conspiracy stopped.

"What's this?" Egerton asked, stepping back again. He

stopped abruptly when one of Anne-Marie's security detail put a hand on his shoulder.

"I should think it's pretty obvious what this is," Cal said, moving to stand beside Beni. "I'll let the agents say all the official things, but gentlemen, you are both under arrest for oh so many crimes."

"And frankly," Anne-Marie said, "I hope you both rot in hell."

CHAPTER TWENTY-FIVE

BENI SAT across from Cal in the helicopter as they headed back to Tildas Island. He was so used to carrying the weight of responsibility so much of the time, that it surprised her how easy it was to see how much the past forty minutes had lightened that load. Not that she didn't think it would have—after all, it wasn't every day that a man escaped being so spectacularly framed without so much as a scratch. Even so, the small smile dancing on his lips and the loose way his shoulders fell, told her just how much the past few weeks *had* weighed on him.

"How do you feel?" she asked through their headsets.

He switched his gaze from watching the Caribbean fly by beneath them to her, and to her surprise, his smile faltered. "I'm glad we stopped them. I'm glad that part is over, but it's all really just beginning, isn't it?"

She reached over and took his hand. Instantly, he twined his fingers with hers. "I wish we could keep most of this out of the public eye, but with all the arrests and the trials that are sure to follow, we won't be able to do that," she said.

He brought her fingers to his lips and dropped a kiss on them. "I know. In some ways, I think quietly sweeping up the mess might be best, but in others, I think the more public it is, the better it might be. It will be good for the people to understand how dangerous it can be when they put party over people —regardless of which party that is."

She rubbed her fingers over his knuckles, and he shifted his gaze back to the window and blue sea below them. The flight was a short one and they only had ten more minutes before they landed.

"That's not all that's bothering you, though, is it?" she asked.

He didn't look at her, but after a beat, he shook his head. "I'll spend some time wondering if there was something that I could have done differently. Something I should have seen but didn't. Some way that I could have protected people like Serena, who lost her career, and Hameed Khan, Joseph Taglia, and Jason Grant who lost their lives. And then there are the young people who were destroyed by the drugs Connaught and Egerton funded. I know, rationally speaking, there's probably not anything I could have done, but I'll still ask myself those questions. Maybe someday I'll stop, but for now, it will be a while before it's not close to the surface for me."

Beni didn't know what to say to that. Again, it struck her that the weight of everything he carried must be unbearable at times. Bear it he did, though. And with a grace and poise she almost couldn't fathom. Unstrapping herself from her seat, she scooted across the seats and shoved herself in beside him. Knowing no words were needed, she leaned into his side and gave him the only thing she had to give at the moment, herself.

He wrapped an arm around her even as Shorty, their pilot, admonished her to retake her seat—which she responded to by telling him to do something anatomically impossible—and the Secret Service eyed her like they might need to strap her down themselves. She ignored them. If she was going to see this thing through with Cal, she'd need to figure out how to pretend they weren't always under someone's watch and now seemed as good a time as any to start.

Her phone buzzed in her pocket and she pulled the device out. Seeing a message from Alexis, she opened the app and read. Then read again.

Sensing her interest, Cal leaned over and she showed him her phone.

"Smythe and Hernandez left the house earlier today for Hernandez' jet. Both were arrested at the airport. Loughlin is on his way to Hemmeleigh for The Summit."

The cameras that had been set up all over Alexis' house prior to the dinner had shown Calloway, Hernandez, and Smythe conspiring to frame Cal. Loughlin hadn't actively participated, but Beni thought they might discover something different the more they looked into the events of the night.

"What about Calloway?" Cal asked, having taken her phone from her.

Bubbles appeared, then disappeared, before they reappeared. *"The fucker is still at my house,"* she wrote and both Beni and Cal barked out a laugh. *"We weren't sure if you wanted to do the honors. If so, we'll wait for you. If not, just say the word and we'll take him in. I think Nora would really like that."*

"What's up with Nora?" Cal asked. "She just got involved in the past two days, what horse does she have in this race?"

Beni looked up into his blue eyes, confused by the question, but then remembered he hadn't been told everything. "The young woman you were photographed with for the fake article?"

He nodded.

"That's Nora's cousin. She just turned eighteen last month. She's been trained in the business—"

"What the hell kind of business have they trained her in?" Cal demanded, straightening in his seat and nearly dislodging her. He grabbed her and pulled her onto his lap.

"Not *that* kind of business," Beni answered. "Apparently Nora and Cyn, remember her from the party and Alexis' boat?"

"How could I forget, she rather enjoyed discussing Calloway's dick," he muttered.

"Well, to be fair…it was rather noteworthy in its lack of noteworthiness," Beni countered. Cal glared at her, making her laugh.

"You were saying?" he prompted.

"Turns out there's some sort of special school in Europe—Switzerland, I think Nora said—that certain families are invited to send their daughters to."

"You are supposed to be making me feel better. This is not making me feel better."

She jabbed him gently in the ribs. "If you'd let me finish…"

He let out a dramatic sigh. "Please, continue explaining about this special school for young women that trains them to pretend to be…oh my god, is it a spy school?"

She grinned. "You make it sound like some sort of work of fiction, but then again, I suppose that works for them. It's so outrageous that it couldn't possibly be true."

Cal drew back to better be able to look at her. "*Is* it true?"

She nodded. "I didn't believe it at first, either, but it is. Nora and Cyn attended at the same time. Nora's cousin graduates in a few months."

Cal was silent for a long moment, his brow furrowed. "How…why…I can't even imagine how that works. I thought you said Cyn was from the UK, but isn't Nora from the Middle East somewhere?"

Again, she nodded. "At some point, someone must have decided that despite the fact spies tend to be lone rangers, they do actually need allies. I guess having them train together and come of age together and know each other in ways that I suspect spies don't generally allow others to know them, must have seemed like a good way to facilitate that."

Tildas Island came into view and they still hadn't answered Alexis yet about what they wanted to do about Calloway. Reaching for the phone, she raised a questioning brow at Cal.

He gave her a flat look but relinquished it. "I want to know more about this school later," he said. "But as for Calloway, I want to be the one to confront him. While I respect Nora's desire to step in, I think it might be better to keep her, and the role she played, out of it. After all, we wouldn't want to risk exposing her as an asset for whatever country she works for or the existence of the school."

Beni studied his face. "You sure?"

Cal didn't hesitate. "I never liked Calloway and you have no idea how much pleasure it will bring me to be the one who finally brings him to his knees."

Beni's gaze searched his eyes for a moment, but when she saw nothing but grim certainty, she smiled. "Then I'll let Alexis know we'll be there in thirty minutes."

Cal followed his security detail into Alexis' house. Her two dogs, Howdy and Red, were tearing around the yard. They'd been locked in the gatehouse with Alexis and Beni the night before and looked to be enjoying their freedom.

Ascending the stairs with Beni following him, he paused at the top of the landing to find Yael, Alexis' head of security, and her husband, Eric, the amazing chef from the night before.

"He asked to use the office," Yael said. "There's nothing in there we need to worry about, so I let him."

Cal shot Beni a questioning look. He didn't know the layout of the building other than the rooms he'd been in the day before. In response, she stepped in front of him and led him down a long hallway that ran the length of the house. Pausing outside a closed door, her eyes met his.

"You ready?" she asked.

He nodded. He wasn't quite sure what he was going to say, but he wasn't known for his debate skills for nothing. Beni raised her hand to knock on the door, but he stopped her. Sensing what he needed, she stepped back, and, without warning, he flung the door open and walked in.

Duncan was sitting at a large mahogany desk, leaning back in a leather chair with his feet propped up on the desktop. He had his phone in his hand and a look of frustration on his face. He startled at their entry but didn't shift his position.

"You're still here," Cal said, stopping in front of the desk.

Duncan grinned. "I am. My flight doesn't leave until this afternoon, although I'm surprised to see you here."

"Why's that?" Cal asked, taking a seat.

"Uh, because I saw the paper, Cal. I'm not sure how you accomplished that last night with all of us here, but kudos to you, I guess? Well, maybe not, since you got caught. Truthfully, I didn't realize you were into that kind of thing. I guess it's always the mighty that fall, isn't it?" Duncan's gaze drifted to where Beni stood behind him. "I admit to being surprised to see you, too, Agent Ricci. I know love is blind and all, but can you really forgive a man for paying for an underage prostitute?"

"You know how I feel about that term, Duncan. It's not prostitution if the girl is underage, it's rape," Cal said.

Duncan's attention landed back on Cal and, for a moment, his former fraternity brother studied him. Then he swung his legs down and placed his hands on the desk, leaving his phone on the desktop. "Whatever you want to call it, I'm sure the press will be having a field day."

"Is this the article you're referring to?" Cal ask, producing the copy Beni had given him.

It would have been impossible for Duncan to have seen the actual paper before this very moment. The remaining three copies—the only others that existed—had been delivered to the resort for Connaught, Egerton, and President Cunningham.

"That's the one," he said, his eyes greedily absorbing the image and the printed article.

"I'm curious about where you saw it," Cal said.

Duncan sat back and shrugged. "Does it matter? I don't know, maybe Alexis' staff had it at the breakfast table. I'd like to say I was surprised, but truly, you are one of the most sanctimonious asses I know that it actually comes as no surprise that you're as much of a hypocrite as the rest of the politicians. Although, I will say, this will crush the American people. I'm heartbroken about that," Duncan said, so obviously not.

"It's interesting that you saw this earlier today," Cal said.

Again, Duncan gave a negligent shrug. "Not really, but whatever."

"I mean it's interesting because only three other copies of this were printed. All of which were delivered to a private resort and distributed to Lawrence Egerton, Anthony Connaught, and President Cunningham. The resort is just a short helicopter ride away from here and we just finished having a little chat with Connaught and Egerton this morning. Anthony says 'hi' by the way." It might have been petty, but Cal couldn't help but add that little dig.

For the first time since they'd stepped into the office, Duncan reacted. His eyes darted between him and Beni as if he sensed the trap but couldn't figure out if he needed to start looking for an escape.

"There is no escape, Duncan," Cal said with a grin that wasn't entirely pleasant.

"I don't know what you're talking about," Duncan said.

"He doesn't know what we're talking about, Nita," Cal said. As if she'd been waiting for this moment all along, Beni stepped up beside him and held her phone out for Duncan to see. Cal didn't know what she was showing him, but it didn't take long for him to figure it out. The voice of a newscaster filled the office, reporting on the arrests of Anthony Connaught and Lawrence Egerton and alluding to a widespread investigation by the DOJ into a conspiracy to bring down the administration. The part about the DOJ being involved surprised Cal—he'd known they *would* be. He just hadn't anticipated they already *were*. Then again, one never knew about these things when Sunita Shah was involved.

Duncan paled as he watched, his eyes glued to the small screen. When Beni finally pulled it away, Cal chuckled at the panic in Duncan's expression.

"Go ahead and say it, Cal," Beni said.

He turned his head and looked at her. She arched a brow and issued a silent challenge. He had never been all that interested in belittling someone, or hitting them when they were down, but in this moment, it did hold some appeal. And apparently Beni knew him well enough to know he was weighing the options.

"I'm not condoning it on a broad scale, but sometimes it really is needed," she said.

He switched his attention back to Duncan who hadn't moved since Beni had showed him the video, though his gaze danced between the two of them. "Do what?" he asked.

"Tell you you're not as smart as you think you are," Beni answered.

Cal chuckled at her impatience. "She's not wrong, Duncan," he said. "You always equated charm and looks with intelligence —that if you had one, you obviously had the other, especially when no one told you otherwise. But the thing is, no one ever told you otherwise because you're more or less a joke. I knew it, everyone in the fraternity knew it. There's not much more to you than a shell of a man with an easy smile, and you were so clueless that you never picked up on the fact that our silence didn't mean we agreed with your assessment of yourself. It just meant that none of us felt you were worth the time to correct.

"And now this," Cal said with a shake of his head. "I guess I should applaud your commitment to the cause, although I'm sure it had more to do with the power you thought you held, and the company it allowed you to keep these past few years, than the actual cause. In fact, I don't actually see you caring one way or the other what administration is in power. I'm betting the only thing you really cared about was whose name you got to drop and whose yacht you were invited onto next."

"I think it's pretty safe to say that it won't be the Wrights'," Beni interjected dryly.

"Definitely not the Wrights', since I suspect he's looking at a very, very long prison sentence," Cal said. "Being convicted of treason will do that."

"Treason?" Duncan asked.

Cal nodded. "That is what they generally call it when someone tries to overthrow a legitimately elected government."

"You know what I don't get, though?" Beni asked. Duncan's gaze snapped to her, but Cal kept his attention on Calloway.

"What's that, love?" Cal asked.

"I hear what you said about Duncan's ego being so big he basically couldn't see what was right in front of his face. But I would have thought his survival instincts were a little more finely tuned. I mean, if he's not relying on his intelligence, *something* must have been keeping him out of trouble and alive up until now."

Duncan swallowed. "What's that supposed to mean?" As he spoke, his eyes drifted down to the weapon Beni had in her shoulder holster.

She chuckled. "*I'm* not going to kill you, if that's what you're worried about. Not unless you do something stupid. But don't you think Connaught and Egerton would have? You're a weak link with a lot of information that could bring a lot of people down. Did it really never occur to you that you were never meant to make it out of this alive?"

Cal could all but see the gears churning in Duncan's head as he parsed through Beni's logic. The heavy pause that followed her comment made it obvious that yes, he never *had* considered he wouldn't make it out alive. In fact, Cal would bet his salary that in Duncan's mind, he saw himself as being taken into the fold by the political elite. That men like Connaught and Egerton would be so grateful to him that he'd be forever welcome at any party, at any dinner, at any place.

"That's sad, Duncan," Cal said. "There have been any number of times over the years when you've struck me as a pathetic man unable to grasp his own mediocrity, but this definitely takes the cake. You know what's most sad of all, though?"

Duncan didn't respond, but he did hold Cal's gaze.

"What's most sad of all," Cal said, "is that even with a modicum of intelligence, you could have done something good in this world. You could have been kind, you could have cared about people other than yourself, you could have *done things*, real things, for your community. But you chose not to. Your preference for basking in the world you made up rather than living in the real one, is, to me, the saddest thing of all."

Beni's hand came down to rest on his shoulder and, together, the two of them watched Duncan. Cal didn't anticipate Calloway would suddenly cave and confess everything, but he did want to give the man a chance to, for once, take responsibility for his decisions.

"There's the sanctimonious Calvin Matthews we all know and love," Duncan drawled with an expression on his face that wasn't quite a sneer, but was damn close. "One of us might very well live in a fantasy world, but it's not me, Cal," he said, spitting out the name. "You live in your ivory tower and ride around on a white horse. You have no idea what the real world is like because everyone kowtows to you, the golden boy."

The words weren't surprising, but disappointment pressed in on Cal and he sighed. Rising from his seat, he caught Beni's gaze. "Shall we call in the agents to make the arrest? I think we're done here."

She nodded and together they turned to leave the room. They were nearly to the door when Beni made a sudden move, pushing him into the wall.

"You don't want to do that, Calloway," he heard her say. Then the sound he'd heard just before being pressed against the wall registered. Beni had pulled her gun from her holster. She had him pushed up against the wall, her body in front of his, protecting him. He had no doubt she'd even be trying to shove him onto the ground where she could cover him better if her hands weren't occupied with her gun and her attention focused on Calloway.

Not wanting to disturb her balance, Cal slowly managed to get himself turned around as the sound of footsteps echoed down the hall.

"Agent Ricci!" a voice called.

"Do not enter," she called out, never taking her eyes off Calloway and the gun he now held. The door was at Cal's back and if they threw it open, it would fly into him and he'd fly into her. Then again, if that meant they both tumbled to the side as the agents and his Secret Service flooded the room, that might not be such a bad idea.

"Get a team outside," she called. "I'm justified in taking this shot, Calloway," she said, her weapon trained on the traitor. "But in deference to Cal's presence, and because I know he'd ask it of me, I'm going to give you an opportunity to put your gun down. He's far, far nicer than I am."

Her restraint went against everything she'd been trained for, and Cal was well aware that she was doing it solely for his benefit. Right now, Beni was pushing aside the fact that he was the Vice President of the United States and treating him as the man he was—a man who preferred to employ violence only as a last resort. Calloway wasn't worth more than the dirt on Beni's shoes, but she was right, he didn't want to see him die.

God, he loved this woman.

As they waited for Calloway to make a move, four agents appeared on the other side of the floor-to-ceiling window behind him. Cal suspected the glass was bullet proof—he knew the Wrights were fanatical about security—but at the very least, if someone shot at the window, it might distract Calloway long enough for Beni to disarm him.

"Get down, Cal," she ordered.

He'd take hell for it later, but he ignored her. "How many agents are outside this door?" he asked.

"Four at the window and four in the hall. That's not counting Alexis' security which would be an additional three," she answered. Then, directing her next comment to Calloway, she added, "I have to admit, that even for you, this seems very poorly planned."

"You said I wasn't meant to live. Maybe I just want to put a rush on that since I have no plans to go to jail. Or maybe I just want to hurt the golden boy. Or hurt him by hurting you," Calloway said.

Cal recognized the hollow look in Duncan's eyes—he'd seen it before in survivors of violent crimes, that moment when they questioned everything and gave up hope. Only Calloway wasn't a victim and the situation he found himself in now was one of his own making. To give him any quarter would be more than the man was worth.

"I think I'll need to have a little talk with my security team when this is all over as to why they didn't search him for a weapon when he returned from picking up the rum and the young woman last night," he said casually.

Catching on, Beni negligently lifted a shoulder. "Probably a good idea. They *were* told not to search too thoroughly, but I agree, a little more thoroughly would have been a good idea.

Oh, and Duncan?" Beni waited for his eyes to rest on her. "Just to be clear, we have video of everything. Video of you slipping the drugs into Cal's drink, video of you bringing the young woman into Cal's room. Video of you making her pose in certain ways. I'd say smile you're on Candid Camera, but we're a little late for that."

Duncan kept his gaze on Beni though his gun was trained on Cal. Cal was no expert on shooting—though he knew enough of the basics—but he was fairly sure that having his attention split wasn't going to end well for Calloway. Not that it was going to end well for him in any situation.

"So, what now, Calloway? Suicide by cop?" Beni asked. "I really hope that's not the case, because I'd hate to foul up Alexis' home with blood and, well, other body parts."

"As I said, I'm not interested in going to jail."

Beni frowned. "I would have thought you'd be able to convince yourself that your charm and smile would be able to get you out of a conviction. You really don't have any survival skills, do you? First, you miss the fact that you are the biggest loose end on the planet for your role in the conspiracy, and then, when you have the opportunity to live—albeit perhaps not in the way you anticipated—you pull this kind of shit, because it's just *too hard* to go to prison." Beni paused, then bobbed her head. "To be fair, prison would suck, but at least you'd be alive. You could, you know, read a lot, or maybe learn to knit with your hands or something."

Cal couldn't help the snicker that escaped him. It wasn't appropriate, but it was also poorly timed. At Cal's reaction, Calloway, whose arm had started to waver the longer he held the weapon, snapped to attention.

"Beni?" Cal prompted.

"I got this. Don't worry," she responded.

It was hard not to worry when there were two guns in the room, one of which was now pointed at the woman he loved.

"It's time to make a decision, Calloway," Beni said. "Will you pick the hard way or the easy way? Oh, what the hell am I saying? You're going to make me make the call, aren't you? Because didn't we just determine that you never pick the hard way?"

Duncan must have sensed her intent to end the stand-off because he shifted his gun a hair lower, aiming at the center of her body, and braced himself.

"Nita!" Cal called.

Just as a single shot rang out.

CHAPTER TWENTY-SIX

"WELL, THAT WAS DRAMATIC," Beni said, walking over to where Calloway lay on the ground, bleeding from the shot in his shoulder. She kicked the gun aside then looked at Cal as Secret Service and FBI flooded the office. "You okay?" she asked Cal, holstering her weapon.

"You shot me, you bitch," Calloway said from the floor.

"Yeah, I shot you," she said, glancing down at the man again before pointing one of the Secret Service agents toward the gun she'd kicked out of the way. "He'll need medical attention, but someone also needs to Mirandize him," she said to the agents in the room. One of the FBI agents from Miami stepped forward. He was a good-looking guy with dark hair, dark eyes, and a dimple.

"It would be my pleasure," he said.

With one last look at Calloway who was writhing on the floor with what amounted to little more than a flesh wound, she spun away and walked to Cal.

"Are you okay?" she repeated her question as she stopped in front of him. He glared at the Secret Service agents who'd surrounded him, and they obligingly took a few steps away.

"What the fuck, Nita?" he asked, pulling her into his arms. He needed comfort, and maybe she did, too, but she was still running on adrenaline and the hug, though welcome, felt confining.

"He never bothered to take the safety off," she said, her voice muffled against his chest.

Cal's hands, which had been running up and down her back, froze. "What?"

She pulled back just far enough to see him and grinned. "I wondered if he had. He wasn't the best at thinking ahead, so it crossed my mind he'd forgotten. It wasn't until you snickered, and he moved, that I was able to confirm it."

"So, you were never in danger?" Cal asked.

She narrowed her eyes at him. "We need to get a few things straight between us if we're going to make this work, Cal—"

He placed his palm over her mouth, silencing her. "We do, I agree, but maybe not here and not right now."

As if to give credence to his words, his Secret Service team surrounded them both as the FBI led Calloway out of the room. They remained protected by the circle of armed agents until Alexis' security gave the all-clear, letting them know that Calloway was no longer on the property.

Taking Cal's hand in hers, she led him to the kitchen and motioned to a stool at the counter. "I'll make us some coffee," she said.

"I feel like I'm the one who should be making it," Cal said, pulling her to a stop.

Beni put a hand on his chest. "You don't know where anything is. I do. This isn't a commentary on how I think you're processing or handling what you just saw, it's purely practical."

"Or I could make it," Yael said, walking into the room as she holstered her own weapon. "We just ran through some extra security checks and the house is all clear. Rachel is already on her way over to start with the clean-up." As she spoke, she walked into the pantry where the coffee machine was located.

"Who's Rachel?" Cal asked at the same time Beni said, "Rachel doesn't need to clean up."

"Black for you, right, Beni?" Yael asked, ignoring their comments. "What about you, Mr. Vice President?"

"Black for me, too, please. Who's Rachel?" he asked her, as they each took a seat on a stool at the kitchen island.

"Yael's mother-in-law and Eric's mom. She manages the house for Alexis," Beni answered.

"And there is no way she'd let anyone else handle the clean-up," Yael said, setting down two cups of coffee in front of them. "The office isn't that bad, anyway. You had a clean shot through the flesh so no bone or anything. The floor in there is tile so it shouldn't be too hard. One of the agents was considerate enough to pull the area rug out of the way so when the blood spread it didn't run onto the silk thread."

With his coffee cup raised half-way to his lips, Cal stared at Yael.

After a pregnant pause, Yael asked, "You guys good? Rachel's on her way and I want to make sure none of the agents give her a hard time."

Cal blinked and took a sip of his drink. Beni nodded. "Thanks," she said, raising her cup in salute.

"I'd say 'anytime' but I'd really rather not find ourselves in this situation again," Yael retorted with a smile.

"Amen to that," Cal muttered.

After Yael left, and his security detail made themselves scarce, it was just the two of them. For a few minutes, they sat in silence, sipping their coffees.

"Did Duncan actually drug me?" he asked.

Beni almost smiled at the confused curiosity in his tone. "He tried," she answered. "Serena had a second glass of rum in the pocket of her jacket. She didn't want to spill it, which is why she was moving so slowly as she gathered the empty tumblers. When Nora provided the distraction, she switched out the glass Calloway gave you with the one in her pocket. It was still drugged—sorry about that—but with a sleeping pill rather than with what Calloway had used."

Cal started to say something, then paused and shook his head. "I'd ask why drug me at all, but I suspect it has something to do with the fact that I wouldn't have been as compliant as I needed to be when he brought the young woman to my room later that night if I hadn't been."

Beni nodded then took a sip of her drink. They fell into silence again as she contemplated how shitty it was that they'd done that to him. She would have preferred if they'd at least been able to warn him, but the opportunity hadn't arisen, and Serena and Nora had simply acted.

It had been the right decision and, thankfully, Cal didn't seem all that upset about it. Everyone—including Cal, himself—knew that he wouldn't have been able to pull off being drugged if he hadn't, in fact, been drugged, when the young woman was brought to his room.

Several minutes passed as they finished their coffees. She'd just set her empty mug down on the granite counter when Cal let out a long, slow breath. Knowing the time for her rambling, random thoughts was at an end, she took her own deep breath and faced him.

The time had come to talk about—or at least start to talk about—the elephant in the room.

Shifting his gaze from his empty mug to her face, he spoke. "I know you were in the Army and deployed more times than I want to count. And I know what you do for a living, Nita. I *know* the career you've chosen comes with certain dangers. But I don't think that really sunk in until just now."

Her heart clenched and her hand tightened into a fist as it rested on the counter. She'd known all along that what she did for a living would be an issue between them. Not because Cal would ask her to stop, but because he'd worry, and she didn't think she could live with being the cause of that worry. He had enough to deal with already that he didn't need to be thinking about her safety every time she walked out the door. Of course, there was always the argument that she could get hit by a bus, but statistically, her job was more dangerous than most and that wasn't something they could ignore.

But she didn't want to give it up. At some point, she might be more open to that option, but right now? Right now, she felt she still had things she needed to do.

"What are you thinking, Nita?" he asked, reaching out and brushing his fingers along her cheek.

Even knowing she had to find the strength to have this conversation she hesitated. Then finally, she spoke. "I don't know how we're going to do this, Cal," she said. "I don't want to be the cause of more worry for you, but I don't want to give up what I do. I love it and it's a part of who I am. On the other hand, I feel like I need to pick you or the job because even if you and I figure out how to muddle through, I'm not even sure the FBI would still let me be a field agent."

To his credit, he didn't jump in and try to solve the problem or convince her that they'd figure it out. If nothing else, his slow response gave her some measure of comfort. He was thinking about it—about their options, about the impact on her, about their future—and he was thinking about it deeply.

"Do you *want* to figure it out?" he asked.

"I do, you know I do. But I don't know how, Cal. Do you see the FBI allowing me to keep working? Do you see yourself being okay every day I walk away from you and head to my job? I know I'm making assumptions about my role in your life, but I don't want to be a distraction to you, Cal. You've done remarkable things in your career, and hopefully you have many more years to keep doing what you're doing. I don't want to take any of that away from you."

"You said yes," he said.

She paused, sifting through the conversation to try and find the thread he was pulling. "What?" she asked, her brow dipping.

"I asked if you wanted to figure it out and you said, 'I do.' You said a lot of other things, too, but you said 'I do' first. So yes or no, Ricci, do you want to figure this out? Whatever might come of it, are you in or out?"

"It's not that easy, Cal," she said.

"Actually, it is. I'm not saying that figuring out *how* we do it will be easy. But the decision to be in or out is, or should be, an easy one."

She studied him as his gaze held hers. Then as she did, something shifted inside her. Yes, they both had demanding careers, but all that noise fell away as she stared at the man she loved. And it was noise. Their jobs were important, but so were *they*— as a couple, as partners, as two people who loved each other. What they had and who they were together was important.

If she *wasn't* in, then she'd be on her own with her career. Her life would probably turn out fine, but he wouldn't be a part of it. If she *was* in, though, then they'd have each other and together they could figure the job thing out—maybe they'd have the same ones, maybe different ones. The important thing she needed to remember was that having each other didn't preclude having a meaningful job with purpose, it just meant that they'd be there to help each other figure out what that purpose might be.

As the seconds ticked by, Beni felt it sink in that Cal was right, it really was a simple question. What followed might not be simple, but the initial decision sure as hell was. Was she better off with him than without him? She might not know what the future would bring, but she knew, with every fiber of her being, that they were stronger together.

"You're right," she said, allowing a smile to show.

He smiled back. "My favorite words. But I need to hear exactly what I'm right about."

"It is an easy decision," she said.

He didn't touch her, but the intensity of his emotions—his love, his hope, his desire, and yes, even his anxiety—washed over her.

"And?" he asked.

She leaned forward until their lips were a hairsbreadth apart. "I love you, Calvin Matthews," she said.

"I love you, too, Benita Ricci, but I need to hear your answer." His lips brushed against hers as he spoke, but he didn't kiss her.

She smiled and leaned in, closing the tiny gap between them. It was a gentle kiss, almost teasing. When she pulled back just a touch, he slipped his hands into her hair and looked her in the eye.

"Your answer, please, Agent Ricci," he said.

"It's Nita to you," she said. "And I'm in. All the way."

EPILOGUE

Two months later

"I'D LIKE TO RAISE A TOAST," Alexis said, holding up a glass of sparkling something as she rose from her seat beside Isiah.

Beni looked around Alexis' patio at all the familiar faces. After two months of wrapping up the investigation and the other responsibilities of the task force, all ten of them were spending their last evening on Tildas Island together. Anika had her back against the armrest of the love seat where she sat with Dominic, her feet up in his lap. Jake was lying down with his head resting on Nia's thighs. Charlotte was tucked up against Damian and he had his arm around her shoulder. As for her, she sat beside Cal, her hand in his, her head resting on his shoulder. Thank god Alexis' patio had a swamp cooler that allowed them to enjoy this last night together outside.

"To us?" Jake asked, rolling onto his back but keeping his drink steady.

Alexis smiled. "That and to a happy Father's Day today."

Everyone looked to Damian who grinned. A month ago, he and Charlotte had told the team they were expecting their first child—a girl they planned to name Harlow, Charlotte's mother's maiden name.

"Happy first Father's Day, Damian," Alexis said. He raised his glass and with a smile, took a sip. "He's not the only one, though," she continued.

Her grin had everyone sitting up. When it spread into a smile, the patio filled with gasps, laughs, squeals (from Nia and Jake), and congratulations. Isiah rose and put his arm around Alexis' waist, pulling her against him.

"As you may have guessed, Damian isn't the only one celebrating a first Father's Day. We're also expecting a girl in five months," Isiah confirmed with a huge smile.

Beni was thrilled for the couple. She and Cal weren't there yet, they might not ever be there, but her friends' joy and excitement warmed her heart in a way she'd never anticipated was possible when she'd first accepted the position with the task force.

Once everyone had given the new parents-to-be hugs and they were all seated again, Cal asked, "Any names yet?"

Alexis glanced at Isiah who nodded for her to respond. "We're going to name her Amara. It means grace, which is my mother's middle name and Isiah's grandmother's name."

"That's perfect, I'm so excited for you both," Nia said with an excited little clap. "Will you be staying here?"

The question hovered in the air between the group. Beni assumed that her friends had been making plans, just as she had, but by silent agreement, none of them had spoken about it. Maybe, like her, they thought if they didn't talk about it, it wouldn't happen so quickly.

Alexis cleared her throat and cast her gaze around the patio. "Actually, the FBI decided that they needed a bigger presence in the region and Shah recommended me to run the office here. I'll keep the current local agents, but I'll get to bring in two more."

That was a development Beni hadn't seen coming. Though

the more she thought about it, she realized it shouldn't have been a surprise. The FBI *did* need a bigger presence in the Caribbean and there was absolutely no question that Alexis would be an amazing leader of that team. Beni wasn't the only one of the group who thought so, and everyone offered up their sincere congratulations.

"So, are we going to do this now?" Alexis asked, once they'd all quieted again. No one needed any clarification as to what her question referred to. Jake groaned, but stopped when Nia nudged him in the ribs.

"Just for that, I think you should go first," Nia said, staring down at Jake who'd retaken his position and was lounging with his head in her lap.

"Really? You ready for this?" he asked.

She rolled her eyes and poked him again.

He muttered something about regretting the pokes later and shifted to his side to face everyone. "I've accepted a position in the Miami field office and Nia has been offered a position at the University there. She'll head their research center and be in charge of merging it with the Caribbean Marine Research Center."

Another round of congrats went around. Nia was a damn good scientist and had only stayed on the island to be close to her family—a family that wasn't worthy of her. Beni was thrilled that Nia appeared comfortable finally cutting the ties that had done nothing but hurt her. And Jake staying near the water was a given—he couldn't live without being near the ocean. It was perfect that they'd both found positions that suited them so well.

"Now, I'm passing the torch to Damian and Charlotte," Jake said dramatically.

Damian shook his head and laughed. "Well, with the arrival of Harlow, I've decided to take some time off. We just put an offer on a house up in Windsor, New York. We both have a lot of friends up there, so it seemed like a good place to settle. Charlotte will keep working and I'll stay home with the baby. At some point, if I find I have the time, and I'm inclined, I also have a friend—a former CIA agent—who now runs a training facility in the area; he's given me an open offer anytime I want to pick up some work."

Damian and Charlotte's next step, like Jake and Nia's, was ideal for them. Beni had heard a lot about Windsor and knew both Charlotte and Damian's best friends lived there.

"And Dom, what about you?" Damian asked, handing over a mock torch.

Dominic looked to Anika and she grinned at him as she answered. "Dominic was offered a spot in the FBI field office in New Orleans, and I just signed on to be the new chief of police in a small suburb about ten miles outside the parish limits."

"I wanted to be closer to my family," Dominic said. "And with the discovery of Anika's biological family living in the same area as mine, we thought we'd give it a go and spend some time there."

That would be a big move for both of them. Dominic hadn't lived in Louisiana in over fifteen years and Anika had only just found out about her large, extended family. Dom had been feeling the pull of his parents and sisters and their families, and had been itching to get back, though. And Anika no doubt wanted to give herself the opportunity to get to know the family she never knew she had.

As Beni smiled at her friends and the news they shared, Cal rubbed a thumb over her palm, then raised her hand and dropped a kiss on her fingers. In the past few months, he'd been able to make it down to the Island about every other weekend, and he'd grown to know her teammates and their significant others. It didn't surprise her at all that she could feel his own joy for these people who'd once been just her colleagues but who had become her family.

"What about you, Beni?" Anika asked. "What are your plans?"

Beni didn't miss the hesitation in Anika's voice. Unlike the rest of the team, her choices weren't entirely her own. Yes, each of her teammates had decided with their partners what their next steps would be, but that would have been a luxury for her and Cal. In addition to their own wants and needs, they'd had to consider things like media attention and even national security.

There had been some tense conversations over the past two months. Intellectually, they'd both known that they'd have to make compromises, not only with each other but also with the Secret Service. Knowing and doing, were two different things, though. Thankfully, eventually, they'd arrived at a compromise everyone could live with.

"The FBI field office in DC has agreed to take me on as part of their anti-terrorism team," she said. "It might be okay in terms of balancing everything we need to balance because it will be a lot more office work than field work, but we all agreed we'd re-evaluate in six months."

She glanced at Cal as she answered and saw the smile teasing his lips. He hadn't had to work too hard to convince her to move to DC, but politics wouldn't allow them to live together unless they were married. It was a battle she'd fought, and lost, and something she grumbled about on a near daily basis. In response to her complaints, Cal usually just shrugged and reminded her that if she agreed to marry him, then the issue would go away. He'd made it very clear that he'd prefer for that to happen sooner rather than later, but he viewed that six-month trial period as his chance to convince her that the pros outweighed the cons. An activity he was very much looking forward to.

"Are you okay with that?" Alexis asked. "I mean, I guess you have to be, but are you?"

Beni had considered the question many times over the past

few months and had found, with each passing day, she was more and more okay with it. She nodded. "I am, actually," she said. "It's not what I imagined my career would be when I joined the Bureau, but I'm okay with it. It doesn't hurt that Stella, Cal's sister, has an offer permanently open for me with her private security firm if the FBI thing doesn't work out."

Beside her, Cal chuckled. Stella had actually lobbied hard to get Beni to come straight to her firm rather than try giving the FBI a go. To this day, Beni wasn't sure if that was because Stella wanted her that much or if she was just trying to do her brother a solid.

"Are you even allowed to work when you get married?" Jake asked, eliciting a punch from Nia. "Ow, woman, what was wrong with that question?" He rolled over and mocked glared at her.

"We've had this talk before," she said. "What are the two things you are never supposed to ask a couple?"

He narrowed his eyes at her then let out a sigh and flopped back onto his side. "Never ask them when they are getting married and never ask them when they are having kids, or if they are pregnant yet. To be fair, I didn't ask when they are getting married. I know they will. Beni won't be able to hold out for long if the sounds coming from their suite that night on Virgin Gorda were anything to go by. Ironic that we chose to go to Virgin Gorda, too, since I'm quite sure there was nothing virginal about that weekend."

Nia closed her eyes and let her head fall back and Beni threw a pillow at Jake. Cal just laughed. The weekend in question had occurred three weeks previously when all ten of them had rented a luxury villa for a short getaway on the nearby island that would guarantee their privacy. It had been a good weekend in more ways than one.

And as much as Jake was a pain the ass, she actually couldn't fault his logic. Chances were, she wasn't going to hold out much longer, but she hadn't mentioned that to Cal yet as he'd have a ring on her finger before she even finished the sentence.

"How about another toast," Cal said, holding his beer up. Everyone followed suit and Jake even sat up to join them.

"It sounds trite, but there truly are no endings, just the start of something new." He paused and looked at everyone before his gaze landed on her. "To some of the best people I know and may your next adventures be grand."

THE END

Thank you for reading EIGHT MINUTES TO SUNRISE! This was the final installment of the TILDAS ISLAND SERIES. Have you read the first 4 books?

Check out A FIERY WHISPER (Charlotte & Damian's story), NIGHT DECEPTION (Alexis & Isiah's story), A TOUCH OF LIGHT AND DARK (Nia & Jake's story), as well as THIS SIDE OF MIDNIGHT (Anika's & Dominic's story)!

Want to know more about the enigmatic CYN? If so, check out my new DOCTORS CLUB SERIES!

A dead body, a dubious admirer, and an explosive conclusion is just another day at the office for Cyn Steele.

Read on for a sneak-peek!

EXTRACT OF
CYN

#1 Doctors Club Series

CHAPTER 1

Cyn flicked her wipers on again, clearing a few flakes of the icy January snow from her windshield. She loved almost everything that came with living in Cos Cob, the waterfront community located a little over an hour north of Boston where she and her friends resided. But she did not like it when the snow fell at the precise rate of being just enough to make it difficult to see through her windshield yet not enough that using the wipers had any impact other than to create streaks across the window. Thankfully, she was only a few minutes from home and would soon be out of the elements.

As she turned onto the coastal highway that would lead her to her home five miles up the way, her phone rang. Glancing at the screen on her dash, she smiled when she saw Nora's name.

"Hello, darling," Cyn said, after connecting the call.

"Are you home yet?" Nora asked without preamble. Cyn might have been gone for sixteen days, but there was no need for pleasantries—she and the rest of the club talked nearly every day.

"Five miles," Cyn answered. Nora was the worrier of the group—well, that wasn't exactly right. She was the caretaker of their lot, and she'd wanted to know when Cyn had landed, when she was on her way home, and when she actually arrived.

"Glad you missed the storm this morning," Nora said, obviously deciding to keep Cyn company for the last leg of her journey. "I'm surprised Logan wasn't backed up with delays."

A nasty winter storm had blown into town the night before and blown right on out by ten that morning, leaving eighteen inches of snow in its wake.

"We landed on time, but it took a bit for a gate to open for us," Cyn answered. "It's good to be home."

"Your visit was pleasant?"

Cyn smiled at Nora's question. Raised in Jordan, Nora was the only daughter of a very prominent businessman who had dealings in about every precious commodity there was. Cyn knew for a fact that when Nora visited her family, it was, indeed, "pleasant."

"We ate and drank too much. Daisy pretty much lap-danced her husband every night—they are trying to get pregnant, and she's taken to encouraging his amorous activities to the extremes," Cyn answered, referring to her older sister. "And Ash was convinced I'd made up all the sudoku and crossword puzzles because he was incapable of completing any of them," she said about her brother.

"Did you?"

Cyn grinned in the dark of her car. "Maybe once or twice. He threw me to the wolves with Mum and Dad, so I had to get back at him somehow."

"I take it they are still waiting with bated breath for you to settle down?"

"They are," Cyn confirmed. "You'd think with Daisy married and getting ready to propagate the Steele line that they'd be happy with that. But, of course, they aren't."

"I would think Ash, as the heir, would be the one they'd harass."

Cyn's mind went to thoughts of her brother as she navigated the curvy road north. Occasionally, she caught glimpses of the Atlantic Ocean to her right, but the woods were thick in this part of the state and the vast stretch of water only peeked through in teasing intervals. As to her brother, Ash might be the heir to the family title and the only one to actually be able to carry on the name of Steele—according to the rules of primogeniture—but her parents had long ago given up on him. And with Daisy married, they had, with Ash's encouragement, turned their sights on her—their youngest.

"Yes, well, we know how logical my parents are." They weren't. Not in the least. Alistair and Aurora Steele might be a marquess and marchioness, and might run a not-insignificant business empire, but at home, you'd think they'd stepped right out of a hippie commune. Which was another factor that made their apparent obsession with grandkids so weird. They'd always encouraged their three offspring to live their lives, stand on their own, and be their own people. Yada yada yada. Falling into the cliché role of desperate wannabe grandparents had thrown Cyn, Daisy, and Ash for a loop. Then again, maybe that had been her parents' plan.

"All quiet here?" Cyn asked as she stopped at the stop sign at the intersection of Cos Cob's Main Street and the state highway. To her left, Main Street stretched eight blocks before turning back into a rural road that wound its way west. But those eight blocks were lined with colonial style buildings, housing everything from restaurants and art galleries to the more practical merchants like a pharmacy, food co-op, and bookstore. While her chosen hometown was always charming, with a recent snowfall and Christmas lights still hanging, this time of year was especially delightful.

"Isn't it always?" Nora answered.

Cyn eased forward through the intersection. The roads had been cleared from the earlier snowstorm, but during her first winter in the Northeast, she'd learned about that sneaky little bastard otherwise known as black ice. "You almost sound a little put out by that, Nora-luv. Everything all right?" Cyn replied as she continued north. Her house was the last house within the city limits and was another mile up the road.

Nora hesitated, then sighed. "Everything's fine. I found a litter of abandoned puppies this morning and you know how I get about stuff like that."

Cyn's heart clenched. Nora attracted strays and helpless creatures like other people attracted mosquitos in the summer, and while Cyn had a hard time understanding how someone could dump a litter of puppies, let alone do it in the dead of winter, Nora would feel it ten times more. "Are they going to...?" She didn't want to finish her sentence, but the chances of a helpless litter of puppies surviving unprotected in this weather wasn't high.

"I have them in the warmer. They seem hardy and hopefully they'll make it, but it's too early to tell." That was Nora in a nutshell—she had a bigger heart than the other three of them combined yet still had an innate ability to stay grounded and pragmatic.

"Well, I'll come by to see them. Maybe Auntie Cyn will bring a toy or two."

"There are nine of them. You better bring more than two. Devil and Six brought cozy fleece blankets and extra bottles, so you have some competition in the *favorite auntie* category, too."

"They beat me there on purpose, didn't they?" As she spoke, she passed the turnoff to Six's house and Cyn shot a glare in her direction for good measure.

"Maybe. Probably." Nora chuckled. "You're always the first one to show up with treats for my strays. I guess the only way they could beat you was when you were out of the country."

Cyn gave a dramatic sigh. "I suppose I'll have to live with

that. I will come by tomorrow, though, and we'll have a good chin-wag."

"Are you home now?" Nora asked.

"Nearly to my drive. Thanks for keeping me company, luv."

"Anytime. See you tomorrow and sleep well."

"I always do," Cyn replied, then disconnected the call. Less than a minute later, her driveway came into view. The state highway curved to the west, and drivers often mistook her driveway for a road because it continued straight. For that reason, she'd put a bright yellow gate fifteen feet up her drive and had her groundswoman keep an area cleared for people to turn around if they accidentally went straight instead of turning with the highway.

As her wheels transitioned from the pitted and uneven state-maintained road to her recently paved one, the cabin of her car quieted. Hitting a button on her Bluetooth display, the flimsy gate opened. It wouldn't really keep anyone out, and it wasn't meant to—*that* gate was farther up her drive—but it was, generally speaking, enough to let the accidental tourist know that they'd made a wrong turn.

Pulling through as the arm opened, she paused on the other side. Watching in the rearview mirror until the gate latched behind her, she then eased her foot off the brake and continued forward. Her jet-lagged body clock was telling her it wasn't quite yet nine, so she wasn't too tired. That didn't stop her from dreaming of her bed and its big, fluffy down comforter, though, as she drove toward the main gate of her property. The one that was actually intended to keep people out. Or, she supposed, in.

She rounded a bend, and the tops of the wrought-iron structure came into view, bringing with it a familiar feeling of belonging. Her house might be big enough to fit her entire family and then some, but it was home.

Smiling to herself, she let her mind wander in anticipation. Soon, she'd park in her warmed garage, then traipse in through her mudroom. Dan, her personal chef, would have a light meal and a good bottle of wine waiting for her. No doubt, the gas fireplace would be on as well.

Thoughts of having a small bite to eat and a nice glass of wine were dancing in her head when she rounded the last bend before the gate. Finally, it came into full view, all twenty-feet-long-by-twelve-feet-high of it. A utilitarian fence ran the perimeter, but the gate itself was a work of art, literally. A local metal artist had designed and built it for her. Sure, many aspects of her life made her need to be extra cautious about security, but that didn't mean that security had to be ugly.

She smiled as her eyes traced the top lines then fell down the center to the big faux keyhole. She was reaching for the button on her Bluetooth display that would trigger the opening mechanism when something caught her eye. She hesitated, squinting through the windshield. Stopped so close to the gate, her headlights were too high to shed any light on the form propped along the bottom and she couldn't quite discern what it was. Switching off the headlights, she turned her fog lights on, immediately illuminating the ground area.

She stilled and stared.

Then cocked her head and stared some more.

When she'd first seen the form, she'd thought maybe one of her friends had left her something and just hadn't bothered driving all the way to the house to drop it. But as warped as her friends were—well, particularly Six—none of them would have left what she now recognized was waiting for her.

No, her friends might still have the capacity to surprise her, but there was no way in hell they would have left her a dead body.

Made in the USA
Middletown, DE
21 April 2023

29255274R00179